Mountain Fast

S.J. Shank

CARTHAGO
NOVA PRESS

Copyright © 2024 by S.J. Shank

Published by Carthago Nova Press

All Rights Reserved. No part of this book may be reproduced, stored in a retrieval system, or transmitted, in any form or in any means—by electronic, mechanical, photocopying, recording or otherwise—without prior written permission from the publisher, except by reviewers, who may quote a brief passage in a review.

This is a work of fiction. Names, characters, events and incidents are the products of the author's imagination. Any resemblance to actual persons, living or dead, or actual events is purely coincidental.

ISBN (Ebook): 978-1-7380556-2-3
ISBN (Paperback): 978-1-7380556-1-6

Cover design by Raven Daly

www.sjshank.com

For Susan

Mountain Fast

One

Pál's knuckles rested on the table. Dry blood filled their creases and flecked his swollen lip. A fissure in the wood held his attention. Like a convict marching to the stocks, he would not look at me. Nor would my brother-in-law answer. I tried again. "Did you know this lad? Was it one or many?"

He stared down with such force his pupils bobbed beneath the lashes. He did not move his eyes from that dark little cleft.

"Perhaps you were simply misunderstood," I said. "It has happened to me. You must be mindful of others and how they take your meaning."

He slid a crumb beneath his thumb.

"At your age, boys turn savage," I said. "Some men never outgrow this."

Pál flicked his head. I could not tell if he meant to shake it or to dislodge a hair from his brow. I waited for him to say more, to tell me I was wrong. To tell me that there was good reason for this latest scrap. That it was not senseless and that he was no ruffian. For a time we sat in silence, just the two of us, alone as we had been these last months. No stew bubbled on the fire. Half a week's dirty crockery crowded the table about our elbows.

Soon I would have to go. I tried one last time. "Did you know this boy? Tell me his name and I will make this right."

Pál's voice broke, "I did not know him."

I leaned toward him and reached for his wrist. He shifted his arm before I could take it.

"A stranger did this to you? Why would he do that?"

He flashed his eyes at me. Despite Pál's new height and the size of his hands, I thought that if I continued to prod, tears might flow. I could not decide if this was for the best. He had come to me an orphan but he was well down the road to manhood. How far, I could not tell, nor why he so easily strayed.

"You owe him nothing," I said. "You must not protect him. Tell me his name and I will speak to his father."

"His father?"

"Yes," I said. "I will not stand for this brute treating you so."

"You have no grounds to speak. Not on my behalf."

He pulled his arms across his chest and found a tower of clutter on which to rest his gaze. There was no chance of loosening that tongue now.

I pushed back from the table and stood. I studied Pál for a long moment. He did not look up. He had Annaka's stubbornness and of late he had developed his sister's talent for pique. It did not matter if I told him to stay indoors today to tend the fire. He would not listen and I could not blame him if he left. This cottage had become unbearable since we lost her.

"Terézia will be by later with our supper," I said.

"My great luck."

"You are in no position to complain."

"Even a beggar would protest eating her tripe." He turned those fierce eyes towards me. This time he did not look away.

"Only those new to their vocation," I said.

"I will not count slop among my blessings."

"Terézia has only treated you well. You must never repeat such nonsense outside these walls."

"Else what?"

I let his childish defiance hang, awaiting a flush of shame. But there was only anger coloring those cheeks. His thrust-out chin did not lower an inch.

"It frightens me," I said, "your ignorance of how far a man might fall."

His smile broadened. I left him grinning like a fiend.

I saddled Fejes and began the short ride into town. Soon I passed through the gates and was climbing the plaster and timber corridors of Veszprém's narrow streets. My destination was the palace upon Castle Hill, where my master, Bishop Albert Vetési, would hand me a letter to deliver. I would depart at dawn, and if His Excellency's correspondent lived in Sopron, I would return in five days. If he had written to Székesfehérvár, as little as one. If Debrecen though, eleven or twelve nights might pass before I was back home again.

The townsfolk squeezed past my horse and jostled my knees. I paid them no mind. Instead I studied the sky, searching for the cause of this unseasonable warmth. The mellow autumn light easily rolled back the chill of long nights, and the quiet breeze whispered no word of rain or snow. Ideal weather for travel. Good fortune for the days ahead, but at that moment I felt no gratitude.

A child darted in front of me, bringing Fejes up short. The boy carried a roll of leather in the crook of his arm. He gave no backward glance at me, and I watched as he rushed beneath the awning of a cobbler who stitched hide cutouts into useful forms. The cobbler marked me and bowed his face, and at his word the boy turned and shouted an apology.

A little apprentice. Five years younger than Pál, and already more advanced in his career.

I had never had such thoughts before my wife died. No one had fixed my future, so I suppose I had expected Pál would find his own way. Now I knew I had erred. I was losing faith that he might find success through chance. He was not fit for a life of accident. Annaka was no longer there to care for him when I was on the road. In her absence, he had taken to tramping through town, seeking out his new friends who passed their shiftless days talking of bold futures, only to pester townsfolk for coin enough for wine.

At the gate to Castle Hill a grizzled old-timer leaned against the wall next to a cold brazier. He appeared to be sleeping on his feet, but the sound of Fejes's clopping hooves opened his eyes a crack. This veteran was named Jakab, the least valuable member of the king's Black Army. He had arrived the past summer, and I gathered he was sent to Veszprém as a sort of exile. It was said he was as vicious as a weasel in close-quarters, but since arriving he had only distinguished himself by running dice games that ended in hard words. That, and his penchant for drink. He was suffering its after-sickness now, I guessed, and had no doubt been assigned this standing post in punishment.

Recognition took and sleep lifted from his eyes though he made no move to right himself. His watchful look lacked any deference or hint of amity. I commanded none of the former, for it was not my rank but only my role as messenger that set me ahorse. As for the latter, I knew him only by his reputation, and perhaps he divined from my own expression what I thought of him. And perhaps he only knew me by my reputation, or more correctly my wife's, for the story of her life and death was well known throughout the town. In the months since, strangers sometimes crossed themselves when they thought my back was turned.

"Has the bishop's visitor from Croatia departed?" I asked.

The veteran stared at me. A vague hostility, like that of a dog whose boundary marking had been crossed, kindled in his eye.

"Has he?" I repeated.

"How the hell should I know?"

I had half a mind to dismount and box the man's ears. That would be a mistake, not least because I owed my calluses to handling tack, where his were earned drilling that he might better kill.

Fejes, knowing what was best for me, stepped forward. As I

passed, Jakab pressed a thumb to one nostril and fired the other like a cannon. He closed his eyes again.

My horse led me to the stable. I left her there with the stable boys before crossing the yard's pavement on foot. From the glowing ovens wafted the smell of the evening's bread. In the palace, the vestibule blazed with candles illuminating a sainted heaven upon its ceiling.

The bishop's apartment was closed, so I set down my messenger satchel to wait, wondering if the maid Sára might wander by to wish me a good day. By some twist, this maid had come up in my last conversation with Terézia, and my sister was so full of details about the young widow I wondered if she had come prepared.

My sister had said that, like me, Sára was alone. She was still young, had kept her figure, as I had no doubt remarked, and her two little girls were the sweetest creatures. And strong. Both had stayed dry-eyed the day their papa went to the churchyard as they held up their mother's arms. Sára came from farmers attached to one of the bishop's manors, simple folk who had not hesitated to take her in when her husband was lost. Word was her grieving was near its end and she was looking to move on.

Perhaps this maid and my sister colluded. All I knew was that Sára always smiled when I spoke to her, showing the tips of her teeth, and that she looked at the floor when she curtsied in a way I found most charming. But Sára did not come along to dust the corridor's statuary this day, and I waited alone, idly twisting my wife's silver betrothal ring about my finger. I exchanged one-word greetings with the clerical secretaries who brushed past, and adjusted my footing as my knees began to ache. I had done nothing wrong, but like Jakab, I was left standing.

The memory of the miserable old dog chased away all thoughts of Sára's slender wrists. Suddenly, and with a sinking heart, I saw how Pál might turn out.

The bishop's door opened. Out stepped a big man who boomed his farewell, the Adriatic still sparkling in his eyes. The Croatian ambassador glanced me over, noticed my messenger's bag, then returned his gaze to study my face. I had become accustomed to this sort of lingering appraisal. He, like so many far and wide, had heard the story of the messenger's doomed wife.

Pál, I realized, must encounter this same look every day.

"András. Enter."

The sun threw fishnet shadows through the leaded glass. The bishop sat alone at his table, poised over rows of letters and charters that covered the surface like overlapping scales. Upon these records he had laid a bounded volume, his lectern forgotten in the corner. I recognized the book as a work of Greek statecraft. He had had me fetch it from the Universitas Istropolitana in Pozsony that summer. Despite the warmth of the light splashing across his broad shoulders, His Excellency wore a fine velvet cape, as red as ripe cherry, for later that day he would preside at the wedding of one of the Essegváry heirs.

He waved me forward without looking up from the tome. His finger slid down the parchment and turned the leaf. He contemplated the new page for a moment before he placed a string, closed the volume and set it aside.

"You travel to Buda."

"Yes, Your Excellency." Four days.

"I would that you hand my missive to the chancellor directly."

"Understood, my lord."

The bishop withdrew two sheets from a leather portfolio and reviewed them. I waited with my hands behind my back as he scratched out a postscript. Needless to say, Albert Vetési was one of the greatest men in the realm. He was once the land's chief justice. He led the king's delegation to Naples. My place as one of his messengers was secure, but Annaka always wanted me to make better use of my position. I had always resisted, until I surprised myself this day by speaking out of turn.

"I have a brother-in-law, my lord. A boy yet, really more of a son."

Vetési's eyelids fluttered as he registered that I had broken my silence. After writing another line, he set aside his quill and looked up from his desk. "Yes," he said. "You spoke of him once before."

Despite my twelve years of service, I squirmed beneath his gaze. The gold upon his fingers, the precious stones at his neck, did not hint at his authority. Albert Vetési had met the Pope in Rome. He owned this city. The county was his.

I was mortified to have broached the matter with my master. It was not my nature to preconceive the path ahead, I just followed it. It had been she who had pestered me to raise Pál's career with the bishop. She had harried me since he was eleven. It had been the great quarrel of our life together. With Annaka's death, I had surely prevailed, yet here I was suddenly capitulating.

It was the latest instance of a strange new habit of mine, as if some rebellious part of me thought to make up for Annaka's absence by acquiring her concerns. I often found myself thinking of tasks outside my domain, matters I had never paused to consider—the washing, grinding corn, batting cobwebs down from between the rafters—chores I now paid a neighbor to perform and towards which I felt a new and vague disdain. I found myself thinking, too, of grander matters—the movements of the Black Army from front to front, whether the revolts in Erdély would spread west, the rumored estrangement between the Archbishop of Esztergom and the king. The affairs of the great, upon which few as powerless as she wasted a thought. Even I did not, though as His Excellency's vehicle, I often passed through the thick of it. I had never cared.

The bishop watched me closely. He showed great patience, even interest, I would say. I had been told that he spoke to Annaka privately in her cell the day she died. Perhaps she had asked him to look after Pál.

No. The bishop had not even intervened to save her. Yet they had spoken, about what I did not know. It was a question I had tried to leave unanswered for it sickened me to dwell upon it.

"He is near enough a man," I found myself saying. "I have no proper trade to pass on to him. It is time he found his place."

The bishop returned his attention to his papers. Instead of resuming his letter, he moved the leaf aside and replaced it with a fresh page. As he wrote, he said, "They need men at Kuszkol. A fortress in Trencsén County. It is comparatively safe. Send the boy to the garrison with my recommendation. The marshal will look after him."

Without a further word I had secured Pál his future. Two hundred miles from home.

Two

WE SET out beneath the vanishing stars of daybreak, the horse, the boy, and I. Up gully streets, up beds of cobble and mud parched by autumn drought. Night still held fast those paths, though some little light seeped from hovels where men stirred morning embers and women laid babes against their breasts. The scarp of Castle Hill rose at our side, a steep shadow, the weight of manmade foundations raised upon its summit.

We walked in silence, as one does on the day of leaving home. This silence was deeper than pending absence and it clung not only about the boy. He brooded and I kept sealed my lips lest I loose a torrent of unspent words.

The previous night, I had not shouted when he had come home late, thoughtless of the meal prepared for him. I had not howled to see him battered and limping. I just watched as he crawled up to his loft and answered none of my guests' queries or pleas. I said nothing as Terézia and the others finally climbed the ladder to lay a hand on his arm, to take their leave of him, one by one.

This day he would meet the men he would serve beside and with whom he would make the journey to Kuszkol, including a knight who would command him. His eye, black and swollen shut, now branded him. Though his bruises would fade, I feared their impression would not. These men could change the course of his entire life. If they saw his quality beneath his scuffs and scratches, they might make a fine man out of him. If they suspected he was too wild, that he would not heel without the whip, they might turn him into a dog.

I watched Pál reach back to touch Fejes's neck. After our journey, he would not see her for months, if not years, if at all again. Nor would he soon see these streets again, the only home he knew. He did not pause to take a second look at the city.

The boy and I were already approaching the castle gate. I struggled not to drop my head into my hands. I had made a mistake. An awful, irreversible mistake. "Pál," I said. "Let us have a word."

He kept walking towards the gate.

"Pál."

He was through.

The sentry looked haggard, his brow lurid in the light thrown by the brazier over which he warmed his hands. It was Balázs, an old acquaintance of mine, who waved us on, calling out Pál for his long face. Beyond, the castle precinct was rousing. At the brewery men unloaded a cart by torchlight. The doors to the cathedral stood open and a servant boy scrubbed its steps.

We stopped outside the stables. A tall fellow jogged towards us. A lean young man, a few years Pál's senior. He tipped his peaked cap.

"Headed to Kuszkol, then?" he asked.

"I am," said Pál.

"Ferenc," he said with his fingers pressed against his chest, as though he might bow or doff his cap. He did neither. After he drew out Pál's name he turned to me. "And are you his pa?"

"I am his brother-in-law," I said, offering my hand. The young soldier had a mannish grip.

"I see. Have you served before?"

"No," Pál said.

"My luck! But who does not love to instruct a virgin? Rest easy, son, Old Ferenc will take care of you." He squinted at Pál's black eye.

"Though it looks like you needed my protection last night." The young soldier winked and burst out laughing. Pál seemed to take the ribbing in good humor, and despite myself, I felt a flush of hope. This Ferenc might be a good companion for my boy. Easy-tempered. Close in age. I hoped this open-handed welcome did not conceal a rotten core.

"Have you served long?" I asked the young soldier.

"Long? Not as long as some, I suppose."

"Where have you been posted?"

"You know," Ferenc said. "Here and there."

"Perhaps I have been to one of those heres or theres," I said. When he did not elaborate, I asked, "Have you been to the front?"

"No, not the front proper. But my old lord had been."

"I see." At my side, Pál said nothing as he scrutinized his new comrade.

"This past year and three-quarters I assisted my lord in collecting taxes around Fonyód," Ferenc said.

"You were a tax collector?" Pál asked.

"You know," Ferenc said. "Beggaring farmers. Threatening to seize their cattle if they do not pay up."

"There is no shame in that," I said. "I am sure you have some tales to tell."

"Oh, aye. One would be surprised at the trickery some employ to avoid paying their dues. I learned to always check the butter churn for spare coin, and if not there, a goodwife's bonnet."

I nodded. He was rather uncomplicated, I thought. Not overwise to the world. Perhaps just the sort of friend Pál needed.

I searched the plaza for the rest of the party.

"Say," Ferenc said. "Have you heard what they say of this Kuszkol to which we travel? It has a rather freakish reputation."

"To which you and Pál travel," I corrected him. "I know very little. It has been abandoned for many years."

"Sixty, I hear," he said.

"I heard the same."

"They say a ghost walks its parapets."

"A ghost?" Pál asked.

I shook my head. "That is just an old story."

"But there must have been a reason it was deserted," Ferenc said.

"There are ruins all over this country," I said. "Most abandoned by those who died long ago. It is impossible for us to know the minds of the dead."

"Not a few have shared their secrets."

"Not a few who?"

"Not a few of the dead," Ferenc said. "Come back from the grave to share their secrets. To prowl their old haunts."

I thought Ferenc must be making a poor attempt at jest, yet he seemed suddenly rather somber. I scanned the plaza again. "This looks like your leader," I said.

They turned to the knight who was striding towards us. Taller than me, wider, but perhaps no younger. His graying temples interrupted the dark of his beard and hair. He wore a black cloak over his mail.

Of the knight I knew a little. I understood Kálmán Kustyer to have roots in the region to which we traveled. I knew he was either a wandering agent or a scholar whose affairs had taken him well beyond our borders. I knew better his father Kázmér—a battle-scarred veteran who stalked the periphery of the king's court like a lean wolf. Kázmér Kustyer had recently taken up lordship of Kuszkol and had spent the last nine months rehabilitating the keep.

"Ferenc," the knight said nodding. He stopped before Pál and took his measure. His face was closed like a fist. "And you are Pál."

"Yes, sir."

The knight continued studying my brother-in-law even as he addressed me. "You are not my last man."

"No, sir. I am Pál's brother-in-law."

He turned. "You are the messenger." His face remained unreadable but obviously he knew my story. "Why are you here?"

"To see the boy off. I will wait upon His Excellency once you are departed."

"Very well. We leave directly."

The knight left us to look after his horse. I thought to pull Pál aside, but Ferenc had begun again his discourse on the wiliness of taxpayers. After a minute Sir Kálmán exited with a stable boy who led a splendid Turkish palfrey, white with a high and curving neck. They were a rarity in Veszprém, though I had seen them often on my travels and had described them to Pál.

"Where is the last man?" Kálmán asked. "I was to have three men."

"We have not seen him, my lord," Ferenc said.

Sir Kálmán frowned and set about inspecting the tack. Pál stared at the horse mutely. His attention did not go unnoticed.

"He is fine, is he not?" Kálmán asked the boy.

I watched the two closely. Pál had never spoken to one so high born. "Yes, sir."

"His name is Kladivo. It means hammer in my mother's tongue. A sultan sat atop his great-great-grandsire. This girl seems keen on you. What do you call her?"

"Fejes."

The knight patted my horse's flank. He did not compliment her. He did not need to. He could see her quality.

"Do you know the ways of horses?" Kálmán asked.

"Yes, sir," Pál said. "I grew up with them."

Kálmán nodded, then placed a hand heavily on Pál's shoulder. He peered into the boy's eyes. Pál did well to not look away.

"I hope you are not a brawler," the knight said.

"No, sir," Pál said. "I received these injuries defending a maiden's honor."

I had to bite my tongue. Pál had not uttered a word to me about the reason for his beating, but I knew enough from his other fights to know how unlikely this explanation was.

I watched to see whether Kálmán accepted Pál's boast. The

knight did not speak for a long moment. He knew Pál lied, yet he did not show any sign of displeasure. Instead, he shook Pál heartily. "I am glad to hear of your gallantry, but now you must choose your battles more carefully. This body now serves one greater. You belong to the king."

"I am eager to serve."

"Where is the third man?" Kálmán asked. "You," he said, pointing at Ferenc. "Go into the barracks. If he is still abed, pull him out by the ear. You," he pointed at Pál. "Go into the mess hall. Haul him from the bench by his hair."

"Who should we ask for, sir?" Ferenc asked.

"He is called Jakab Kun."

Jakab. The name soured my mood like the spray of window-thrown slop. I knew a few Jakabs on the hill. The only one who was a soldier was that old wastrel so often assigned lowly tasks on account of his ill discipline.

"I am here," croaked the familiar voice from the direction of the barracks. A shadow separated from the wall and ambled stiffly to meet us. We watched the features of the veteran resolve in the weak light. He adjusted the strap of his dingy pack.

His eyes sat like pits in tired prune skin. They darted around and came to rest on me. They narrowed. Mine narrowed in reciprocated contempt.

"You were to muster at first light," Kálmán said.

"I beg your pardon, my lord. It is only the cook asked that I give the boys a hand with rounding up some piglets that had escaped the butcher's pen. Did you not hear the commotion? He said you would understand."

That was two men who lied to Kálmán in the span of five minutes. I was gratified to see the knight less inclined to let Jakab's invention pass. "Vetési promised me three able men," he said. "I have half a mind to leave you behind."

"I can only beg your pardon, sir," Jakab said. "But I think you will find I serve well enough. Been a soldier for over thirty years.

Tough as old leather. I even served under János Hunyadi at Nish. Almost lost my ear to black powder." He grinned and pushed forward a mangled lobe.

"You served under the king's father?" the knight asked.

"Aye, sir. A real gentle fellow, that one. He wreaked bloody hell on the Turk, but he looked after his men. Gave us each a taste of the spoils." He shrugged. "I have served well for years. Asked for little. Devoted my life in return."

"That may be so," Kálmán said. "But next time I will not be kept waiting. The quartermaster should have our provisions ready. Let us be on our way."

Pál touched Fejes's mane one last time before he began to trail the others.

"Pál," I said. "Let us make our farewell."

I do not know if he would have stopped if Kálmán had not said, "Go on."

Pál came back and stood before me. "Have you rehearsed your parting wisdom?" he asked.

"For what it is worth. Listen, Pál. I want you to heed your commanders. Do as Kálmán says and do it well. The same for Kuszkol's lord. If you are unsure, seek the advice of Ferenc. Never that scoundrel Jakab. Do not befriend him or think you can come to depend on him. He is loyal only to his vices. If he chooses to disdain you, then welcome his scorn. He may spread rumors about you. Behave yourself and your uprightness will be the best defense of your name."

His face grew troubled. He had probably hoped he could outrun his sister.

"I know you will do well," I said. "You may not yet feel like a man, but you are near enough, and I think you will make a fine one. A man molds himself. Keep faith with your masters and they will keep faith with you."

I was rambling. I stopped and took a last long look at my boy.

Annaka had never given me a son. I never asked her for one. She had given me Pál. I remembered the first day he arrived in my cottage after our wedding. A subdued child with sharp eyes and nose, like a falcon waiting upon the huntsman's glove. Wary, a little uncertain of his place. He had let go Annaka's hand only after she pushed him forward to peer into the empty bins and circuit the garden, gone to seed. Finally he clambered into the loft and called his sister up. I followed to find them crouched beneath the rafters as he asked her in a quiet, astonished voice if he would truly have the little space all to himself.

The years before had been hard for them. Annaka had cared for her little brother since their parents had fallen to plague. She had been fifteen, he three. They were the only survivors of a family of eight. She protected him when cousins grudgingly took them in and gave them a place in the cowshed.

In those early days, I would come home from my journeys and he would hop onto my knee to listen to my wild stories of clever foxes stealing letters that they might learn the king's news or as I read about Great Alexander's own fabulous travels. His sister would linger a few yards off, leaning against the post, listening and keeping half an eye on the steaming pot on the hearth. I never wanted more.

It was only years later that I tarried that final mile home. Pál was often as not away with his playmates, and when I stepped through the door I would find only her. A thin line where the pixie smile had faded.

"Do you ever feel that my sister has not left us?"

He spoke so cautiously. I laughed and reached out to brush the hair from his brow. "Little Colt!"

He recoiled. I let my hand drop, unsure what had earned his startled expression.

The men came tramping back to us. Ferenc held out a sack of rations for Pál to stow in his pack. Kálmán mounted his horse and said, "We are off." He nodded curtly to me and urged his horse forward.

The men hoisted their packs. I took Pál's hand. He was quick to pull away. He flashed a last bewildered glance at me before hurrying off to join the others.

I watched as they passed through the gate. The knight riding above them and ahead. The men already falling into a trudging gait. I waved as they began to descend the road. Only Jakab looked back and flashed a gesture I was hard-pressed not to return.

"András!" I turned to the voice and heavy footfalls. Father Lajos, the bishop's secretary, came running, flapping his hands at me.

"Father, is His Excellency ready to receive me?"

The red-cheeked cleric could not have run far, but his chest rose in panting breaths. "He is still abed, but he has prepared a letter for your delivery. You are to leave forthwith."

I took the envelope and tried to read the inscription in the weak light. "Kuszkol?"

"Yes, I believe you are to travel in the company of Lord Kustyer's son. Has he departed? Oh dear."

I stared at him stupidly, uncomprehending like one of those woodcutters in the old stories who finds a sack of gold in the woods.

"With Sir Kálmán? What business has His Excellency in Trencsén County?"

"I would not presume to speculate. I suggest you not do so either."

"Of course. But . . . did His Excellency leave any further instruction?"

"Yes," the cleric said. "He bids you not to dawdle. He will need you back in Buda by calends."

"Anything else?"

"He said also to tell you, 'Godspeed.'"

Three

Pál knew to hobble on in silence. That Kálmán would refuse him if he asked to rest and, worse, mark him for a weakling. That Ferenc and Jakab would bay like idiots if he spoke of his misery and wield it as a needle to prick him.

I would have gladly traded places with him and let him ride on Fejes's back, but it would not be right. I could only keep a close eye on the boy. I could only watch as he ground his teeth with every step. As he tried to hide his limp and the longing looks drawn out by the boggy ditches we passed. I guessed he wanted nothing more than to throw off his boots and plunge blistered feet into dirty water.

The others witnessed his suffering and did not spare him their mockery.

"I think our Little Colt has hurt his hoof," Ferenc said.

"Keep up, lad!" Jakab said. "Do you think those country girls are getting wet at the sight of you gimping? I have seen pregnant ewes with more swagger."

Pál laughed them off. To no avail. Their jeering continued. Kálmán ignored them until I called for a rest. The knight agreed, pretending it was not for the boy's benefit. We stopped at a crossroads where some farmers had left stumps that served as stools. Pál grimaced as he took a seat.

I crouched at his side. "Can you hear those waxwings? They are making such a fuss over those wild grapes. And look there to those harriers skimming the reeds. It seems more spring than autumn. The last warm days of the season."

"I suppose," he said.

"What think you of our journey so far?" I asked.

"The town of Pápa was less splendid than I expected."

"Is that so? Why say you that?"

"Its steeples and towers seemed rather near the ground."

"Pápa is not the seat of a bishopric," I said. "You cannot compare it to Veszprém."

"The women were no lovelier than back home."

"I have never noticed that."

"Ask me again when we get to Buda."

Jakab snorted. I lowered my voice. "We are not heading in that direction."

I took up a switch and traced our route in the dirt. I showed how we would come to the Duna, make the crossing, then continue northward into the mountainous uplands, following the course of the Nyitra and over to the Vág, up narrowing valleys until we arrived near the border of Moravia and Poland, all the way up in Trencsén County.

Pál said nothing.

"But where is Krakow on your map?" Ferenc asked. "Will we not see the domes of Constantinople?"

"Men like this messenger have never seen a Turk up close," Jakab said. "At the first sight of those devils, they slink off, clutching their messenger bags like dolls."

"You make much of your exploits against the enemy," I said, "yet I suspect you have no understanding of their kind."

"And you do?" Jakab asked. "Have you made such careful study from afar?"

"I have broken bread with a Turk."

I glanced at Pál to see if he remembered. A few years back, I had passed an evening in the company of the bey's messenger. When I had recounted this to Pál afterwards, the boy, still whiskerless then, had hung from my every word. The Turk had told me that they know of Great Alexander in the East. That they tell tales not found in my book or any other in Christendom.

"If that be so," Jakab said, "then you must be one perfidious bastard. Do you know how many good men I have seen butchered by those sons of bitches?"

"I recall our own countrymen butchering good men not so long ago," I responded.

"The rebellion we put down in Erdély last year?" Jakab asked. "That was bad business. Those fools should never have broken with the king. But, by God, even their rats were starving. A man can only be taxed so much."

"Enough." Kálmán's voice snapped like a whip through our squabbling. He spoke not as peacemaker. "We move on."

We moved on. I rode alongside Kálmán in silence, or sometimes a few horselengths ahead on my own, as the footmen bragged and taunted one another behind us.

Over the next few days, Pál's limp improved and his misery seemed somewhat alleviated by the conversation that grew between the men. I listened as Jakab told of the blood he had shed, the booty he had won and lost, and the misbegotten babes born in his wake. I gathered he had Cuman ancestry, but he said only of his own family that it had been so long since he had seen them that they would no longer recognize him. He was old for a soldier. I thought he must love the road little better than Pál, but he never fell behind. True to his word, the man was all leather.

Ferenc, whose achievements were few, told them about his childhood in Zala and the dovecote his grandfather had built next to a churchyard. Very seriously, he told them he had never once eaten the flesh of the birds raised there because they housed those restless spirits who were not content to lay beneath the clay until Judgment Day. How they warbled, to the attentive listener, of calamity and the Lord's harsh mercy.

I was grateful that neither asked about Pál's family.

It was only after we ferried across the Duna, I would say, that Pál truly began to understand that he had left home. Kálmán happened to speak to a passing soldier in the Slavic language, and I noticed how keenly the boy listened. In Veszprém, a few words of German might impress a merchant's daughter, but you need not speak other than the mother tongue. But we were nearing the Upper Country, where in the remoter corners, his ignorance could render him mute.

Pál was surprised to learn that I also knew the language, picked up on my years on the road. When we broke for lunch, I taught Pál a few sayings, like *som smädný*, which means "I am thirsty," and *na zdravie*, which means "To your health." Later, Jakab was happy to teach him the few oaths he knew—this was the first time Kálmán turned in his saddle since we left Veszprém, and his frown shut them up.

Pál became even more attentive when a troop of soldiers came down the road, marching in formation about a wagon draped in the device of our king. Kálmán called for us to stand aside. I told Pál that it hailed from the mint in Körmöcbánya, and that the chests were full of Upland gold. He craned his neck and watched it recede behind us until it was a speck on the horizon.

We entered Nyitra with a few hours of light remaining to us. We marched to the castle where Kálmán said, "We leave at daybreak." He then left us to pass his evening among the well-bred in their paneled halls.

We threw our packs down on the barrack floor with time on our hands.

"Pál," I said, "Remember I told you my mother named me for Saint András Zoerard? His bones rest in the cathedral. Come with me to see his shrine."

"I ought to rest," he said.

"It is not far. Come with me. Let us have a little excursion."

"Run along to church, lad," Jakab said. "Unless you care to join me. I am off to sample the vinegar."

Pál nodded and the three of them set off for the mess.

I wearied of Ferenc's timidity and of Jakab's nasty smell, but I found myself trailing behind them. The mess was full of twitchy and melancholic men who not so long ago Pál would have avoided. We found a spot near the wall and settled down to drink.

Halfway through our first cup of wine, Ferenc had already grown sullen, "I do not understand why we even need garrison Kuszkol."

"We are at war with Bohemia," Jakab said. "Perhaps you have heard."

"Are there Turks in Bohemia?" Ferenc asked. "Surely the threat from our southern border is greater. From what I hear, our own king started this fight."

"Keep your voice down, lad," Jakab laughed. "You must not second guess the wisdom of your masters so volubly."

"These Hussites in Bohemia are heretics," I said. "Through our king's mercy we hope to save their wayward souls."

"Heretics. What does that even mean? Are they not Christian men?"

"Aye," I said. "But they pervert the faith."

I was surprised when Pál spoke up. "The Hussite claims it should not be the priest alone who consumes our Savior's blood during the Eucharist. That the chalice be raised by all parishioners alongside the host." He had come by this knowledge from Annaka, no doubt.

Ferenc sipped his wine as he pondered this. The veteran stretched beside him. "I hope we are not going to talk salvation all night."

"It seems to me," Ferenc said, "that there is a certain balance to the Hussite's thinking. Their error seems not so grave."

"But it is," Jakab said. "The Holy Father says so."

"That may be," Ferenc said, "but have we not more fearful

enemies? The Hussites may have become muddled, but surely the German Emperor can correct then. A little Bohemian queerness seems a small threat next to an Osmanian siege engine, and it is our walls the Turks will scale next."

"You will hear no argument from me," Jakab said.

"I have heard it said that even the bishops are urging the king to turn his forces south. That his counsellors argued this past autumn—"

"You have made your point," I said, glancing at Pál as I did. "But as Jakab says, there is perhaps little profit in voicing your doubts so frankly. Or in spreading such wild rumors."

"All wars are fought for the spoils that might be prized from the fingers of the dead," Pál muttered.

"Ha!" Jakab thumped the table. "The greenhorn speaks the best sense of all." He turned to the Zalaman. "I think you are unnerved about Kuszkol's reputation. Do you honest to God believe in ghosts?"

"If you had seen how my grandfather's doves fell silent at every funeral," Ferenc said, "you would not doubt the dead are watching us."

"Then why did you volunteer for a posting at Kuszkol?"

Ferenc dropped his head. "I did not."

"I see," Jakab said. "Well, I am sure those old stories are worthless. You know how soldiers like to talk when the sun goes down. Too much idle chatter, always expounding on events far removed and decisions beyond our ken. Like why the powers that be should have left a border fort like Kuszkol sitting empty for sixty years. No wonder the Up Country was left overrun for so long. It just seems like the place must be peculiar in some way. Who is to say?"

"What exactly do they say about Kuszkol?" Ferenc asked.

"They are just old stories," I said.

Jakab carried on as if I had not spoken. "There are different accounts, depending on the company one is keeping. The one I know best is told in the mess." Jakab looked about him as if to spot eavesdroppers, then continued in a low voice. "The story goes the last commander there went mad."

"Mad? Then we have nothing to worry about," Pál said. "If old Kustyer is anything like his son, I cannot imagine him letting a day pass without saying his prayers, let alone allowing his sanity to stray."

Jakab shrugged. "Maybe. Kuszkol is situated in a wild, wild place. High in the mountains. They say that when the snow piles thick and the air grows still, even the birds are loathe to fly lest their flapping disturb the mountain's peace. Imagine the vastness of that place, way up high in the sky. Totally silent. And cold."

"And perchance ghost-ridden?" Pál asked.

I sipped my wine and held my peace. These men were Pál's comrades now. Perhaps it was for the best that this fellowship grow.

"Oh, there is a ghost, boy," Jakab said. "The story goes that the last lord of the place took to his bed and did not leave his quarters for days. His men understood him to have a fever. Maybe it started that way, but lying there, shivering beneath his quilts, watching the shadows creep along the wall, he noticed one day that the shadow at the end of his bed did not dispel when the morning came. He knew the shadow well for it was his own. The shadow told him what to do."

Jakab raised his hand to preempt another interruption from Pál. Ferenc leaned forward on his elbow and asked, very seriously, "What did the shadow tell him?"

"He said this lord must rid the mountain of his men. That only he was welcome. So, the lord rises from his bed, tells the men all is well. Then he goes to his captain, in all confidence, and tells him to keep an eye on so-and-so, because the man has been stealing rations. Then he goes to so-and-so's lieutenant and says that there are rats in the storeroom, so get so-and-so to clean it out. When the captain, who thinks that so-and-so is a thief, finds him removing whole baskets from the stores, he clobbers the poor bugger! On and on it goes, the commander issuing orders and counterorders, spreading lies. All so he can divide the men from one another. He tells one

György that Gyula cheats at dice and to keep an eye on him. He tells Gyula that György is an imperial spy and to keep an eye on him. Then he starts to mete out little punishments. He tells the men who were repairing shingles they were lax so commands them to work through the night. He places a dead chicken in the cistern, then decries the water is poisoned and has the men replenish every drop.

"What common soldiers do not understand is that our betters stack our effort and allegiances one atop each other, like a tower. When the wrong man buckles, the whole house comes down."

"I should think few of our betters are so fastidious," I said.

"I beg your pardon, friend," Jakab said. "Are you telling this tale, or am I? And what do you know about it? I speak of the army, not your messenger corps. I speak of the front, where real men stare down death every day. Now, as I was saying, this lord was a master builder, though a demented one. Finally, he nudges the men just so, and the men fall upon one another. So-and-so is beaten to within an inch of his life. So-and-so's mates answer with knives. The place goes whoosh, like tinder. Order disappears. Factions form and fracture. Men begin to stalk one another through the halls and galleys. Others desert. Word must have gotten out, because the Lord of Lednic finally sent a troop in to clean out the whole rotten lot."

Ferenc gripped his tankard's handle. I found this little game tedious, but Pál leaned back on his stool so the Zalaman could not see him smile. Jakab kneaded Ferenc like dough.

"Now that is just one story," Jakab continued. "In the officer's mess, they tell a different account over their dumplings and jam. They say that Kuszkol's shadows began to walk among the common men first. Each one hounded by his own shade, whispering madness into his ear. You can imagine what happened next." He lowered his voice another notch. "Mutiny. The officers that survived the initial treachery retreated to the keep, where they held out for a time. Eventually the men found a way in, but not before the commander managed to light the beacon. In this version, too, Lednic sent a troop to wipe the men out."

Jakab dabbed at a crumb and licked it off his fingertip. When he turned to wink at Pál, the boy had to feign a cough to mask his hilarity.

"This is bad," Ferenc said. "We will not survive the winter."

"How is this?" Jakab asked. "I told you, this is just old gossip, lad! You cannot let a few tall tales fuss you. I did not think you would become upset."

"This is just a silly tale," I said. "There is no reason to be frightened."

"The messenger is right," Jakab said. "Besides, if you think the stories about Kuszkol are bad, you should hear about his wife."

"His wife?" Ferenc swung his face toward me. "How could your wife compare to that?"

I returned his steady gaze.

"Go on, Pál," Jakab said. "Tell Ferenc about your sister."

"She has nothing to do with Kuszkol," Pál said, his shoulders sagging.

"Well, no, not Kuszkol," Jakab said, "but her story is no less horrific, from what I hear."

Jakab had toyed with Ferenc's gullibility, and now he made cruel sport of Pál's and my misfortune. I rose from the bench. "Come, Pál. Let us go."

"What is he talking about?" Ferenc said.

"Tell him, boy," Jakab urged. "There may come a day when we need to put our lives in each other's hands. We must have perfect trust."

"I have nothing to say about her."

"What is it?" Ferenc asked. "Did she see a ghost?"

Jakab gripped Pál's wrist and said, "You cannot keep secrets from your brothers, lad. I understand your reluctance, but if your comrades find out you have not been forthright, well, they might just figure you are a touch tricksy yourself."

I placed a hand on Pál's shoulder. He made no move to join me. The firelight gleamed from the clay cup between his fingers. It seemed the hall had grown more hushed, that all those bored and tired men listened.

"They say she was a witch," Pál said.

"A what?"

"They had to burn her," Jakab said. "Is that not so?"

I found I could not speak. Not once since I lost her had anyone dared speak so brazenly about Annaka. Beside me, Pál tried and failed to smile. "She was never tried," he said. "She died in a fire in her cell."

"Is this a joke?" Ferenc asked. He found the truth about Annaka harder to believe than Jakab's stories.

"Not a good one," Pál said. "They made a mistake."

"They say witches are compacted with Lucifer."

"Enough," I said. I felt too sick to say more.

"No one accused my sister of being a good Christian," Pál said, "but she was compacted to no devil. People came to her to have their fortunes told. That is all."

"And no doubt to hex their enemies," Ferenc said.

"No," Pál said. "Before they turned on her, our neighbors would sometimes ask her blessing."

"She blessed them?" Ferenc asked. "Did she fancy herself a saint?"

"It was a terrible mistake," I said. "My wife told people what they wanted to hear so they would leave her alone."

Ferenc turned to Jakab. "You knew and did not think to tell me?"

"It was not my tale to tell."

Ferenc set the cups rattling when he stood. He glared at me and Pál in turn before marching out of the mess hall.

"Never mind him," Jakab said, patting Pál's arm. "That boy is a sniveling coward. He will not last in the army. Not a fraction of the time I have served."

"Come, Pál." I stepped away from the table. "Jakab trifles with you."

Pál did not even look at me. "Why the hell did you tell him about my sister?"

"Easy, boy," Jakab said. "I do not take kindly to having another bark in my face. I swear, I did not know he would react like that. Forget that spineless dupe."

"Pál."

"I meant it when I said we must not keep secrets from one another," Jakab said. "The truth is like the threshing floor. It might damage the stalk, but there is no quicker way to separate wheat from chaff. Ferenc will be a false comrade. Now you know."

"Pál," I said. "Let us go."

He continued to glare at the veteran as if I had not spoken.

"Look at you!" Jakab said to him. "You are full of piss. Good. Listen, this swill is as sour as your face. Let us find a real winehouse. Do you play dice? Not half as well as I do, I bet. Let us find a game."

"Pál, this scoundrel means you only ill."

Jakab finally acknowledged me. "That is no way to speak of a friend."

The boy muttered. "I can handle myself."

"Come on, then, lad!" Jakab said. "When I first saw that shiner of yours, I thought I was dealing with a man. Was I wrong? Are you just another little girl like that Zalan puss?"

"I am no puss."

Jakab stood. "Then unglue your ass from that bench, boy. It is high time we pried wide this town's pleasures."

When Pál finally limped from the mess, it was not by my side.

Four

I ROSE and shut my eyes, piling hair up off my neck that the breeze might touch the trickling sweat. I needed to stretch, to cast off the aches of crouching and scrubbing and murdering stains with that paddle. Oh, that I were born to swing a morning star! To blow holes in others by hand cannon with such a magnificent crack. I stretched, knowing the eyes of boys were on me, those scamps who ogled from the line of elderberry, who gathered every glimpse of knee and skirt-hugging bend like fatwood to ignite their night fevers. I let them be. I let them think I stretched for them, they were just children. I let ugly Borbála think it too, the untouched cow, whose paddle sped that she might tut-tut in time, as she squatted on her rock, her damp finger creeping to scratch at fleas that crawled beneath her braids. There was a hawk wheeling. There were salamanders wriggling through the pebbles near my feet, fronds waving from their heads like the plumes of knights. The life of that stream was short but dear to me. It rose in the hills, it rushed to its annihilation in the shimmering lake, so near. But there were other streams and it was in those others where I dreamt I steeped my feet. I dreamt of those streams like you dreamt of doorsteps between trees and the paths beyond, deer tracks to empires, the affairs of sultans and popes rattling in your bag. Like your dream of the wandering king who rambled in conquest beyond life's edges, to its beginning or its end, whose beloved never saw home again.

I dreamt these streams would free me. No despair, none, I deny it now and then and when I dreamt your dream. I dreamt your dream would free me. I dreamt your dream to be.

Five

I awoke short of breath. My mind full of bright-edged shadows, my feet so heavy I thought they were bound. I could not remember why. I knew only that the scowl I wore upon rousing was another shadow thrown from the wild lights that had dazzled and infuriated me through the night. That I scowled for the same reason my tongue tasted of imprecation, like I had spent the wakeless hours spitting from another's mouth.

The dreams came first, during those first months following Annaka's death, when I would awake in a sweat, groping at the empty expanse beside me, at the pillow from which she used to watch me fall asleep. Only later came the stray thoughts, and worse, the stray words.

I once asked Pál if he heard me talking in my sleep. He stopped mending his shirt, torn in his latest brawl, and lost himself in the cracks in the tabletop. "I do not know."

"I think you heard. What things did I say?"

One of his new tempers seized him. He rose without leave or farewell and quit our house for the day.

My first coherent thought that morning in Nyitra was that I

must ask again. I rose in the dim hall, strange men sleeping on all sides of me, to seek him out. I found him at the end of the line of pallets. He snored beside Jakab. Neither had taken off their boots when they had finally staggered in. I took the oxblood stain in Jakab's beard to be vomit. Pál drooled from a fish-wide mouth.

Pál was not a horse. He was not Fejes. I knew not how much rein to give, or if it was even possible for me to guide him. That peevish ne'er-do-well Jakab had humiliated Pál as much as myself in the mess hall, and yet my brother-in-law chose to make merry with his insulter.

Worse than any hurt this caused me, I was concerned. Pál would be slow to rise this morning. His head would ache. God forbid he should complain. Before now he had tarried because of weary feet. That was pardonable even if it inspired no mercy. To delay because of the wine fever, though, would only provoke Sir Kálmán's wrath.

Perhaps I should have hauled him up and dunked his head in a basin of water, but instead I walked away. I checked my satchel, broke my fast. I visited the stable and flipped through my Alexandrine and remembered how it felt in my hands that first time Father Péter had exchanged it for a Bible through which I had been struggling. The weightless heft to it. Like the wind that always threatened in those days to blow me over the horizon. A memory all my own.

I sat and twiddled my wife's ring until I judged by how the light fell slantwise across the pavement that enough time had lapsed. I returned to my companions and found I had missed the worst of it. Pál and Jakab stood blearily before Kálmán. At least Pál had the decency to hang his head. Jakab scowled miserably and shuffled as if he needed to run to the privy. As for Ferenc, he stood apart from the other two. Full of watchful reproach.

". . . our king. He demands not perfection, only perfect loyalty."

The knight paused to glare at the men.

"Only perfect devotion to his mission as the eastern bulwark of Christendom. You stand in his stead where he cannot. *You may not falter.*"

The knight fancied himself more priest than warrior, I thought. He believed he was an equal on matters of ritual.

I shook my head to clear the stray thought.

"I will not hear again that you have missed the reveille. If I hear of this, I will dock you a month's pay."

But to hear the knight speak to my boy, this self-deceiver, this deluded seeker who did not return from Jerusalem empty-headed, who sat up with those dusty anchorites, those proud sons of Szaladin, those few inheritors of Salamon who know the true history of the Flood that he might secure the secret he carried, to hear this featherless peacock utter ultimatums to my boy flooded my veins with bile.

"I will not hear again that you have touched wine until Advent's end. If I hear of this, you will touch no more until Easter."

Yet how was Pál to learn if not corrected? Pál must learn that throwing his lot in with the veteran would bring him grief. He would amount to nothing good if he did not learn to serve.

"I will not hear again you have played dice for the rest of our journey. If I hear of this, your first days at Kuszkol will be spent in the pillory."

But this ghoul, this worker of strange devices . . . no. Stray thoughts. I swooned before their onslaught. I pinched my nose and squeezed my eyes to drive them from my mind. Woe to me should the voice escape.

"I will not be lenient."

For the voice had such will. I bit my lip to stifle the words that rolled inside my cheeks, that buzzed like wasps upon my tongue, that buffeted against my teeth that I might let them fly and let them sink their sting. I clutched my fist on nothing and I ground my teeth lest I say anything but, "Sir Kálmán."

He broke off his reprimand and turned to me. "What is it, man?"

"I have seen to the horses," I said. "They are ready to go."

Pál was a puzzle I knew not how to solve. I had chafed at Annaka's hectoring that we foist ambition upon the boy. I had said a man must find his own place in the world. But now Pál was in the world, and I feared he knew not where to begin his search. Maybe he could not until we parted. Maybe he lacked the wisdom, or worse, the will.

I did not know. I was no model for him. I was still a child when I began to find my own place. Almost by accident, I crossed a threshold. I was small, perhaps six years old. My mother had brought my sisters and me to gather firewood in the forest. I was a poor worker and had grown deaf to my mother's admonishments and my sisters' challenges to make a game of gathering the most. I turned over stones and picked lichen from logs. I sulked, longing to return to our hovel where I might drag my toy horse through the same dust again.

Then one day I noticed the lay of those woods. Two beech trees, a little way from where we foraged, stood a yard apart. It struck me how their straight boles rose like doorposts. How their roots crossed like a doorsill. The trees formed a doorway, and a powerful question became suddenly lodged in my breast. What lay beyond?

So I passed between the beech trees, and what lay beyond was the forest. The same green roof, the same carpet of fallen leaves and fissured boulders with mossy caps. Indistinguishable from the glade from which I had wandered. Yet this discovery did not disappoint me. It beguiled me, rather, and so I pressed on. This was the first time I became lost.

When I finally heard my sisters' voices, when they passed me between their embraces and pinched my cheek, I shared none of their relief. All I thought as I gazed over their shoulders was that a threshold lay between any two trees, that no matter in which direction I walked, I would tread upon a path. From that day onward, I wandered.

I skirted my chores whenever I could. I felt no duty to help my mother feed us. Instead, I disappeared, sometimes not returning until the next day, dew-soaked and shivering. I followed deer tracks and streams and gullies. I would seek new vistas over new hills and new faces in new towns.

Other boys would grow up to be expert with the lathe or the plow, the mallet or the sickle. But even from that young age I understood that my tools would be different. My guarantees must be the clouds and birds, and what they foretold about the morrow's weather. My guarantees must be the stars, and what they told about the course I had set.

I learned other things, too. I never had want for company, for I found the world was full of people. As I never begged, strangers were glad to answer my questions. Thus, after a summer of speaking with the sexton in a neighboring town, I earned my first soup for carrying a message from the church to the gristmill. I became known as the message boy, and soon I was bringing home heels of bread.

It was one of my early patrons, Father Péter, an old parish priest with a palsied hand, who thought to teach me my letters. At first he wanted me simply to draft his notes, but soon he thought I might be more useful if I could pair sense to the letters I was mastering. In this way I came to know Latin. As his eyes dimmed, I began to read to him the scriptures. At the end of each reading he never tasked me to meditate upon the verse, but instead told me tales of his own boyhood in the monastery that these lines had stirred, a beginning now so much harder to imagine as he neared the road's end.

But his favorite tales, and mine, were the stories I read from his prized possession—a slim volume recounting the exploits of Alexander Magnus. I would read a page, whether on Nagy Sándor's encounters with the men who bore the faces of beasts, or his building of the iron gates to hold back Góg and Magóg, and afterwards we would marvel at the vastness of God's creation and how clever and gracious was that bravest of kings.

The passage we returned to more than any other, however, hinted at his fallibility. The account of Nagy Sándor's travels through the Land of Darkness, whose shadows concealed the Water of Life.

The king never found that fountain, and of all the lands he visited, this darkened country was the only one he did not conquer.

"See how in the pages that follow his disappointments mount," Father Péter said. "It is after this he falls short of reaching either the heavens or the bottom of the sea. Among these failures, his beloved Bukephalosz dies, and there was naught Sándor could think to do but return to Babylon to die himself."

I sat, a shoeless boy, chin cupped in hand, beside the stooped preacher in companionable silence. "He had ridden as far as pride might take him," I said.

Father Péter nodded, for I had absorbed the lesson. "Even in his youth, his pride was marked. Indeed, there is another story not found in this book wherein a famous wise man of that age tried to instruct Sándor of pride's limits. This was before Sándor left Greece, when he was already flush with triumph and beloved by all for his charity. He came to stand before this wise man, who was old like me and who was enjoying the October sun, and he proclaimed himself and said, 'Great sage, name what you would have of me and you shall have it.' Imagine this offer, from the mouth of a king. And this wise man, who wore the drab rags of a mendicant, said, 'I would that you move out of my light.'"

Father Péter grunted. "Every one of us is as flawed for we are each born a sinner. Sándor was not perfect, but even so he was as virtuous a man as could be found in his pagan times. Outside the pages of the Bible, there is no better model for living."

Father Péter fell into thought, staring into a corner whose depth his cloudy eyes had ceased penetrating long ago. Even when scrutinizing man's foibles, he managed to give encouragement. The priest was incapable of malice. I first realized this about my benefactor on that long-ago day. Perhaps that is why I asked the question I had dared not ask before. "Do you think I might one day become great like Sándor?"

He smiled, as though he had been awaiting the question, and reached out and pat my head. "Oh, my dear little wanderer.

Alexander is a fine example, but you must not mistake me when I say you will never be great. You are a peasant boy, and though Christ loves you as well as any prince, the judgment of mortal men will never be as kind. Your place is a step below the great. That does not mean you can never share in their glory. Be faithful to your sire, and you will find your place in your master's affections. Serve faithfully, and he may love you as well as his own pampered son."

I was a twelve-year-old boy and had fancied that my itinerant ways possessed some grain of nobility that was out of others' reach. Maybe those boys who trained to become plowmen and smiths found no fault in their future lives of obscurity, but to be told I would amount to nothing more was a hard lesson. "No songs are sung of simple folk," I said glumly.

"No, none worth singing. But what good is a song? Think of those faithful sons of Macedon who followed their king to the ends of the earth. They served well and they shared their king's splendor. They wore gleaming mail, ruby brooches and partook of the finest morsels from his table. Forget not that they were at his side when Sándor saw all those sights no civilized man had seen before. They beheld those same sights themselves. Think, too, of lowly Bukephalosz. Just a horse, you might say, but did Sándor love any creature better? That creature carried a king upon its back."

Weeks after this conversation Father Péter nodded off to sleep for a final time. I did not learn of his death until after he was placed in the dirt. Kneeling in the churchyard, tears dripping from my cheeks, the deacon laid a hand upon my shoulder and pressed into my hands the priest's bequest. The book I still carry with me.

After my tutelage under Father Péter, I wandered further afield. I met more folk who were willing to give me a meal or more often a coin, until one day I traveled beyond our hills and discovered the plain at the heart of our country. An endless field that knows no fence or border. The grassland that ripples beneath the shifting Pannonian sky. Gazing outward, gazing eastward, I thought of priest and king both.

Even then, I found my way back home. I fed myself and I helped to feed my family. Still, my wandering never sat well with my mother. She could not accept that for me the day's bread was an afterthought. She said I put too much faith in luck, that there would be a day when I would go forever astray. I did not believe her. For every path leads, inevitably, to some other place. There is no luck in that.

Six

Beyond Nyitra, we lost the sun behind early winter clouds and became accustomed to riding through sleet and rain. The forest had swallowed the road and reared above us. It was nothing to me. Neither drought nor blizzard has ever slowed me, but a gray malaise hovered over us, threatening our spirits. It was not just the weather and the knight's discipline.

For a time, I rode at Kálmán's side. I thought it best to hear every word he spoke to the men. These were few indeed. The men's banter also flagged. Whenever I turned to look at them, Jakab glared while the others never bothered to acknowledge me. Not for the first time, I wondered if I had trapped Pál by securing him this post. I had thought the knight could be a good master for him, but some men were tyrants.

"Do you think you will have a quiet winter?" I asked Kálmán.

"We travel to a place of quiet."

"Have you been there before?"

"My family holds land in that valley. It has profited us little for long years."

"But of course. Your father holds command of Kuszkol. You must know it well."

Kálmán's smile cast no light. "I have visited twice before," he said. "Once as a young man. Once again last winter."

"What did you find?"

"An empty fortress." He then addressed me in the language of those parts. "You speak my mother's tongue well," he said.

"I speak a bit of everything," I answered in kind. "I have traveled across the king's realm and some ways beyond it."

I could not tell if Kálmán nodded, or if his head merely moved with the motion of Kladivo beneath him. I could tell the men behind us were straining to listen.

"They are fine people hereabouts," I continued in the tongue of that hinterland.

His lips moved beneath his beard. "Tell that to the Saxons at court."

"I have noticed how . . . what is the word . . . taciturn some of the local folk become when you tell them we are bound for Kuszkol."

"It has an evil reputation. You must know this."

"I have heard stories."

He shrugged. "When God loves a country so well it is only right that men live in fear."

"I have heard it said that you have traveled to the Holy Land."

Kálmán turned to me. Perhaps I had finally bested his patience.

"Yes," he said.

"You must have heard stranger tales than what they tell of Kuszkol."

The knight said nothing.

"Did you travel overland or by sea?" I asked.

"Sea. I set out from Syracuse, to Crete, to Cyprus, then down the coast of the Levant. Why do you ask?"

"I enjoy hearing when others tell of their travels, that is all."

"Then I will tell you that the Holy Land is depraved. The work of the Crusaders has been undone. A few Christians still huddle in their churches, their worship more alike the Greeks' than the Romans'. But it gives less heart than one might suppose to see the cross in that land where the True Cross was raised. Those churches are flickering candles in the darkness."

"You describe a ruder country than I imagined. I am surprised you found it so benighted. It was great even before the coming of Rome."

Kálmán looked at me quizzically. "Before Rome?"

"I know that Alexander conquered those lands. And far past them too, far past Babylon, all the way to the banks of the Indus."

Kálmán laughed. "Alexander Magnus. That was a pagan king."

"A pagan, yes," I said, "but enlightened. He planted the wisdom of the Greeks everywhere on his eastward journey even as he learned the secrets of the magi and the gymnosophists."

"You mistake wisdom with error. You speak of a time before the Holy Spirit's descent on Pentecost."

"I suppose. I thought perhaps you might admire him, since you have traveled so far."

"I concede, there is some wisdom in the East. And perhaps those wonders they say Alexander discovered are to be found, somewhere beyond Chaldea, where I have never ventured. But wonders are worthless if they are the works of Lucifer. Less than nothing next to the good news of the gospel. The only miracles that interest me are those performed by our Savior and our blessed saints."

"I do not disagree," I said, though certainly I did.

"I may have spoken intemperately. I know your master is much interested in what the Greeks have to teach us. I do not question the wisdom of His Excellency. He is a learned man."

"He is a fine master." When Sir Kálmán did not respond, I said, "I came to his service when I was twenty-five. I knew some irregular years before that, but I have given him no cause for complaint since." I furrowed my brow. Best I forge ahead lest he think on Annaka. "The boy," I gestured over my soldier. "This is all new to him. He is good-hearted."

"He is a soldier now. He is not irredeemable. Tell me, messenger, why are you here?"

"To assure you he is no rascal. If he has stumbled, then know the blame is mine. I have been lax in my discipline, but he can learn."

"I ask why you have you joined my party."

He faced forward again. "You know already I have a letter to deliver."

"You are His Excellency's agent."

"Less than that," I said. "Surely less."

"He sends you only to give his regards to my father?"

"I do not know the content of his letter. He does not discuss his mind with me."

"They are old friends, my father and your master," Kálmán said.

So I knew well. The elder Kustyer was one of my master's most regular correspondents. "Is that so? Then you must know my master better than I do."

"That may be so," he said, switching to the common tongue for all to hear.

We rode in silence after that.

All of us were bowed beneath a skin of ice. It was another day and a half to our destination. For the rest of this day we were to climb, up to the crest of a ridge from the valley bottom.

We ascended the tangle-root path. Jakab made use of a staff to punt himself up and both Kálmán and I dismounted to guide our horses by hand. When Kladivo lost his footing and nearly lodged his hoof in the stone, the knight's face grew grayer than the sky. When finally we reached the level road cutting across the hillside, Kálmán said we would seek shelter and wait out the storm.

Sunset was not far off and the promise of hot drink and rafters from which to hang our hose and glazed cloaks spurred us forward.

We cleared the trees and came upon a great farmhouse. Woodsmoke whipped from the chimney and the broad doorstep that remained miraculously dry beneath the eaves' generous dripline. I could sense the others' desperation to find shelter within. Even so, we approached cautiously. A strange fringe hung from those eaves like globs of fat. Not fat, decorations, encased in ice like the peaks of our hoods.

"What the hell are those?" Jakab asked for all of us.

"Charms," Ferenc said sullenly. "The Feast of Saint Lúcia is but days away. The darkest night of the year, when witches are said to prowl."

Kálmán handed Pál his reins and stepped forward to rattle the door handle. When it did not yield, he pounded. His knuckles rapped next to a garlic braid.

After a spell the owner opened the door. An immovable freeman, broad of brow, neck and belly. He glanced at our party, which had pressed itself into the wall's lee, and made no move to step aside. Kálmán addressed him in their mountain tongue. I studied the talismans above my head as the knight explained our need for shelter. Dried bouquets of goldenrod and yarrow, I thought. Tatty mugwort wreaths and undyed yarn that I guessed were meant to entangle forest imps. The smell of fire-turned meat drew a growl from my stomach. I listened as the knight spoke soothingly, his inbred authority pitched to inspire rather than to cajole.

"No."

Kálmán stood blankly before the unexpected denial. The freeman crossed his arms.

"We but ask for a place near your fire. Somewhere to dry out, to wait out this storm." Kálmán gestured at the wind. "I will compensate you."

"Have the Bohemians crossed the border?" the man asked.

"The border?" Kálmán said. "No, what have you heard?"

"As I thought. You are headed to *Kuszkol*." The man snarled the name as though it belonged to his blood enemy.

Kálmán was taken aback. Few, I am sure, ever dared speak to him so dismissively. Beside me, the veteran edged closer, his grizzled head tilted as he tried to follow the conversation.

"From Kuszkol we will bring some order to these valleys," the knight said.

The farmer grew sterner. "That mountain was forsaken with good cause!" His jowls quivered as he spoke. "What use is there in rousing it now?"

When the knight pressed his palms together and shifted to conciliation, I knew it was hopeless. This tree stump of a backwoodsman was not going to share his hearth with us willingly.

I wondered if the knight would insist. But his countenance did not turn steely. I remarked the restless shifting of the other men as they read the situation as I.

"What about his stable?" Pál blurted.

Kálmán's sideway glance could have pinned him to the wall. I placed a hand on my brother-in-law's arm and muttered, "Shush."

"We cannot stay out in this weather," Pál said. "Ask about his stable."

The freeman sized the boy up and switched to the mother tongue for all to understand. "No, no, no!"

Kálmán spread his hands. The peasant stepped back into the warmth and began to close the door. "Will you not reconsider?"

The door shut in the knight's face.

Kálmán snatched the reins from Pál's fingers and marched back into the frozen onslaught. The boy was stunned, not so much at Kálmán's treatment of him, I thought, but that the knight had not commandeered the place. He opened his mouth and I could see he would give voice to some foolishness. *What good was being a lord if one could not take whatever one pleased?* I squeezed his elbow to forestall the question.

We had no choice but to continue. All concern for comfort was set aside as we pushed, pulled and pleaded with the horses to climb the treacherous path. We slipped. We slid. The men swore oaths and were reprimanded for using the Lord's name in vain. Even I found it awful. But when the forest began to fill with gloom and there seemed to be no end in sight and I began to wonder whether I could manage to build a fire, the road improved. "We are close," Kálmán said, and so the men found the reserves to forge on. Shortly after this, the trees cleared again and we could see we had risen to a saddle between two summits. Below us a dark valley and, black against an ashen horizon, another ridge. The lookout stood stolidly before us, a squat building that might be called a tower if the attic in its pointed roof counted as a second story. Its windows were as lightless as the space between the trees.

We entered. It smelled as though many a shepherd had sheltered his flock inside. When I got a fire lit, we saw this was the case. Jakab and Ferenc kicked desiccated muck out the door as I tended the fire and Kálmán muttered about dereliction in disgust.

I took Pál with me to settle the horses in a stable set between the back of the tower and a great swaying fir. The stable was breezy but its four walls still stood. We wound grass into knots and stuffed the largest holes about the doorframe.

"How are you?" I finally asked.

"Cold." With another word, this would be the longest exchange we would have had since Nyitra.

"You will be warm tonight."

"I could have been warm two hours ago," Pál said.

I ignored this. "By this time tomorrow you will be safely tucked away in Kuszkol. It is just on the next ridge. If it were better weather we might see the torches on its watch towers."

He stuffed another hole with wound grass.

"The horses will be fine tonight," I said.

"Why would the farmer not lodge us?"

"That man . . . he was an ingrate, was he not?"

"Why?"

"Why? The people of these valleys are not much pleased with the king. They do not approve of the re-garrisoning of Kuszkol. They think it better to let the fortress crumble to dust." Pál's look was such that I felt the need to continue. "You must understand it is a delicate matter. Kuszkol is fed and provisioned by the folk of these valleys.

Most are willing to transact with the king's men, even if they disapprove. Some are not."

"The king is the king," he said.

"He is, yet he must exercise caution, and even more so his men. All these wars. He is leaning hard enough on the little folk. It does no good to provoke them further. Kuszkol inspires strong feelings."

"Because of its reputation," Pál said.

"It is a strange history, though misremembered, I do not doubt. There was once a town there. You know the stories by now. But they are just daft old tales. Phantoms do not haunt these mountains. There is no such thing as a ghost."

He found this declaration less than adequate. "Is there not?"

"No. Have you ever seen a restless spirit? I have not."

He looked away.

"Regardless," I said. "It is the king's land and it is his right to use it. There is a war, after all."

"The border," he said.

"It is less about defense than about the cost of war." I took his silence to mean he did not understand. "The king faces threats on all sides. If it is not the Sultan in Bulgaria, it is the Emperor in Germany or that apostate in Bohemia. Yet he does not succumb because our Black Army is the greatest fighting force in all Christendom. But it is expensive. He can raise taxes. He has done so often enough in the past, but there is a limit to how much he can wring from the people."

"I still do not follow," he said.

"You know of the troubles in Erdély last year. The towns rebelled after the king's latest levy. Perhaps you paid no heed, but Annaka was obsessed by this. She would bore me to sleep talking about it."

"What does this have to do with Kuszkol?"

"That mountain yonder is said to be threaded with gold. The king means to secure the valley and to re-establish the town that once stood at its foot."

Pál looked up, as though he could see through the wall to the next ridge. I remembered how he had watched the mint's soldiers bound out of Körmöcbánya, and wondered if the heft of the chest they escorted still weighed down his thoughts. Gold meant opportunity. Gold meant patronage, largesse, and excess. Gold meant purses full to overflowing.

"Is there still a mine?" he asked.

"There must be. But never mind that. I am speaking thus that you might understand the dispositions of those about you. In the weeks ahead, if you are ever uncertain, speak to Ferenc or perhaps someone else you come to trust. Think twice before you press your superiors for answers."

"You mean I must not pester Kálmán," he said.

I gestured at Kladivo in lieu of the knight himself. "You must take heed of him. He is a man of few words."

"I must do better to obey," he said.

I studied the wad of grass I had been holding the past five minutes. "I am glad you understand. You must learn what he expects of you. You must not speak out of turn. You must never question him or flip his words on their head or spin them around to find their loose ends. A servant who squabbles with his master will not long serve."

"I must put my faith in him," Pál said. "As you put your faith in the bishop."

"Just so," I answered. "I have been faithful and the bishop has been good to me."

"You hold an honored position."

I finally placed the grass stuffing. "I do."

"One which you would do anything to retain."

"Retain?" I asked. "What do you mean? Why would I ever leave His Excellency's service?"

"Indeed, why would you ever loosen your grip on the hem of that crimson robe?"

I turned away from the drafty wall. I am sure I was scowling. "What is this about? Why do you speak so poorly of my master?"

"Because that bastard killed my sister."

"Pál! Who told you this?"

"No one need tell me. She died in his prison."

"No, Pál." I drew a breath and wound my fingers in Fejes's mane. "No. It is false. You misunderstand. His Excellency felt no animosity toward Annaka. He did not even know who she was. Not really."

"He knew she was your wife, and still he arrested her."

"And he has not held it against me."

He gripped my arms, "That villain killed my sister and you are grateful he still flings his coin at you?"

"Mind your tongue. His Excellency did not kill her. The fire was an accident. She was never even tried. No, do not speak. It is your turn to listen. What is more, the bishop has not forgotten my suffering. Or yours. You have his munificence to thank for your position. You should be grateful as well."

He stepped back unsteadily. For a moment, I thought he might use those balled fists.

"What you must understand," I continued, "is that what happened to Annaka was inevitable. I know the gossip they told of her. Terézia tried to tell me. His Excellency bore no grudge against her. He is a very learned man. I doubt he believed the charge. I am sure that were she tried, she would have been found innocent."

"He waited until you were out of town to arrest her."

"Justice cannot wait for one man. He could not be seen to be favoring me. I am just another member of his flock."

"He betrayed you."

"He spared me."

"You are not allowed not to hate him."

"*Hate* was your sister's word."

"It was her best weapon."

He did not wait for my response. He pushed past me and through the door.

I was left blinking at the chinks in the wall. I would have let Pál lose himself in the darkness, to find whatever comfort it offered, had not Fejes shifted beside me, as if to rouse me from my stupor and tell me to follow.

The wind and sleet lashed as severely as at any point in our journey. Worse than the storm's rage was the cold certainty that Pál had not retreated to the others. He would not want to sleep in the same cell as me this night.

I returned to the path. The light from the tiny lookout bled around the door and closed shutters. Below the valley stretched, dark and unknown. How easy it would be for him to dive into its murk, I thought. To lose himself as in a bottomless pool.

But he had not gone so far. He stood upon the path like a statue cut from black rock, seized by the sight from across the valley.

Opposite us on the next ridge, Kuszkol revealed itself. Against the wind, against the frozen torrent that fell, a steeple-high pyre raged against the night.

Seven

I DID all that I did so I might speak. Thus he and I agreed to no grief on that day that I leaned back and beyond me saw not the timbers atop me nor the dark sky above me, only the glow that shed from my sleeves and my hems and my hair flying up in brilliant strands.

Eight

We huddled about the open hearth. None of us saw the flames that danced before us, only the great beacon that had seared itself into our minds as we stood gazing dumbly at the impossible sight across the valley.

How? More importantly, why?

I studied my comrades. Sir Kálmán leaned forward, his hands planted on his knees as though he would rise at any moment. He looked somehow paler in the golden light, the shadows entrenching more deeply into the creases of his face. I had never seen him so severe. Across the valley, his father had ordered the fire lit and was contending with whatever troubles it presaged.

Jakab's lips were moving and his hands fidgeted with a stray lace. The old dog muttered to himself as empty smiles flit across his face. Ferenc sat with his shoulders hunched and his eyes darting. He leapt at each sputter from the fire or strike of a tree bough against the shutters.

As for Pál, his face was a placid mask and it reminded me of nothing so much as that evening he had laid in a fever six months after he had moved into our house. Even Annaka's poultices seemed to have little effect. That night when we sat holding each other, gazing at the boy's face, so like this, was the first time I heard her rail against the angels. That had been the first time I realized I would die for this boy.

Even as I watched and remembered, the mask dissolved. His eyes narrowed, keener than that night his spirit almost fled him. This expression, too, was lost the moment he looked up, startled that I had been watching him.

"But what could it mean?" Ferenc asked. His beseeching tone seemed to implore good tidings.

"What has a beacon fire ever meant?" Jakab replied.

"An attack?" Ferenc said. "In this weather? How fervent must the heretic be to attempt such a thing? I thought they were master tacticians."

It was a sound point. Kuszkol sat atop a steep slope. It was hard to see how a sneak attack would be profitable in this weather, in the night, in this terrain. Unless, of course, their plan hinged on treachery.

"No, we all know the reason," Ferenc said. He cowered as he said it and I wondered at the manic force of his unease.

"I do not," Jakab said.

"It is just like decades ago," Ferenc said. "The ghost has come to move among them." The ghost. I sensed Kálmán bristling at my side. "All the accounts agree his arrival was heralded by madness and the lighting of the beacon fire. The commander must have—"

"Watch your tongue," Kálmán growled.

"But in the stories—"

"Damn the stories! I will hear no more of it!"

I saw few hints of wisdom in Ferenc's many words, and in that moment of fright I believe he must have forgotten Kuszkol's lord was Kálmán's father. "I would gladly we spoke of anything else, but the beacon is lit and we know not what it portends."

"The beacon," Kálmán said, jabbing a finger across the fire, "is either a warning or a plea. We do not know which. Either way, we must find out."

We must find out. Of course he meant to march us to the fortress and see for ourselves.

"We should summon help," Jakab said.

"If the men of Kuszkol are in distress, it is either too late for them or they can wait out the siege," Sir Kálmán said. "We will approach and learn which. Others have seen this fire and will report to Lednic. We are not the only watcher this night."

Pál turned to me. I did not mean to, but I must have smiled. He turned away in disgust.

"We go forward," Kálmán declared.

"Do we dare?" Ferenc said.

"We go forward and we discover for ourselves the meaning of this beacon. Though you are not acquainted with them, the men stationed there are your comrades and you owe them a debt of solidarity. They need your loyalty now."

"Our loyalty? They have never been our comrades," Ferenc said, rising from his crouch.

"Easy, now," I said. I had seen many a spooked horse, and could not help but hold out a staying hand.

He paid me no heed. "If the place has been overrun by ghosts or turned feral, we must stay clear."

"The fire has been lit. That is all we know." Kálmán rose to face Ferenc across the fire. "Now sit down and keep silent. I have heard enough."

"Enough? You are the one speaking madness now—"

Kálmán seized Ferenc's tunic at the throat and hauled him forward, so that the young soldier's feet were dragged across the burning logs.

"I have said enough, and by God, it is enough." He threw Ferenc aside like a drunk barring his way.

I marked how Pál had moved from sitting to squatting, like a wary hare.

"What is your plan then, my lord?" Jakab asked. I watched as Pál's eyes drifted towards the door.

"Our plan is to push onward. If need be, we shall scout from afar. If can be, we shall approach and do whatsoever we can to provide them relief."

Beholden to some reckless humor, Ferenc asked, "You think a ghost will so readily reveal itself to our inspection?"

The fist that struck his mouth flew with a lazy precision, like an arrow that drifts, inevitably, to stick its target. Ferenc was thrown backwards and tripped over our packs to land hard against the wall. Pál shuffled half a foot closer to the door.

Ferenc groaned. The trees beyond the walls scratched at the walls. From the stable I could hear the horses whicker.

"Have any of you another word?" Kálmán asked. "Any of you? Old man? Nothing? What of you, messenger?"

Kálmán eyed me with the indifference of an upraised axe.

"I suppose . . ." I said. The others leered at me in the fire's glow, as if I had the final word. It seemed important to set a good example for Pál. Even so, if it had not been Jakab's eye that I caught as the others waited to hear what I had to say—if the veteran had not regarded me so scornfully—I might have spoken otherwise. "I would know better if I might discharge my duty. I have a letter to deliver."

"Your letter," Kálmán said quietly, as though to himself. He drew a breath and examined his knuckles. "Nothing changes," he said. "On the morrow we cross the valley."

The rain stopped. For a time, the sun shone. These were the only blessings we were to know that next day.

We broke our fast in silence. We broke camp in silence. We filed down into the dripping forest without a word.

Halfway through our descent into the valley we came upon a village that boasted a church and a water wheel, but little else to commend it. Half the villagers came out to call to us, while the other half hovered near on their thresholds, the better to step inside and bar the door.

"Wherefore the light in the night?" one man called. "What passes on that terrible peak?"

"We will learn this very day," Kálmán replied.

"Will the king protect us?" called a second man.

"What have you provoked?" called a third.

A fourth said, "Heaven forfend!"

There was nothing more to say, and so Kálmán did not answer them. We passed between the few houses and the pig pens and the crowd did not make to follow us any further down the road. Nor did any call out *Godspeed* or *God bless*. When I looked back, the men of the village were already talking among themselves. I raised my hand in farewell, and those women still glaring at us replied with thumb stuck between fingers in the sign of the fig.

It turned out there were no other villages in that valley. The path became even less worn. On the final leg of our journey we traveled through a wasteland. Here, new woods had risen on fields left untilled for generations. What few pastures existed were left uncropped, for no shepherd would bring his flock to range this close to Kuszkol. Still further, and the forest grew ponderously deep. We forded streams and stopped to take our bearings where the paths forked. The forest was as empty as the one Adam must have found when the Lord forsook him and cursed our ancient father to stumble into the world.

Thus, we progressed through the wilderness, catching sights now and then of Kuszkol on its crag above us. We would stop to squint, Kálmán longer than the rest of us, but we saw no signs of life in the mountain hold. Even the beacon that had roared had been reduced to a tail of smoke in its senescence.

Ferenc was the first to spot the wreck of the last village. A wall, dingy, rising between the trees. Kálmán dismounted to study the ground but could make out no evidence of an invading force having passed this way. We crept forward, wary that a scout may be watching, and listened hard for bird whistles or other tells that we had been spotted by the enemy's scouts.

We heard nothing, and the further we advanced the less I believed any scout would take up position here. Many of the houses had collapsed roofs, while the walls of every other seemed to be leaning. The windows were blank. The plaster was splotched and the walls' wicker bones peeked through. The trees grew up and around the village and told a tale of all that might be lost to Man and how quickly the forest might conquer his works.

This is no ruin, I thought. This is a corpse. One that had not been left to rest.

The decrepit buildings provided a hundred opportunities for ambush. I am not certain it was this knowledge that caused us to draw our weapons, or simply the utter emptiness of the place.

We had not yet crossed the ditch that marked the village's boundary when a cry flew from Pál's lips. We all dropped to our haunches.

"What is it?" Kálmán hissed. "What did you see?"

"A man," Pál said. "A man in black."

"Where?"

"Past that pile of chimney stones. In the village proper."

Kálmán stared at the place. From our crouch it was impossible to see. He motioned for us to withdraw down the road a hundred paces. "We best hobble the horses," he said.

We retreated further back, to where we could make out no buildings between the trees, and I will admit it was a relief to be surrounded by only forest again. We were invisible, or nearly so. As we looped the reins around a young birch, Jakab pointed to the fortress that loomed above.

We left the road and crept back to the village. Kálmán had slung a quiver on his back and he proceeded with an arrow nocked as his cape dragged across the forest floor. Jakab walked beside him, rigidly but with pluck enough in his wiry arms that he seemed deadly. He held his sword before him. Pál held the short blade I had gifted him, point thrust forward. As I watched him, I became acutely aware that should a real warrior pounce upon him, he would no doubt bat it from Pál's hand as simply as a man a child's club. I sidled closely at the boy's side, wielding a simple knife.

As for Ferenc, he came in the rear, as he had the entire day. He muttered a prayer to himself until Pál told him to stuff it.

We were soaking by the time we sighted the ruined walls again. We stepped through icy puddles and pushed through brambles that sloughed their watery mantles on our cloaks even as they snatched at us with their thorns. I struggled to hear any sound besides the constant dripping. Nothing. I wondered if the tang of woodsmoke was from the enemy's cookfires, and how I might distinguish it from the beacon's long final exhalation, which had filled the forest for half the day.

We approached the northern flank of the village, down and up again through the ditch to take our pause behind a stone wall. We were well out of sight of the road now. Kálmán peered over the stones for a spell before leading us to an old gate. We entered and scurried forth to press our backs up against one of the houses.

Kálmán cocked an ear. I did likewise and heard nothing. He peered around the corner, then quickly pulled back. He raised a hand that we not speak.

He dropped to a crouch, pulled back on the bowstring, and peered around the corner again. He stepped out, leaned silently on one knee, and lowered his cheek that he might gaze true down the shaft of his arrow. Kálmán shifted to the other knee. He pulled the string taut and made a tight fist where he gripped the fletching, save for his little finger, which splayed outward as if seeking purchase on some passing midge.

He had the perfect shot.

Then he let the string slacken and stood without loosing the arrow.

"This must be the work of our comrades," he said.

He motioned for us to join him. We stepped tentatively around the corner. He pointed to where it took some moments to recognize the bend of an elbow and a shoulder in the gap between the trees. The man he had sighted stood stock still. He was well disguised in that village, for he wore a tunic the very shade of the wall against which he leaned.

Kálmán was now walking forward. "No one has been here," he said, waving at the street ahead with the horn of his bow.

Jakab seemed to agree. "No tracks."

"But, that man," Pál whispered.

"It is no man," the knight replied.

We passed the intervening trees and finally beheld him.

It was a man. Or rather, it was a man's form. Drawn in outline only, in charcoal, on the crumbling plaster of a house.

"This is what you saw," Kálmán said.

"It must be," Pál answered. "Though I thought he wore all black."

"What is it supposed to be?" Ferenc asked. He had followed so meekly that I had forgotten he skulked behind us.

"Target practice," Jakab said. His rough laugh seemed forced. "The men-at-arms probably drew him on a lark."

"If they filled this shape with arrows," Ferenc said. "then why are there no holes?"

"There are more over there," Pál said. We turned, and on a wall that we had passed a threesome of human figures stood. Outlines of two men and, disconcertingly, a woman.

We continued down the road. It had once been the high street of this village. Somewhere beneath the knee-high weeds we now trod upon cobbles. The houses on this street were taller. Many two-stories. This was not a village at all, but a town. If anyone still dwelt here, it would have been the biggest we had seen in three days.

Abandoned. Sixty years past, along with the fortress.

The charcoal figures crowded the walls here. Tens, hundreds were sketched, all in outline. Featureless, though each distinct enough that it was possible to discern many builds of men, and of women, as well as children sketched among them in their dozens. I could not fathom the purpose of these drawings, let alone the effort Kuszkol's soldiers must have expended in drawing them.

As we walked between them, it was difficult not to feel they waited upon us. That they had gathered, even, to observe our procession, as though we should heft the relics of some saint upon our shoulders. On we walked until we came to a plaza that seemed more woods-choked garden.

"That is him," Pál said.

Among all the silhouettes, one stood apart. This one was shaded black where the others were empty, and solid where the others were insubstantial. No face was drawn on it, no eyes or mouth, but it was too easy to imagine these had been blacked over.

Pál could not have seen it from the road.

Kálmán turned and surveyed us. Grimmer than before, I thought. "Where is Ferenc?" he asked.

"What?"

"Where is he?"

We were surprised to find he no longer dogged us.

"Perhaps he went back to the horses," I said.

"Not by my leave." Kálmán studied the ground. "Back this way."

We retraced our steps, away from the coal-black figure. As we retreated down the street, I turned back more than once to make sure it had not moved from where it stood among the others, singularly, like a man among scarecrows. We retreated all the way back beyond the wall and through the ditch, through the trees and back to the road.

"He must be with the horses," Pál said.

We gained pace. Within moments we saw that the boy was wrong.

"Coward," Kálmán spat. He unhitched Kladivo and hauled himself up into his saddle.

"Where is he?" Pál asked Jakab.

"That idiot deserted." The veteran jabbed a thumb back over his shoulder. "He probably thinks he saw a ghost back there."

Kálmán wasted no time. He had already whipped Kladivo into a gallop. He left in such haste he still clutched the bow.

"The poor bastard," Jakab said. "What a dolt." He leaned against a tree.

"What is the purpose of those drawings back there?" Pál asked. "Have you ever seen their like?"

Jakab shook his head.

"András?"

"No purpose is my guess," I answered.

"Yet someone took such care. Do you think . . . perhaps . . ."

The silence stretched. I was wearier than the day's exertions warranted. At last, I said. "I think this past hour will hold fewer lessons for you than the next."

So we passed the next hour waiting. We did not talk. For several minutes Pál paced listening for any hint that Kálmán had caught up with Ferenc. Jakab stamped his feet on the wet earth, while I did my best to divine meaning in the blanket of cloud that sealed us off from the sun. Knowing it was out of the question, Pál began to talk about lighting a fire. I had thought his blistered feet were healed, but he complained the wet had aggravated them. Jakab fished a scarf from his pack to wrap around his neck.

"This will soon be over," Pál said. "Ferenc will be found and we can take some satisfaction in his humiliation. Then we can reconnoiter the fortress and find there is nothing to be done and then we can leave this empty place."

But it was already afternoon. We would easily make Kuszkol by nightfall, but afterwards, if we trudged all the way back to the lookout, we would not arrive until midnight. It was more sensible to pass the night on this side of the valley.

Finally, we heard a horse on the path. We watched as Kálmán emerged from between the leafless trees, black-clad and erect on his horse like some self-righteous friar. The mud that smeared across his cheek only added to his haughty air of tribulation.

He did not look at us until he was within ten feet, and then he spared us only a glance, apparently as captive to deep thoughts as we had been before he returned. Ferenc lay senseless across Kladivo's haunches.

"We are finished here," he said. "I would not care to hear you speculate on what we have seen on those walls."

With that he pressed his heels and Kladivo began to walk again toward Kuszkol.

"What is going to happen to him?" Pál whispered to the veteran.

Jakab sighed. "Need you ask, boy?"

"This is not peacetime," I said.

"The noose?"

I placed both hands on Pál's shoulders. He shrank from my grip. "Best you not ask again."

Nine

No sentry hailed us. No arrow shot from those grim parapets to silence the voices that failed us, faltering in our throats.

Kuszkol's ramparts cast a shadow even on that sunless day. Its mass pulled our eyes upward, up past walls blackened by a lichen that had crept across its face like a pox. Up past murder holes and unmanned crenels, up to the glowering late autumn sky. Grass sprouting from the mortar proclaimed the fort's long decline.

But Kuszkol should not have stood empty. We should have heard voices, the complaints of horses and metal crying out from the smithy forge. There was none of that. There were no desperate cries, no croaking exhortations that might explain the flames we had witnessed, the beacon roaring skywards into the night. The smell of ashes lingered, but there was no warmth in the place. There was no light.

The knight dismounted and strode into the passageway. At its end he placed a hand against the gate. Jakab squatted by the side of the road. He stared at the frosted pebbles beneath his feet. He wanted no part of the mystery we now confronted. Ferenc had finally stopped weeping. He lay gut-netherwards across Kladivo's back, ankles bound to wrists, a gag spilling from his mouth.

As for Pál, he raised his eyes to mine. He did not find reassurance. I had none to give. I swung out of my saddle and joined the knight before the gate.

"What now?" I said.

The knight studied the voids in the ceiling. There were no defenders above waiting to crush us. After a long hesitation, the knight rapped softly against the wood.

I almost snatched his hand from the door, but he had let it drop. He bowed his head and listened. I could not tell if his face was stretched by indecision or by fear.

No one appeared on the walls. No voice called asking for us to declare our allegiance. Kálmán did not knock a second time. Rather, he pressed lightly against the great wooden panels. They did not give way.

"And now?" I asked.

"Now we must find another way."

He did not acknowledge my sideways glance. I had lost my chance to naysay him. The weather was turning. All through our ascent up the mountain, my old friend the wind pursued us, seeking beneath our billowing cloaks and down our collars like the fingers of mobbing urchins. We had made no provision for retreat. Our rations would hold for a day or two longer, but not the daylight. We would find no shelter on the winding path before nightfall, nor in the quiet forests that draped the mountain's shoulders.

The horses were restive, unnerved by the mountain stillness, or perhaps by some threat their animal wits comprehended better than our own.

"Perhaps we could spend the night in this gate passage," I said. "It is not unlike a cave."

Jakab nodded. "Aye. The messenger speaks some sense."

"We enter," Kálmán said.

"But the way is barred."

"We climb."

The sheer stonework offered no manageable ascent, no matter

how strong one's fingers. I studied the wall and its vacant posts, imagining what Kálmán's father had found when he had reclaimed Kuszkol earlier that year. An open gate, surely.

Kázmér Kustyer had gone some way in sloughing the fort's decrepitude. The parapets stretching south of the gatehouse were hidden by a new wooden shed running the length of the ramparts—a hoarding from which defenders could rain arrows down on the heads of their foes. On the gatehouse's northern flank, beams sprouted at intervals in a line beneath the battlements where the hoarding was yet to be affixed. A rope hanging from one of the beams bowed in the wind.

The knight took a hold of the line.

Jakab and I met each other's eyes, both realizing that the moment to call an end to the lunatic venture was slipping us by.

"Now who will lead our escalade? Pál, your limbs are less weary than ours. Go on."

Pál started, for I think he understood only now what poor use the knight meant to make of us.

"He is a boy," I said.

"He is mine to command," Kálmán answered.

Pál reached a hesitant hand toward the rope. I took it from his grasp and said, "I will go."

"Then do so freely," Kálmán said. He was not dissatisfied.

I looked up the rope's shaft. It fell vertically from the beam. I would have no use of my legs to brace against the wall. A snowflake fell, spiraling in time with the swaying line.

"I will do it," Pál said. He made no effort to seize the rope from me.

I took a moment to test the rope's knot met my satisfaction and began to climb.

I was no weakling, but in the balance, my years tipped closer to forty than to thirty, and within minutes my arms and neck burned. My legs, gripping the rope, were dead weight. Long-standing aches from years spent in the saddle began to speak up. I huffed and puffed and in short order I was forced to pause.

I had diligently avoided looking down or at the wall, out of reach, but now I did and with dismay I found I had made it only halfway to the beam.

I kept going. Though it felt like some cruel jeweler threaded wire through the vertebrae of my neck, though my arms had become so enflamed that I could no longer feel the pain. A little traitor in my brain whispered that my hands were about to release of their own accord, but I continued to climb.

My goal neared. The cantilever jutted from the weathered stones. In the recesses of that pitted wall rock doves had bred for generations, the story of their years written in the white filth that painted the stone. I need only reach those stones and I could rest.

My knuckles scraped newly-planed wood. I clung to my rope more tightly and closed my eyes that I might not fall now that I had only feet to go. The men below were silent, and when I opened my eyes again I looked not down, but outwards.

A vast wilderness lay below me. The solemn ridges of spruce and fir and their denuded brethren were inky on that gloomy day. On the valley's far slope I spied the thin tracts of cleared land, black from autumn plowing and muddy yellow where only the sickle had passed. So too could I see villages, whose thatch roofs sat clustered without pattern like leaves frozen in river eddies.

Following the snaking line of road that led to Kuszkol, my eyes fell upon the town at the mountain's foot. Between the walls of those houses that were missing roofs, beech saplings spread their boughs with the pride of conquerors.

I quickly looked away. My wife's silver ring flashed against the leaden sky. The fingers of one hand ventured about the wood, and before I could reflect, my second hand loosed the rope and hooked about the beam. Next, I brought up my legs and sidled towards the wall like a scamp playing squirrel in a tree. Without grace, I righted myself and shuffled towards the wall, my fingers at last finding a hollow filled with dead grass and broken shells.

I clung to the stone and pulled my legs up. One foot beneath me, a knee drawn against my chest. And then, with as little faith as any man sent first up the ladder in a siege, I raised myself to standing. I had no white rag to wave. I planted my fingers on the stone and pulled myself up, my eyes rising not to find blood-stained planks but an empty wall walk. I saw no pale face leering from the gatehouse door, nor from the windows of more distant towers. I slunk over the parapet's edge like a newt over a tree root, forging ahead, in denial that this could be the moment I was pierced by cruel talons.

Thus I came to be first among us to stand within Kuszkol's walls. My gaze swept across the lower bailey, prepared to behold a slaughter.

There was none. The only break in the gray was the white of drifting snow.

I assayed the fortress. The lower bailey was ringed by a curtain wall that provided the castle's outermost defense. Within those walls, a main body of defenders were meant to live and toil. From the walls, I could see the two-story barrack hall, the kitchen and stables, and the chapel's peaked roof. Another courtyard sat uphill, across a chasm. I remarked that this upper bailey's bridge had been drawn. Within that upper yard one would find the granaries, a second cistern, and the keep—the fort's final redoubt. The keep was built on higher ground still, its back pressed against the summit's final ascent. I had a clear view of its black windows. I saw no evidence of life.

Above the keep lay the summit, the beacon mount.

The immense silence of the place, the countless vantages above me, hastened me into the gatehouse. I entered and stepped into incredible cold. I had expected to find shelter from the wind, but Kuszkol's stones had captured the frost. Behind those walls, winter had already arrived.

In the floor, beside bins containing a whole armory of crossbows and arquebuses slung against the wall with quivers and horns of black powder, and braziers in which to heat sand and oil to pour upon the enemy, I came upon the murder holes. Through their apertures I spied Pál's troubled face, and I thanked God that no madmen had awaited to rain fury upon us.

But surely someone waited, somewhere in Kuszkol.

A staircase twisted down. I descended, knifepoint forward, as the soles of my boots scuffed the wooden risers. There was no smell to the place, nothing, as if the wind had scoured the stone clean.

I descended and for a full minute observed the bailey from the shadows of the doorway. The chapel door, which hung open, from some worshipper's forgetfulness. The archway to the kitchen, whose chimney belched no smoke. Still no one. I crept out, and stood for several moments longer before sheathing my knife and turning my back on the impossibly quiet yard. I was utterly exposed. But if anyone watched, they were well out of sight. I heaved upon the heavy timber barring the gate. I managed to lift it but could not bear its weight. With a curse, I let it slip from my fingers to bounce against the cobbles.

One panel of the door swung inward, Jakab straining against it. Behind him, Kálmán waited in the gatehouse passage, hands on hips. Pál stood beside him holding the reins of the horses like the knight's own squire.

My Fejes bobbed her head and shifted. Even my touch did not calm her. The knight's palfrey too, was twitchy, and that beast had seen more blood spilled than I. I wondered what they sensed, what they smelled in that crisp, empty air. What they heard rumbling through the stone.

Pál stared at the courtyard, and with a taut voice, he whispered, "It is empty."

"It appears," I said, and perhaps because he reminded me so of the shivering little boy who would stumble into our bed when the wind howled at night, I added, "Try not to be afraid."

Pál turned to me and scowled.

Ferenc began moaning and testing his bonds again. His eyes were red and dripping from the strain.

"A Christian's strongest shield is prayer," Kálmán said. He fell to his knees and clasped his hands together and did not deign to look more upon us. His conviction was not strong enough to raise his voice above a whisper.

I waved for Pál to kneel alongside me. Instead, he joined Jakab, who was leaning against the gatehouse wall. Once the knight had intoned *Amen*, the boy spoke. "What is that?"

"What is what?" Jakab asked.

"That sound," Pál said. We immediately began scanning the empty yard.

Kálmán rose. "I hear nothing."

"Nor I. Methinks you hear the wind," I said.

"The wind? Are you deaf?"

"Silence!" Kálmán snapped as he stepped forward into the yard. We hewed close to the walls and flinched with every resounding step of the iron-shod hooves. Most of the structures that ringed the court were fashioned of the same cut stone as the walls. Unlike the ramparts, the masonry was in fine repair. The barracks were newly built log and plaster. The hayloft atop the stable looked new.

Still the place felt a ruin. Utterly deserted. This was impossible. Someone had barred the gate from within. Someone had begun the long task of reversing decades of neglect. Surely such signs meant Kuszkol must be inhabited still by strong, hale men. I studied the buildings and their blank windows and open doorways. This place was intolerably empty. None of us had yet dared voice the question that had crushed the last of our faint hopes. Where was everybody?

The horses were determined to dispel the notion we would discover some harmless cause. Their fretting worsened and the mood was catching. The knight retrieved his bow from his saddle holster. I swept my gaze along the walkways and towers, while Jakab marched forward, his lips tight, the face of one who recognized thinning odds.

"I hear it now," I said.

I could not place it. The sound was maddening. It was strident yet sickly. Inconstant yet drawn out. There was suffering in it.

Kálmán nodded. "The stable."

Kladivo tossed her head and would not be calmed even when the knight pulled the horse's head near to his lips. Kálmán told Ferenc to cease his mewling, then sketched an unusual ward against evil in the air, the action reminiscent of a priest's, before nocking an arrow.

I put my faith in his bow. We edged nearer the stable.

Twenty feet out and even Jakab now heard that which tormented our horses. A frayed, reedy rumble. The ebb and flood of low agony, like the lapping of some tortured lake. We stopped mid-stride to exchange glances, wondering with mouths hanging open, until at last we recognized the sound. Ragged breathing. Wheezing from bellow lungs. Long, mournful groans.

The stable's doorway was dark, like all doorways at Kuszkol. As we neared the threshold, a heavy, bestial reek struck my nose. I inhaled the rich stench of horse urine. Kálmán halted his progress. I thought he was struck by indecision, but he motioned for us to proceed.

"Go on," he whispered.

"You will not join us?" Jakab asked.

"I will cover you from here."

I would have preferred he guard our backs from a closer distance, but I knew better than to question him. Jakab was less successful at concealing his irritation, and he earned a frown. Kálmán sighted an arrow on the portal we were about to enter.

We stepped into the gloom of the stable.

The room was long, lit only by slivers of gray light that leaked through the closed shutters. The wooden pens ran the length of the back wall. It was a place of rasping breath, stinking of dirty stalls and failing flesh. A place of woe.

In the first stall we found a draft horse crumpled on folded knees. It had dipped its head down and to the side, as if in its final delirium it imagined itself a swan and sought to hide its massive head beneath a wing. Its mouth hung open like an empty mitt and as the massive chest labored, pitiful little clouds steamed from its nostrils.

How it must have suffered. I wanted to leap the rails and drape my arms about it. I wanted to curse its groom for ever leaving its side, but the others were already moving on.

The horse in the second stall had toppled over. Frost rimmed its nostrils and its tightened lips that looked as dry as shoe leather, as well as the length of its fine lashes that shielded eyes that would never blink again. I continued on when I pictured its second eye open, pressed against the stone.

In the third stall, a young mare loosed a hollow, wretched moan. I had never heard such from a horse before. She was lucid enough to track our approach, but when we finally arrived at the boards, her eyes closed and did not open again. It looked as if the horse had pawed at the fence boards, gouging new furrows in the wood. Perhaps it had thought to batter them down. Her efforts ceased when her hoof had become lodged between the planks. Thus the creature had collapsed, one foot stretched up and outward at a plane that nature would not countenance. The leg must have broken as she fell to the ground.

My guts were churning, but still I followed the others. On it went. Horses, curled and splayed in the varied guises of the dead and dying, their majesty eroded as the truth of their being was out—that they were just flesh-draped sinew and bone.

"The troughs are dry," I said.

I pointed to how one beast's flesh piled in unhealthy ridges behind its neck, how sunken seemed its eye.

"Who cares?" Pál said. "What will we do to help them?"

"They died for want of water." Kálmán startled us all. He had joined us without our notice. His pinched face matched his tone.

"How could one day without water bring them so low?" Jakab asked. "The beacon was lit only last night."

"They have not drunk in days," I said. "The neglect of these creatures stretches back to long before they lit their beacon."

We walked the aisle. Nine stalls. Four horses dead, three still struggled to draw breath, and the condition of the two remaining was unclear without closer inspection. Near the end we came upon what must have been the pride of the stable. A once-fine dappled roan with a braided mane, most likely the commander's own. It lay on its side, in its filth, its tongue thrust out like black dough.

We were reluctant to speak.

"What can we do for them?" Pál asked.

I pressed my lips together.

"You know horses," he said to Kálmán. "What can we do?"

The knight did not immediately respond. He stared with the same disbelief we all felt. I studied the once-lovely beast and realized this creature must have belonged to Kálmán's father. "We must end their misery," he said.

"End?" Pál asked. "How?"

"With mercy in your heart." The knight looked at me meaningfully. "See to it."

I tore my gaze from the travesty in the stall as I grasped his words. "Me?"

"We must try to save them," Pál said.

"It cannot be done," Kálmán said.

"We have not yet—"

But Kálmán was already walking away.

"Jesus Christ," Pál said.

The boy stood with both hands on the boards. Below, thick pipes juddered in the poor mare's throat. The work assigned was ugly.

Pál pulled his eyes from the ruined creature. "What can we do?" he asked.

"Nothing," I said. "One thing." He noticed that my hand already rested upon my knife's hilt. "Why not help Jakab carry one of these troughs into the yard?" I said. "There must be a cistern hereabouts. If it is frozen, gather snow to melt."

He gripped the rails tighter. "We can save them, if we try," Pál said. "Márton must have taught you some useful lore. I can help you."

"You cannot help," I said.

Jakab lifted one end of a trough. "Come on, lad. Give me a hand."

"Please, András. We can save them."

I knew he was thinking of that other time. That other horse and that other lost chance for mercy. Yet I pointed at the door. "Go."

"God damn it," Pál said. "You will not even try? What is wrong with you?"

"An end comes to all creatures."

"But you must try."

"A time to surrender."

Jakab abandoned the trough and took Pál by the arm. "Come on, lad. Leave András to his task."

But the boy refused. He would not turn away when I wandered the length of the stable and removed an apron from a nail. Nor when I donned the leather smock and drew my blade. He watched me hesitate, until at last I roused myself and stooped before the mare. Pál turned away only at the last, only when he saw my knife dimple her neck.

Ten

THOSE DEAD HORSES. Even now I shake my head.

I did what I had to do. I did as my wife would have done, perhaps even acted as she wanted me to, in some farsighted, perverse scheme. It felt like I had made a mistake.

When he came into my life, my boy had close to nothing, beyond his sister and what he had found beneath my roof. What he had found were my horses. Ökör and her foal Fejes.

When he was still a little lad, he would spend every spare moment with them in the stable that leaned against my cottage. This was long before he befriended those idlers in town. I taught him to care for the horses. How to clean their hooves and where to search for ticks. Whenever I had a few spare hours, I would take him out to see Márton, an old horse doctor who had dedicated a long swath of his land to a horse run. At Márton's farm we spent many afternoons pacing our girls through different gaits, steering them around posts, and then doing it all again bareback. Afterwards, the two of us rested beneath a little lean-to where we always used to take our lunch and I told him tales. Of how the Duna blazes with reflected torchlight once the sun sets in Buda, or of the thousand-head cattle droves on the plains. He listened so attentively, so expectantly, I suspect he was always waiting for an invitation to join my next journey.

Ökör failed in the years after Fejes's birth, but even once her foal became my regular steed, I kept Ökör, cherishing her. And so did Pál. Annaka tolerated the expense and the chores when I was away, but towards her end, as an abscess grew on Ökör's leg and she nipped at whoever changed the poultice, Annaka lost her patience.

Bitterness had already crept into our marriage by then. "That dumb beast has seen more of this world than I ever will," Annaka said. I did not argue, for she was not wrong.

Perhaps she begrudged, too, the need to share Pál's affection with a lame animal. Beyond her brother and me, she had never expressed attachment to anyone or anything. She had little time for weakness. One day when I returned from a journey I found the croft empty and Pál's eyes redder than I had ever seen them.

Annaka lifted her chin and told me she had taken Ökör to the slaughterhouse. Without permission, without Pál's consent.

How I roared. How she thundered back, scorching me with her fiery tongue.

She called me a pillar to which she was chained, and which she had grown to despise. She spoke to draw blood. But remembering the row afterwards, the memory that endures is that of Pál on his little stool between us. He had grown too big for it, so his knees came up to his chest and his hands touched the floor. During the exchange he raised his voice only once. I remember not what he said, but it was in my defense. Annaka, in white fury, turned on him. She said she did not trust the boy's judgment, then ridiculed his years-long mooning over the neighbor's daughter, a girl we had all known since she was catching frogs. Annaka called her a clacking mortar who lacked even the courtesy to rinse herself between poundings so eager was she to receive the next pestle, though perhaps there was a slyness to her age-old methods, for she was destined to yield so many red whelps from between her chafed loins it was as if she planned to conquer Veszprém via its breeding stock, and this was impressive, in a way, this recumbent ambition, so maybe one day she could bring herself to call her sister after all, even if on a stream of spew through cupped fingers, that cack-spattered sow, that breathtakingly common, wet gap of a girl.

This was the first time Annaka trained her savagery on Pál. It was the last. She came to regret this moment more than any other, but it was too late. Her tongue left its scars and we all knew our best days together had passed.

Afterwards she was ofttimes despondent. She reproached herself, but as was her way, she cast her net carelessly and snagged me in her recriminations. She blamed me for encouraging the boy's love for short-lived beasts. She mocked my soft heart and said when it next came time to kill, she would stand aside as I closed the stable door and walked away. I said nothing, or went out, and once or twice, I did my feeble best to fend off her hectoring.

Annaka attended less to her housekeeping and spent her days dreaming, or listening, as she called it. She looked forward to the boy's future. She spoke of him having a military career and linked his fortunes to the movements of great magnates in Kolozs, Szatmár, and even Bohemia.

It is true I never indulge in thinking about the future. My new vice is to become lost in the past. This is my failing, but I preferred to let the boy be a boy.

I would not say joy was banished from my hearth that day, but something perfect was fractured. When she folded into my arms at night the break ran between us. Perhaps the intimacy I have felt with her thoughts since her death has been her way to mend the rupture. She has changed me again, but I am hers to change.

Eleven

I WATCHED Pál from the stable's doorway. I had no doubt he was thinking of Annaka as he whispered to Fejes and blinkered her eyes with his palms. Fejes turned her head my way nonetheless when I stepped into the yard. Pál did not.

"You have finished?" Kálmán asked.

"I was swift."

"Then lend me a hand." I helped the knight slide Ferenc from Kladivo's back. The young man squirmed on the flagstones as Kálmán sawed through the rope about his ankles. He left the wristbonds and gag in place.

"Stand up," the knight said. He pulled the soldier to standing. "Be quick about it." No sooner had Ferenc got his feet beneath him than Kálmán gripped his arm and led him stumbling into the darkness I had just left. None of us followed them into the stable. From within came the sounds of scuffling and more whimpering and finally the knight's rebuke, "Need I hood you to teach you calm? Be still."

I looked about me at the desolation and tried to imagine that Kálmán would hang the young man. I did not like Ferenc's chances.

Moments later the knight returned to us, alone. He barred the stable door and looked long and squarely at each of us, daring us to speak our minds. "The stable shall be his cell until the trial. Now on with our inspection. To the barracks first."

We led the horses clopping towards the new building. The barracks had a wide double door that opened without resistance. Plenty of light and a breeze passed through the open shutters into a lower floor devoted entirely to storage. Hemp sacks held dried peas, rye flour and turnips. A dozen hams hung suspended from the rafters, and shelves of butter jars and sauerkraut lined the walls. It smelled vaguely of sawdust.

We ascended the stairs to the second floor. The room was warmer, for here the windows were covered in parchment. Opposite the door, a gaping stone hearth spilled ashes. At the room's western end, a table stood amidst six stools. Atop the table, a chess board with pieces laid out and awaiting the first move. At the room's eastern end, pallets lined the wall. Orderly, save for one, which had been torn open and gutted. Straw lay strewn across the length of the floor.

We stood silently, none of us daring to guess at a possible cause. It took little to imagine how much worse our discovery might have been.

Kálmán swept his foot through the straw. "We will stable the horses below," he said. "Take that broom and clear the floor, lad."

Pál stared at the empty beds.

"Have they retreated to the upper bailey?" he asked.

"I know not what we will find," the knight said. Kálmán then set us our tasks. After sweeping, Pál would forage for kindling and firewood, for the log box was bare. Jakab and I were to make a circuit of the lower bailey to check for survivors.

"We should stay together," Jakab said.

"The sun will soon set," Kálmán said. "We must prepare for the night."

"We will be safer together."

"We will not discuss the matter further." Kálmán retrieved a small green book with elaborate stitching along the borders. He opened it close to his chest, as though to keep us from looking over his shoulder. "Tonight we will need protection," he said. "My preparations cannot be rushed."

The knight began to walk slowly about the edge of the room, one hand brushing the wall as his eyes swiveled up to the rafters and down to the floor, inspecting carefully as though looking for signs of mice.

"What do you hope to find?" I asked.

"I *hope* for peace to finish my task."

"But what defect do you expect to discover in these walls?" Jakab said.

The knight said nothing. He returned his attention to his book, muttering to himself, reciting verses from what I supposed to be his psalter. He paused his ambulation when he noticed how we stared. "The floor must be clear!" he barked. "Now out with you!"

Pál snapped to and sought out a broom from the corner. Jakab and I made haste down the stairs.

My instinct was to keep Pál close, but crossing the vast quiet of the courtyard again, I was glad to leave him safe beneath the barracks' roof. Midway across, Jakab said, "We should never have come to this godforsaken place." When I did not respond, he continued. "And what is the point of him dragging that fool Ferenc here like an animal?"

"Not an animal, a criminal."

"A criminal. I have no love for deserters, but even so it takes a weevil heart to blame the pup. Look about us! And why set him apart and bound? Why this talk of a trial? To make an example of him? To whom? No one is here."

"We are here."

"Aye, we are that. To our folly. I say that when the sun rises we must leave." He looked closely at me. "I say we must force the knight to his senses."

"We will see what the morrow brings."

"The morrow? Bah! I can hear your knees knocking. Stop feigning courage you do not possess. Stop trying to please that reaper and stand with me on this. If not for your own hide, think of your boy's."

I did not answer. We continued on to the smithy. Tongs, hammers and rasps hung where the farrier had left them on a sideboard. The anvil on its block sat stolid and inert. All was in order.

Next we entered the kitchen. Here the cook had abandoned his work partway through preparing a meal. A row of unbaked loaves had been left to leaven and then to freeze on a shelf. In a cauldron above the remains of the burnt-out fire, the pottage had turned to ice. Aside from the busy work of rats, there was no sign of life. Neither of us spoke of it.

At the far end of the bailey, the fortress makers had little improved upon the mountain's ruggedness. The yard narrowed to a twenty-foot ledge overlooking a steep drop. Here the rock was cleft deeply by a chasm that served as a natural moat separating the lower fort from the upper. Sheer walls fell away. Dwarf pines sprouted from cracks like gnarly arms reaching through prison slats. At the fissure's depth the night already pooled.

Across the gap, a second gatehouse awaited, its drawbridge raised.

We stood at the edge, feeling the pull of the long drop and the remoteness of the far gate, two or three man-lengths away, and we both knew, as we had known since arriving at Kuszkol—there was no prospect of ever entering the upper fort by our own efforts.

Jakab grunted. Satisfied, I knew, for we were bound to leave in the morning. Kuszkol was abandoned and whoever had raised the bridge and lit the beacon was beyond us. If they lived, they were huddled in the cold, no fires burning, prepared to starve through the phantom siege.

I was less certain. Staring at the narrow windows in the gatehouse, the slits by which defenders could easily fell us as we considered the gap, apprehension prickled through me. Kuszkol was not empty, I thought. We could not know if someone watched us.

We turned from the moat without a word.

The last building in our round was the chapel.

It was an old structure, built of stone, but the walls had been re-mortared and its deeply pitched roof was newly tiled. If it were sunny and there were men all about, the sight of the chapel would have cheered me. But today was not for high spirits. No candles burnt on the altar. Dark lanterns hung in the niches. The only light admitted came through the smoke holes in the high, narrow gables, and through the open door.

We tarried upon the threshold. A hint of incense still lingered in the air, but I doubted worship had been the soldiers' final concern. In the center of the nave, a messy heap glistened on the tiled floor. The pile was made of cast-offs from our missing comrades. Arms and armor, let dropped in a confused jumble. Daggers, maces, glaives, greaves—even a decorated breast plate from a knight's suit. The chapel was supposed to afford refuge, but this pile of discarded weaponry spoke of surrender.

No enemy from without could have forced Kuszkol's defenders to abandon their arms before they retreated to the keep. Not that we had found any evidence of raiders.

A suspicion darkened my thoughts. What if the beacon signaled nothing at all? What if it was no more than gibberish, the final howl from a mouth dripping slaver?

Jakab entered the chapel. He rounded the pile warily, as if he crept about a deep hole, until some glimmer caught his attention. "Now what is this?" he asked. I could not see where he pointed. Jakab squatted beside the pile and began to push aside gauntlets and greaves, causing a minor din.

I finally entered and stood by as he searched, though I had no interest in the pile. Had Jakab not started to paw through it, I would have held myself back. I would never have picked up the dagger.

The blade still had a fine edge. It was recently oiled. Plain, but perfectly serviceable—and cold. I underestimated how so, for it hurt my hand. It was not like holding ice. It burnt, reminding me how I once plunged my hand into the drill hole while winter fishing on Lake Balaton to untangle my line. Even through the dagger's leather-wrapped grip, the cold penetrated through my hand. I quickly returned it to the pile.

Jakab continued to dig, though I noticed that he used his cuffs to protect his flesh from the metal. I picked up a helmet, careful to take it up by the leather chin straps, and regarded its front. An ashen cross had been signed upon the brow. I returned it to the pile and flexed my hand.

"I see you, my beauty," Jakab said. I looked in time to see him pluck a ring from the floor. He held it up to the light. Silver.

He slipped it onto his finger before he gritted his teeth and quickly pulled it off again. He cradled it in the hem of his cloak and studied it more closely.

I knew better than to speak. Spotting spoils among carnage was a skill honed among many veterans, like the hunter's talent for discerning scat in the undergrowth. Our superiors did nothing to discourage plunder, for it was seen by all as a just reward for those who have endured the front line. Then again, I had never heard of looting one's comrades.

I said only, "They might yet live."

A moot point, one I was not sure even I believed, but one that caused the barest hesitation. He looked up from the ring, secreted it beneath his tunic and continued with his quarry. A moment later he came upon a second ring. Then a third, and a fourth.

I studied the ring that I wore—my wife's betrothal ring. It gleamed upon my little finger even in that dim. Jakab was right, I decided. We needed to leave at first light.

I wandered to the door and waited for him. Eventually, the veteran quit his searching and studied the ground between his feet. I listened to the sudden hush.

We interrupted the silence. The stone walls around us, the miles of stone below. This peace was not meant to be broken. Something had happened here. Something would happen again.

Jakab rose from his squat, "Open your eyes. You know we must go."

"How?"

"How? We pick up our packs and we retrace our steps. If we leave now we can make the mountain's foot before night falls."

"Sir Kálmán will never be convinced." I studied the clouds that gathered over the valley.

"The knight be damned," Jakab said. "We cannot risk the dreams we might have here. If we must desert, so be it."

"So be it?"

"So be it. God damn you, look at me when I am speaking!"

I turned to him. "You may be right."

"May be? I am right."

"But we cannot leave."

"We must!"

"Can you not smell it? Can you not see it in how coal streaks the sky? A storm is brewing. It would be our deaths to be caught outside this night."

He stepped beside me to gaze at the snow-laden clouds. Then he spat an oath, which helped not at all.

Twelve

You never knew whom not to trust.

Thirteen

It was a relief to return to the barracks after the chapel. Among the neatly stacked and shelved provisions, the product of human hands not yet blunted by the high mountain wind. Jakab searched a corner of the storeroom. On a barrel top he had collected smoked sausage, a butter jar and eight apples. Our supper this night. Pál had come in with oats for the horses. He buried one hand in each mane.

Jakab stopped his rummaging and said, "We should not sleep here tonight."

"I am not sleeping outside," I said.

"Did I suggest anything so foolish? I am saying we should retreat to the gatehouse."

"We will have no way to block the open doorways and windows," I said. "Think how cold it will be."

"Think how safe it will be. From there we can slip over the wall in case they come."

"In case who comes?" Pál asked.

Jakab let the silence stretch. "Perhaps the Bohemians," I said.

"The Bohemians."

"Listen, lad," Jakab said. "We do not know what has passed here, but you can bet we are not safe. Nay, we are worms on a hook. That is all you need know. We are only here because our masters have wagered our lives. We, the men who have already died here—the great think little more of us than they do of those poor horses. They saddle us up, ride us out. When they turn their attention away, we may count it a blessing. Unless they have left us hobbled where hunger or wolves can pull us down."

"It is not as dire as that," I said.

"Is it not? I can name a dozen men whose gore I have wiped from my brow, all for the glory of the king. Can you?"

"Jakab is right," Pál said. I held my peace, wary to contradict him. He turned towards the stairs.

I made to follow, but Jakab hooked my arm as Pál began to climb. "Did your wife teach you no tricks?" he whispered at me. "No charms against sprites? Stop dithering. Now is the time to put them to use."

I pulled myself free and made for the stairs. The way at the top was blocked by Pál, who watched from the threshold.

Kálmán was still walking the edges of the room, but now he was reading aloud from his psalter and dribbling water from a little brass vial. It recalled to me the time Terézia had brought a priest to splash holy water about my new cottage shortly before my marriage.

"What are you doing?" I asked.

He finished another line of prayer and crossed himself. "We need protection."

Jakab swore beneath his breath.

"Protection against what?" Pál said.

Kálmán did not answer. Instead he continued around the western wall, along the south to the quiet hearth. He closed his book and said. "I mislike your tone."

"This is a bloody exorcism!" Jakab spluttered.

"It is a precaution," Kálmán answered. "Though I am a layman, I act with the blessings of the Church. By now you know the mountain's reputation is not unearned."

We each stopped our shifting. Kálmán squared his shoulders. This was a hoax. But no, Kálmán knew nothing of humor.

"You say Kuszkol is truly *haunted*?" I asked. I could not believe I uttered these words.

"The rumors are only that," he said. "Yet they have been constant over this mountain's history. None who study these matters can so easily dispel them out of hand. An unclean spirit has long dwelt about this summit. We must not be cowed by it."

None of us dared move a hair. Kálmán walked to the middle of the room while we watched. He gestured with his book beyond the walls. "This mountain falls within the king's domain," he said, "and it is his will that it no longer be shunned from his realm."

The words bubbled out. "Nor would you be estranged any longer from your family's estate." I could not stop them. I only managed to twist my tongue enough to slur them.

The knight's head snapped my way. "What did you say?"

"I said nothing."

"You spoke of estrangement."

"No," I said. The others furrowed their brows at me. All save Pál, whose ears were sharpest. He looked upon me with open amazement.

"What did you say?" Kálmán pressed.

"I remembered a favorite line from my Alexandrine and spoke out of turn. Go on."

Kálmán's eyes did not leave me. "I was saying that this mountain has for too long lain fallow. The king would diminish the wilderness within his realm."

"He would have his footmen lock horns with devils?" Jakab asked.

"The task is not meant to fall on you. I have trained and I have sacrificed to ease the way. I have studied techniques once known to the greatest practitioners. Saint János Khrüszosztomosz, Pope Szilveszter II, King Salamon."

The voice bulged in my throat again but I grit my teeth and

released little more than a hiss. It went unnoticed as Jakab threw up his hands. "What now? Salamon who spoke to *ants*?"

"I speak not of fables," Kálmán barked. "We live in a new era. Knowledge, long sunken beneath the carnage of history, has been raised. Lost ways have been recovered. We command wisdom not known since before Caesar, but which the ancients could only misapply for want of the light of Christ."

"You are not even a priest!" Jakab exploded.

"Yet I am sanctioned. This is more than one can say for those horoscopists the king so fancies. I have studied the problem and I believed the threat at Kuszkol long spent. I journeyed here this past February and spent three days. I prayed. I bore the cross to every corner and saw no evidence of any disturbance and judged the threat was no more."

"But you were wrong," Jakab said with no effort to hide his contempt.

"I was wrong," Kálmán said. "But not for want of effort. I tell you, I scoured every crook for a sign of the spirit. There was none. I told my father it was safe."

"Were there no drawings in the village then?" I asked.

"Not so many of them. No."

Jakab cast about himself as if for some flotsam to bear his weight. I felt the same need to hold on to something. I had never heard one so highborn speak so blithely about hobgoblins.

"The ghost is real?" Pál asked.

"Ghost," Kálmán said. "I will not name it such. Let us call it an *immundus spiritus*. If by real you mean embodied, then again, I do not concede. Phantasms leave no footprints in the snow. This does not change anything. We have come to join our comrades, and they are missed. Our task now is to recover them." None of us had a proper retort for the lunacy of this statement. "But first I would have you join me. Come. Let us form a circle."

"A circle?" Jakab asked.

"A circle. Come now. Come. You stand here. You there and you there."

We looked helplessly at one another as we took up our positions before the hearth. Perhaps if we had another accusation to let fly we might have delayed the moment, but we were sluggish from the admissions that already filled our bellies. As it was, the knight approved of our stance and turned to me. "You are conversant in Latin, are you not?"

"Yes."

"Know you the words, *vade retro me satana*?"

I did not want to admit it. "They are Christ's own."

"Verily, they are. You could repeat none sweeter in this moment. You shall speak this phrase as the others speak the following formula in the vernacular."

He turned to the Jakab and Pál. "Are you listening?" They each nodded dubiously. "You two will repeat after me, 'Get thee behind me, Satan.' Do you follow?"

"We have it," Jakab said.

"Now raise your crucifixes before you and together we shall drive the evil from this place." He retrieved a worn wooden cross about the size of a bridle from his pack and returned to find us all empty-handed. "Do none of you wear the cross?"

None of us could answer yea.

This flummoxed him. "If your comrades are cut from the same cloth as you . . ." He removed the crucifix he wore about his neck and passed it to me. It seemed wholly insufficient. "Now you must speak with conviction. No spirit can withstand the invocation of our Lord. Let us begin."

"Get thee behind me, Satan," the others said.

"Vade retro me satana," I said in time, as Kálmán squeezed tight his eyes and raised his cross and I raised the crucifix pinched between my fingers.

"Again," he said.

"Get thee behind me, Satan."

"Vade retro me sata—" The words felt misshapen on my tongue. Ill-phrased, though I had read these words myself to Father Péter and knew them to be correct.

"Again," Kálmán said.

"Get thee behind me, Satan!"

"Vado retro—" The nailed feet of the crucifix in my hand were pointed skywards, the crown of thorns towards the earth.

"Again."

"Get me behind thee, Satan!"

"Vado retro—" I bit my tongue.

Jakab and Pál and I exchanged a look. I do not know if they had heard my error, but we each knew something had gone amiss. Kálmán did not appear to notice.

"One last time."

I abandoned Latin and mumbled with the others "Get me behind thee, Satan."

We waited as Kálmán then continued with a lengthy prayer calling on all of Heaven's hosts. As I listened to him implore their intercession, I remembered we had left poor Ferenc strapped up in the stable. I did not imagine the saints might favor men like us.

At last, the knight intoned *Amen*. He wiped his mouth on his sleeve when he was done.

"Why was the beacon lit?" I asked.

He kissed the cross in his hands and slid it back into his pack. "We will need to ask our comrades."

"They have locked themselves in the upper yard."

"That is my guess."

"Then let us call to them."

"The Lord has surely heard us today," he said. "But let us remain wary."

"Of your own father?"

His face could have dispelled any spirit. "I would rather not rouse their curiosity. They may yet suffer. Let us wait."

"If not now, then when?"

"Once I am sure I have cleansed this mountain."

"How will you be sure of that?" Jakab asked.

But Kálmán had returned his attention to his book. "Get that fire lit," he said. "The night's cold is already advancing."

There was no wood. Pál had forgotten to fetch it. He set off down the stairs before the knight could upbraid him. I followed but he did not slow for me. In the yard, our footfalls were muffled, as if the mountain had already swallowed us.

"I beg you take heart from Kálmán's efforts," I said.

"I take no heart from them."

"Kálmán says his methods will protect us."

"*Protect us*. Annaka once said prayer was the preserve of the doomed."

"That is fair, I suppose. It all bewilders. He is not an easy master, yet I think him a good man."

"Have you always placed such blind trust in those who abuse you?" he asked.

"Abuse? That is a harsh judgment."

"Not harsh enough. That tyrant sets himself above us on his hillock of faith. I would think you would know better than to heed men like that."

"You would blame him for his piety? Alms flow from piety."

"For God's sake, he is the very sort of man who condemned her."

"Hush," I said. "This has nothing to do with our Annaka. That was then. This is now. And perhaps," I said, presenting the flats of my hands, "perhaps we need whatever protection he offers."

Pál continued on. "They dragged my sister away in chains. She clung to the door posts, and it was *they* who used the Lord's name vainly when she let go and they all tumbled backwards. Now the knight drones on and on, saint by saint, as if vain words could save us! Trust whom you will. I will not."

I followed him into the kitchen. He peered within and beheld a sight that momentarily banished his other thoughts. There was a half-sliced onion upon the table. It spoke of a moment that clove the cook's life in two—a before and an unknown after.

"There is more he is keeping from us," he said. "He knows everything about this place."

"That might be so," I answered. "But think of all those missing men. Would you not see them safe? Or would you rather abandon them?"

"We will find them only to share their fate."

We continued to the woodshed. It was nearly bare, holding at most a third of a cord. This was astonishingly delinquent on the cusp of winter. We picked through the logs without further conversation. Later we returned to the kitchen to retrieve a pot and the iron hook from the kitchen hearth.

I placed my hand on his arm. Pál glared until I removed it.

"In the morning," I said.

"In the morning what?"

"We will go. We will not try to find those men. We will go, but not until the morning. A storm is coming."

He raised his face to the clouds and their promise.

"And how will you convince that zealot to go?"

"The upper fortress is unreachable as long as that bridge is raised," I said. "He will have no choice but to go. For now, take heart in what he has done to protect us. I feel comforted after hearing his prayer. Do you not?"

"His little priestly playact made you feel better?"

"I feel better. I truly do."

He was shaking his head and about to disparage the knight's efforts again, I thought, when he caught himself short. He suddenly swiveled around to face me.

"When is the last time you spoke to a priest?" Pál asked.

His tone had changed. "I am an episcopal messenger," I said carefully. "I speak to priests every day."

"I mean, when is the last time you asked one to pray for you?"

"You know I am merely a part of their apparatus. Are you saying you would like to pray again? We can. I have been neglectful of this aspect of your welfare, perhaps."

"Have you ever heard a priest pray as Kálmán did today? Since Annaka died?"

"No."

"And now you say you feel better?"

"We can pray again if you like."

Pál licked his lips. He was working himself up to voice his true mind, I thought.

"You spoke out of turn today," he said. "This is a new habit."

I felt my brow cinch. "That was improper of me."

"I heard what you said."

"I said nothing of consequence."

"You mocked him."

"I did not mean to. I should have kept that to myself."

"You never used to say such things."

Why was he asking me this now? I had no answer.

"Annaka spoke thus," he pressed.

"Your sister was an expert at speaking out of turn."

"I know what has been happening to you."

I put my hand on my neck, missing the braid I used to tug. "This has been a trying year."

"She is no longer harmless."

"Pál . . ."

"Her will has always been stronger than yours."

I had no answer to that.

"So I ask again—do you truly feel better? Did Kálmán's expulsion work?"

I dropped my eyes to the frost-etched floorboards. "You think you understand, but I am . . . sometimes . . . this is alike a dream."

"András. Look at me. Did his exorcism work?"

His questions assaulted me. I needed to refuse them. I felt suddenly sapped by the day.

"Was it you who spoke out of turn?" he asked. "Or she?"

"Me, of course."

"What about the horses. Did you wield the blade? Or she?"

"The horses?" I blinked. "The horses. I have been meaning to speak to you—I hope you know how sickened I feel."

More than one sentiment crabbed across his face. "And yet you wielded the blade."

"I regret it," I said.

"Why? Could you not curb yourself?"

"The deed was ugly. This place demands the worst of us." I looked across the bailey. "We cannot leave Ferenc in the stable overnight. He will be frozen dead by morning."

"Ferenc? To hell with that jittering pillicock. I ask again—did Kálmán's rite mend you?"

Little Colt's heart was growing hard. I felt my face twitch into a smirk that was never mine.

He retreated a step. "Look at how you hold yourself." His voice was hollowed out by strain. "The way you heft that pot in your elbow. The way you place your weight on your hind foot, as though hanging back, as though to laugh at all. You do not even stand like yourself."

"Pál, we cannot leave Ferenc to suffer."

"He has earned it."

I studied my boy. What had happened to him? Sometimes I too wondered with whom I spoke. "You only play at being so unkind."

I did not join him when he began striding back to the barracks.

The voice chased me all the way to the stable. It filled me with black dread and a joy begotten of bubbling light. Oh, how wonderful, these long strides, the great arcs of my swinging arms! I filled my lungs, so deep, with air that was foreign to me. How my heart ached to skip and cartwheel and laugh and laugh and laugh!

I slipped the ring over my knuckle. I rolled it around, pinched between the thumb and forefinger, not quite off. I felt the terrible chill in the air. If I chose, I could release it, let it tumble to the ground, let it bounce away. I had come close to removing it two or three times these past months. Always I had slid it back in its place. As I did this time. I made a fist, the ring secure. I had made my point. The voice was silent again.

The chill passed. Above me, a dove flew to and fro between the eaves. I watched it for a ten count before carrying on to the stable's gloomy doorsill. I found the young man as I had last seen him. Head bowed and weeping. At the sound of my footfall, he flinched and held me in his wild-animal eyes. The light was poor. It was only when I crouched before him that I saw his battered brow. Someone had struck him.

I removed the gag. No thanks poured out. He held his peace.

"Has Sir Kálmán treated you so poorly?" I asked.

"Kálmán? It was your own bastard brother that beat upon my face!"

"Pál?" The last of the manic delight ebbed from my limbs as I bent to saw through the rope tying his wrists to the stall. He could scarce stand on his own, his legs had cramped so badly. I pulled him to his feet. "Why would Pál mistreat you?"

"How should I know? He is a nasty one, he is. The worst of you lot."

"When did he do this?"

"When? After you all left and I was alone. Where are you taking me?"

"To the barracks. We will spend the night there. A storm is coming."

"But why stay?" he groaned. "Can you not feel how this place covets our bones?"

I saw no profit in telling him of Kálmán's admission. "Maybe you should pray."

"I have been doing nothing but! I have prayed someone would release me. Will it not be you? Let me go."

"I cannot."

"Please! I beg you."

"Ferenc, lad. Be calm."

"Calm! Will you not free me?"

"No."

"I will pay you a groschen! Or better yet, come with me. A curse lays on this mountain. You of all people must know of what I speak."

"Me?"

"You escaped your wife's cunning, but how many times can one man defy his rightful doom?"

I struggled to quell my indignation. Pál had not misjudged this fool. Men like Ferenc flung that word *doom* around far too freely. Such men wet themselves at the sound of thunder, shook their fists at neighbors when they forgot to secure the hutch and all their rabbits escaped. Men like Ferenc had hurled doom at my wife like stones, until one struck true.

"I have no power to free you," I said.

"He means to hang me."

I did not answer.

"And what is my crime? The will to escape damnation? Cannot you feel the ruin of this place? These stones gathers spirits like a web gathers flies. If I die here, I will never know peace. You cannot side with that fiend."

"I have sided with no one," I said.

"He will never let you leave, not until he has found his father. And he is duplicitous. Kálmán knows more about Kuszkol than he lets on. Who prays before crossing a threshold?"

"I prayed with him when we entered."

"He has secrets," he whimpered.

"All men do."

"Did you not see how he acted in the village?" Ferenc lowered his voice as though Kálmán listened outside the door. "He had seen the likes of them before."

"The likes of whom?"

"Those drawings. Those . . . villagers."

Again, I thought better of telling him Kálmán had admitted as much. "What makes you say that?"

"He was so calm."

"He is a soldier."

"He was the only one among us who would not speculate on their nature."

"That is not so."

"It is!"

"You are Sir Kálmán's man. I will spare you what comfort I can, but I cannot usurp his right to rule you."

He slumped into me after this and began to drag his feet, forcing me to bear his weight. I agreed his outlook was not good, but even so, this seemed petulant. I brought him into the storage room, and was glad to ease him down against a post.

"You would see me hanged for my common sense?"

I gave him my answer when I rebound his wrists.

"You will be fed," I said. "If you can keep hush, no one will think to gag you again."

I left him with the horses.

In my short absence, the shadows had deepened in the corners of the hall. Jakab crouched before the fireplace, his muttered oaths too easy to interpret. "I cannot get the damned thing lit," he said.

Pál shifted beneath my gaze. Could he really raise a hand against a helpless man? Perhaps it had been an accident or some misunderstanding. His pride prevented him from even acknowledging my questioning look. He stomped over to Jakab and snapped, "Give it to me."

Jakab passed the boy his tinderbox. Pál was a good fire starter. He had learned from me, and I am the best I know. It is a skill I honed after years of huddling in darkened woods and ditches while on the road.

I stood back and watched as Pál struck the flint and a spark landed on a nest of moss. He blew gently. It did not take. He tried again, and this time a point of incandescence ate through a thread of moss, and began to spread up, as a ribbon drinks dye. But the fire did not take. He tried a third time and failed.

He shook his head, and swore in the manner of Jakab.

"I need that fire," Kálmán said. He had paused in his ambulation and watched with a forbidding scowl, clearly troubled. As were we all. The shadows were gathering. The thought we might soon be flooded by darkness alarmed me, and it was growing colder. There would be snow. The wind was rising again. I wanted that fire.

Finally Kálmán said, "András. Have a go."

Pál threw the tinderbox at the floor so its contents went spinning. He did not pick them up. He stalked off to the table in the darkest end of the room.

I withdrew my own tinderbox, for I preferred not to use another's. I struck a spark and held it in the char cloth. It was fragile. I fed it moss like mush to a baby. It did not flag. I piled a scaffold of straw and whispered my encouragements, and the little flame heard. It raised its head and began to climb. The fire took.

"Come here," Kálmán said.

I turned. He waved me over to where he stood near the wall with his vial, surely empty by now. I approached.

"Your hand. Give it to me."

I held out my hand, unsure what he wanted. "This," he said. He pinched the ring I wore. He turned it a quarter way around my knuckle.

"It is the ring I gave my wife upon our betrothal," I said. "I have worn it since her death."

"It is silver," he said.

"Yes."

"For a moment I thought you wore gold."

"No."

He moved his grip so that he might squeeze my palm. "Your hand is warm."

"What of it?"

"You have just come from outside."

"What is your plan for Ferenc?"

He let my hand drop. "He will have his trial."

"This hour calls for clemency."

"You may make your case at his trial."

"I think I will not be the only one to speak on his behalf."

Kálmán glanced from me to the others. "At the trial we shall hear what you have to say."

"When will that be?"

"Once we have attended to matters of greater concern."

"I have brought him from the stable. I left him bound below."

He turned away. "I know."

Night fell fast after that, and still Kálmán prayed. The shadows deepened. At last he was finished and we made supper from Jakab's findings. Afterwards, we slumped on our stools and watched the fire seethe, not commenting on the day, or on the sound of the wind picking up outside.

"They are gone," Jakab finally said. The knight did not even look up from his thawed wine. "Or surely unreachable," the veteran continued. "There is nothing to be done."

"No," Kálmán said. He did not say more. He was not going to say more.

"The beacon has been lit," Jakab continued. "A force from Lednic can be expected by tomorrow, the next day at the latest. We might retreat to the village and await their arrival."

Jakab spoke sense. Kálmán needed to listen. But it was clear by the way Kálmán did not so much as blink an eye, by how Jakab raised his voice, that the veteran would not succeed in convincing him.

"No," Kálmán said. "Absolutely not."

"This is no place to keep vigil," Jakab pressed.

"If there are survivors," Kálmán said, "they must be found. You saw the state of the horses."

His words sketched a sober picture. That there might be men unable to help themselves, awaiting rescue, or death in its stead. Perhaps beyond help already, but still alive.

"We cannot help them," Jakab said. "But we may yet help ourselves."

Pál shifted on his stool. He was fiddling with straw, twisting strands into loops.

"Twenty-five men were garrisoned here," Jakab continued. "Where are they?"

"We each have a duty," Kálmán growled. "Not one of us has been discharged."

It was no use. Jakab should have swallowed his growing indignation then and have gone to sleep. We needed to wait for morning no matter. We could have this same conversation after a few futile hours of daylit searching.

But Jakab did not stop. "I am to report for service," he said. "Report to whom?"

He might as well have told Kálmán his father was dead. The knight bolted to his feet, sending his stool clattering across the floor. The knight stood tall above the veteran.

Jakab did not rise to the challenge. He swished the wine in his cup, then flung the dregs into the hearth. "Then again," Jakab said. "Why not throw more wood on the fire? We are but humble, bowed sticks."

Kálmán remained rigid, but his voice held such a keen edge the threat cut by his next words seemed anything but idle. "I already have one admitted coward on my hands. Must I treat with another?"

Jakab snorted, then rose and met the knight's eye. "I am to bed." He pushed past Kálmán and carried his blanket to the other side of the room.

For what remained of the evening, we sat in silence.

The knight crossed his arms, his dour lips beneath his beard as grim as the sword he had leaned against the chimney. In his black cloak he looked more than ever like a priest—one with larger cares than the curing of our souls. He did not meet my eye or raise his voice at Pál, who fidgeted in his seat. I could not tell if the veteran's words had affected him. I thought not. He kept himself apart because we and he were of two sorts, despite our shared plight.

As for my brother-in-law, he twisted straw about his knuckles and made knots which he flicked into the flames. Where Kálmán looked like he might collapse inward beneath the weight of his frown, Pál looked like he might spring forward, so restlessly did his eyes search the ground.

I wished we were alone, that I could speak to the boy about his treatment of Ferenc. Not that he would hear me out, not here. And what could I say? That he could be a better man? My fear was that Kuszkol was only drawing out his truest self.

Pál stopped fiddling with straw when he discovered me staring. Only then did he rise and go to bed.

This was beyond my ken. I was lost. We all were.

Kálmán retired shortly after. I took first watch and sat listening to the fire and eventually my companion's rhythmic breathing, jumping every time the wind rattled a shutter out in the yard.

I fretted about the day ahead. I knew Kálmán would insist we stay and find a way into the upper fort. This prospect tormented me. Jakab was not wrong. To our betters, we were fodder to their cause. Kálmán would certainly sacrifice us to recover his father. He must even regard himself as expendable.

I laid awake, spinning the ring, savoring the warmth where the silver met my flesh. I wondered what she would make of our lot—she who had never strayed more than ten miles from Veszprém. She would have reached some conclusion by now, one different from my own.

Fourteen

Pál was born the year Constantinople fell. The year a millennium of argument between Christian East and West was finally settled, not by yielding churchmen but by the unbending Turk. The Turk leveled the gates, slew or deported the populace and replaced them with his own faithful. The Sancta Sophia has been emptied of her relics, and the musulman now sits beneath the dome to contemplate his faceless god.

Whether anything was lost, I cannot say. All I know is that since I was a young man a shadow has lain across our future. One day this city will burn. All my age know it. Whether it will be the Turk or the Austrian, it hardly matters. The day Constantinople was lost, my generation learned the world can come undone.

They called it New Rome, but that city had been Greek since Alexander civilized it, since before Christ was born. They remembered the past differently in the East. Better. And when the city finally succumbed, the exiles that could afford the journey west, the bearded priests and philosophers, came clutching tomes of lost learning. So it is that we partook in the Turk's spoils.

Where others shuddered, these stories of calamity always made Annaka laugh. She liked the idea of an emptied church, of holy wisdom fled. She found even greater mirth in watching the faces of those horrified Christians, who so lewdly bent their ears to the stories until their eyes shone in the glow of ravished nunneries. Those same who defended the work of our princes to raise the heathen on pales, even if equal numbers of our own country folk rise among them.

She laughed more heartily, though, at those nostalgics who lamented the dream unfulfilled of rejoining East to West. Those worthies among whom I silently courier the bishop's word.

My tale concerns Pál, and my own mishaps on that mountaintop, but I have let the flood waters of memory rise and now they overflow and I am stranded again with thoughts of my wife. In this telling I seek not to absolve myself. I suppose it is my attempt to be truthful, and I cannot truthfully recount what passed at Kuszkol without speaking of her. My wife is as central to what happened on Kuszkol as anyone.

Was she wily? Yes, she was. I have met none wilier, man or woman, and I say such not to disavow her for she will ever be my wife. This is not to say she plotted our fates. Or perhaps she did. Maybe she understood all along. Perhaps it was less me she trusted than the future she had invented when she so knowingly stepped across my path. In the end it cannot matter because for a time she brought us joy and she brought me the boy.

After watching Pál grow, I understand better now how young my wife was when we first met. A maiden in full bloom, but near enough a child that a gulf already yawned between us.

I was a courier by then. My wandering was more regimented than when I was a boy, but it also led me further afield. By then I had walked beneath the gilded vaults of the Venetian basilica, seen the Duna empty into the sea, and I had whispered a prayer at the shrine of Saint András Zoerard, who had died fasting in his cave and after whom I was named. This pilgrimage was for my mother, for it had been her dying wish. My sisters were married, and my only home was a space on the floor of the bishop's hall.

I knew nothing of the girl. She was one of many fair faces about town, and I had never spared her a thought before she stepped before me. I was returning from another trip to Szekszárd. It was spring and many a farmer was goading their oxen through the mud. A green haze clung to the branches where the new year's buds unfolded. Ducks filled the shallows of shining Balaton, busy with their nesting.

I remember nodding to the archers on the wall as I passed through the city gate, and then looking down to see the girl. She approached with an open hand. She meant to pat my horse's shoulder.

I pulled on the reins and let the girl stroke the horse. I studied her wide-set eyes, her round chin and the fraying braid that fell from her neck.

"Can you imagine bearing another across so many leagues?" she said.

"Do you suppose I am so burdensome?"

"I do not doubt at times you are."

I smiled at the girl, whose face hovered so unexpectedly near my knee. I could have reached out to touch her head as easily as she felt Ökör's flank.

"She has not once complained," I said.

"Have you cared to ask?" Her eyes flared like a twist of grass catching fire. Then she turned and walked away. I sat astride Ökör and watched her go.

That night, as the bishop's other servants snored around me, those eyes caught fire again and again in my mind. I wondered whether she had been lingering on the road before I even passed through the gate, whether she had been waiting for me. I recalled our few words over and over, and though I could not find the fault in my speech, I despaired, sure I had offended.

I was posted in town the next week, which meant running errands for the clerics, much waiting on the bishop as he harangued or charmed his guests, and the occasional watch duty on the city walls. While up in the watchtowers, it was my custom to keep my eyes fixed on the treed hills beyond the fields, for after a few days in town I longed to wander again. But that week I turned my back on the sheep and plowmen. I watched the streets below, hoping I might spot her, or even, I fancied, find her staring up at me. I spotted a man climbing from his lover's window, but no girl.

The days passed and I took to the road again and her spell on me loosened. This was a time of great uncertainty. Emperor Frederick incited rebellion in the west, and Serbia, cowering in the shadow of another empire, desperately pleaded our king's support to fend off the Turks. I traveled to our capital and visited the king's hall. There I saw our realm's most august persons, heads bowed in conference. I recall that Kálmán's father stood among them. The bishop had other, better spies, but he would interrogate me upon my return, and so, when I passed through Veszprém's gates, my mind was already cast ahead to that meeting.

There she stood, her eyes downcast, rolling a pebble beneath her foot. In her hand she held a basket of lovage. At the sound of Ökör's hooves she looked up and seized my attention. All thoughts of the bishop dissolved.

"Off to market?" I asked, pointing to her pickings.

"Maybe. It depends. I am unsure I will find a buyer."

I stared stupidly, thrilled by her coquetry, yet horrified at my own oafish tongue, which I could not move, for I had no great history with women. Already I sensed she would best me in any battle of will. For all that, I smiled, for I was sure I had not misunderstood her meaning.

"Escort this maiden to the scales," she said.

"With pleasure," I said. I dismounted and for the first time we stood next to one another. She was near a head shorter than me, and this close I could smell the herbs in her basket and a hint of lye. She had flecks of ash in her hair and on the lobe of her ear. "My name is András."

"I know."

"What else do you know about me?"

"You are a courier. Twenty-eight." She took my left hand and examined a scar across my knuckles. "Unmarried. Long known as an eccentric, but vouched as reliable."

"An eccentric?"

I saw again that flare in her eyes that had kept bright my nights. But before it properly warmed me, she dropped my hand and sped off ahead of me.

"You have me at a disadvantage," I called.

"I should hope so."

I tugged Ökör forward. As I did, I noticed an old grandmother standing sentry on a doorstep, a broom grasped in her knobby fingers rather than a spear. Her eye was as disparaging as any tollkeeper's, and I wondered if the girl was ignorant of the look. I discovered the answer when the girl called good afternoon to the crone before looping her arm through mine.

"You must tell me your name," I said.

"Must I? I gave you five weeks to discover it."

"I thought it would be sweeter to hear you tell it."

"Now I know you to be lazy, too. Sloth is a sin. I will not hold it against you. Perhaps you will learn it in the course of our game."

"Game? Fortune rarely favors me when I cast the dice."

"If you do not play you have no chance of winning. Besides, to win this game you will need less fortune than wits."

"Wits. Then you must at least verse me in the rules of this game."

"No, I think not."

"Then this contest is not fair."

"No, but the prize will be worth it."

"Might I have a little peek at this prize beforehand to inspire my play?" I had meant to be provocative, but my words sounded both coarse and stupid.

She laughed at my clumsiness, which I supposed to be a hopeful sign. "I was speaking of my prize," she said.

"Ah, then it is a game you play alone, and it is to torment me. You may pick off my wings, but first you must tell me your name."

She withdrew her arm and chose a sprig of lovage from her

basket. She bent the stem and threaded it through the brooch that pinned my cloak. "Will you forget me so easily if I do not give you one?"

Over the girl's shoulder I saw another dour face turned our way, and I wondered if I might hear from my sisters. They would call her minx and warn me against her.

"No, I will not forget," I said.

A chicken crossed our path. The girl stomped toward it, and it flapped off squawking. "Do you suppose the foolish hen knows the name of the other fowl that peck these streets?"

"But of course," I said. "And so might we if we spoke the language of chickens."

I thought this clever, and she must have liked it well enough, for her lips parted in a smile that warmed me. "Very well," she said. "Since you so admire the chickens, you may call me 'Cluck,' and I will call you—" and here she laid her fingers on my chest and drummed twice, "'Cluck Cluck.'"

She took her leave abruptly, swaying as she went, and made no effort to hurry from my hungry view.

More than one old woman shook her head.

The strange girl haunted my thoughts. I invented errands that took me into town that I might walk the streets, searching for a glimpse of her braid. I lingered at the city gates and prowled the market square that her hand might pluck me from the crowds. I walked the banks of the Séd that her voice might call out to me above the groaning waterwheels. I came to know the city better than I had since I was a child and rambled close to home. But I saw no sign of the girl. When the bishop's house warden asked me how often I need confer with the vellum merchant, I knew I was possessed.

I journeyed again to the capital, and on my return I was so eager to pass between Veszprém's gates that I nearly lamed poor Ökör. I remember stopping a mile beyond the wall to wash my face, run fingers through hair and beard and to forage for caraway to sweeten my breath. I looked so fine when I rode into town that one of the men of the wall whistled. But there was no girl.

Until the next day. I found her sitting with her back against the wall of the convent of Saint Katalin, among the women who hawk their wares there. On a reed mat at her feet she had laid out a dozen embroidered handkerchiefs, fanned out like a hand of cards. I stood in her sun. "Hello."

She looked up and smiled. "At last a pretty face."

A seller's hoarse voice rang out, exhorting a passer-by to peruse her goods. A felt-capped vintner pulled up his cart to study her smoked fish. He must have passed a salty comment, for half the line of women hissed and tossed pebbles at the man, who whipped his oxen forward with a laugh.

"Do you need my help to fend off these brutes?"

"We would better like your denárs."

She had said we. I noticed then the little boy who dragged a twig through the dust at her side. I studied the child and saw the resemblance between them and wondered if I had misjudged the girl's age and circumstances, until she said, "This is my brother. Cluck Cluck, bid good day to Pál. Pál, bid good day to your deliverer."

The boy shaded his eyes and said, "Good day," before turning to his sister. "Is his name really Cluck Cluck?"

"Call and see who answers."

"Cluck Cluck!" the boy said.

"Yes?"

The boy giggled into the girl's sleeve and said, "What will he deliver me? Pastries? You said I might have one."

The girl brushed the boy's hair from his eyes and said, "If you are good, pastries and more. Though I daresay, your sister must to be good, too."

I grinned, certain our conversation was going well. I waited for her conspirer's smile, but she still groomed the boy and ignored me. I waited, only to realize she humored me. Her disposition that day was a little grim.

On the other side of the wall, nuns laughed into their veils. "Is something amiss?" I asked.

She nodded at the butcher who stood in his stall across the street. "That man said the filthiest words to me as I was rolling out my wares. He speaks that way to all the girls here."

The butcher was speaking with a patron beneath his awning. The man's arms were thick from cleaving bone, but he had at least ten years on me and moved with stiff repetition, so I guessed he would cause me no trouble. "Shall I have a word with him?"

"Speaking to him will stop nothing," she said. "His wife knows he is as foul and detestable as the offal he feeds his hogs. Bruise his eye, but he will keep his stall and his wife, for she knows it is he who keeps her and her children, and thus she remains silent. He has raised her up for she was once as lowly as we girls who sit here, and now she is regarded by all as decent. Her husband forgets neither tithe nor tax, and the customs-agent praises his blood pudding. And what is more, the butcher's wife is herself wayward for she has been lifting her skirt for the bone carver who buys their refuse, and she thinks she loves the man. But the boneman is using her for gratification for he is little more than a dog trained to walk on two feet. Worse, he is a killer. When he was young he and another boy went angling beneath a bridge, near a place where the kingfishers make their nests in the clay. The boys' lines became entangled and they raised their voices against one another, and soon their fists and then a wet rock came into his hand. The stream ran red and the boneman, seeing what he had shaped, loosed the other's collar and let him float away. The corpse drifted for two miles before it became snagged in a reed bank near the path to Lókút, and nobody ever found it but the rooks and the crayfish, who shared a merry feast, along with the water bugs who gamboled across his brow, but the dead boy's mother, she was heartbroken for she knew naught but that he went missing in the woods. People are afraid of the forest but chiefly it is other people one must fear between the trees. The story never escaped and the murdering boy never did brag though back in the day some of the young folk whispered rumors. I guess he has since done well for himself. Perhaps he is not so hateful, and maybe he is doing more good than harm by giving a part of himself to the butcher's wife on the side. He makes her smile. Who can say?"

"I am hungry," Pál said.

I was speechless for some moments, waiting for the girl to break the threads of the bizarre and squalid yarn which ensnarled me. I longed for that sharp white smile, but instead she held her peace.

My eye dropped to her mat. The handkerchiefs, I saw, were coarsely cut from old, yellowed linen. The stitch about the border was poor. "That is a memorable tale," I said "How came you by it?"

The sun had moved, so that when the girl looked up to me she shielded her eyes. "I listen."

"But you said the story has never been told."

She shrugged. "Almost never, and I listen hard. You listen, too, do you not? Though you are more of a watcher."

"I suppose I am."

"With all those powerful people, the knights with their estates and their gleaming helms and such. You watch how they wage war with their words and plot savagery over roasted goose."

She had not stopped fussing with the boy's hair, and as I watched, my heart continued to fall. I had imagined the girl differently, as a little wisp, a poplar seed floating in the forest that I might clasp in my hands and keep to myself. But I saw that hers was a life of obligation and tribulation. I had successfully made myself a life free of the complexities that mire others, and it did not please me to see she was so commonly burdened. More discouraging was to find she bore a touch of melancholy about her. The singularity of her person which so entranced me was raised on crooked timbers. Something lilted within. My mother, too, had been given to desperate moods. This was one reason I had found it easy not to return home at night.

"I must take my leave," I said.

"Wait," she said. "Perhaps I have misjudged you. You are not a watcher, but a seeker. You are always looking."

"Am I?"

"You were looking for me today."

"Perhaps I was."

"Yet I feel your gaze already slipping. You are too restless for your own good. Others have told you and they were never wrong. Well, keep your eyes on me a little longer, Cluck Cluck. Look at my face, because you have found me."

I did as she commanded. I looked into her eyes. She widened them, and the effect was as if they had lit. Suddenly I was dazzled and beholden. I was falling into their black depths, and for a moment I felt afraid that I plummeted into a well, but I saw no bottom and it seemed I need not fear the stinging cold of deep water for she harbored only flame. A flame that would shelter me, one I might set myself within. I glimpsed the promise, the joy that awaits the victim upon the altar, the joy of immolation.

She looked away, which left me dizzy. She began to roll up the mat with her gathered linens, none sold. The boy leapt to his feet, eager to be on his way.

"Where are you going?" I asked.

"It is time we took our leave. I will see you again, horseman."

They walked away, and as they did she withdrew a rolled crêpe from some fold of her skirt like a conjurer, which lit up the boy's face. I remained standing, contemplative yet in turmoil, certain my future days had changed.

Fifteen

I was slow to wake, like a bear rousing from its winter torpor, untouched by the cruelty of the season. I was warm and disinterested in shedding my mantle, knowing in my muscles that my very stillness had preserved me from the winter storm.

The scrape of a stool pulled across the floorboards pried my eyes open. I listened to the clink of wood and crockery, a ladle pouring wine. I could smell the fennel seed steeping, and the fire as it consumed its morning repast.

"The storm is over?" My voice cracked. I sat up on my elbows and let the chill air intrude upon my nest.

Kálmán sat hunched before a popping fire, a blanket draped across his shoulders. In the glare, I could see how the night had deepened the lines about his eyes, as if his sleep had been more ordeal than rest.

He did not reply. I listened to the day. Beyond the walls the world was hushed. Though the tempest had passed, snow still fell.

I rose and stretched. Jakab snored, his blanket grasped in two fists beneath his chin. Pál's bed was a tangle. He had risen and stepped out. I pulled forward a stool and served myself wine. I blew steam from the surface. It conjured an image from my fading dream. Smoke rising after a thunderclap, from cracked timbers or perhaps the links of an iron chain that raged in my grip.

My wife's ring caught the fire's light. A pleasing gleam in the dark before day's break. The week before I set off for Kuszkol my sister Terézia had told me I would soon need to remove it. Her reasoning was sound, but I demurred.

"When I was a child," Kálmán said. "No one spared a thought for the North. I would name my father's holdings, and no other boy would know the whereabouts of which I spoke. They would ask if my father was from Poland. A foreigner." Kálmán grunted.

I said nothing. Through my itinerant career, I had traveled the northlands less than any other corner of the kingdom. Though its towns prospered, this country was yet a hinterland. "The forest is deep in the uplands," I said.

The knight's gaze flicked up to meet mine for the first time that morning. "The forest cannot be tamed. These are old woods. We mountain folk have learnt to live among them. The South is horrid. Too much land has been cleared. It is naked, and men are so eager to revel upon it that they, too, lay bare their basest natures. Men are voracious. So sordid they gladly corrupt themselves, everyone a born whore. I mean no offense. I speak of my kind, not the humble."

I said nothing. It was not my place to tell him the South was full of light.

"The riches of the North dwarf that of the South," the knight continued. "This place is the closest thing in this degenerate age to Eden."

I studied the scum on the surface of my wine. I could scarce follow his rambling this morning. I wondered if he was yet to shed night's stupor, or if perhaps he had a touch of fever. He did not look well.

"I do not know what happened to these men," Kálmán said. "But you must not forget to whom we are sworn. You are oath-bound to the king's loyal cleric in Veszprém, and he has sent you to Kuszkol. I must know I can depend upon you."

I formulated a response, but before I spoke the sound of a rustling blanket turned our heads. Jakab sat up and stared at the knight.

Kálmán knew Jakab had been listening, but he was unabashed. "I need to know I can rely on you both," he said. "We must have faith in our orders."

"I have never failed His Excellency," I said.

"Today we will enter the upper fortress," he said. "We will find a way to cross the gap."

"The men are sure to be there," I said. It was not quite a question, and he did not answer. "Is it likely they will welcome us?"

He leaned forward and used a stick to reset the logs in the fire.

Jakab asked, "Where is the boy?"

"He will be downstairs with the horses," I said.

"He had last watch last night." Jakab stretched. "Perhaps he is having a chat with Ferenc."

I glanced at the knight. "Have you been out to see what the storm has brought us?" I asked.

The knight glanced up from his steaming cup. "No."

"I had best have a word with Pál." As I stood, Kálmán straightened and the stupor left his eyes like a cloth drawn from a table. I crossed the room and went downstairs.

Pál was not tending the horses as I had presumed. Fejes snorted as I laid my hand on her neck. "Pál—are you down here?" The horses' trough was dry. On the floor, a thin layer of snow fanned before the doorway.

Ferenc was gone. He had left the rope, still looped in my sham knot, upon the floor.

I opened the door onto a changed courtyard. Enough day had crept into the sky that I could make out the bailey before me. At least two feet of snow had fallen, and still it fell in drowsy flakes. No tracks disturbed the white field.

Ferenc had to have left hours ago. Which did not explain the absence of my brother-in-law. I closed the door and looked behind the sacks and bins in the corners of the room. As a boy, Pál often slept in the hay with my horse. I found no sign of him. "Pál?"

I returned up the stairs faster than I had gone down. Perhaps he had been sitting at the table the whole time, at the far end of the room, keeping silent in some boyish trick. Maybe I had simply not noticed him recessed in shadow.

Kálmán stared expectantly, as did Jakab amid his blankets.

Pál did not sit at the table, nor in any dim corner of the second floor. He was nowhere to be seen.

I took a breath. Just one breath before I would let the crack open within my breast.

A breath is no shield against inevitability. The crack yawed wide. I knew what had happened, and there could be no purging the knowledge.

Kuszkol had taken my boy.

"Ferenc has fled," I said. "Pál is gone as well."

Kálmán and Jakab rose and donned boots and cloaks and followed me back downstairs and into the bailey. I ran on ahead, blundering through the snow.

"Slow down!" Jakab called. "You are spoiling his trail."

"I see no tracks." I turned towards the knight. "What happened to him? Do you know?"

The knight regarded me for a long, aloof moment, and shook his head.

"There." Jakab pointed at a slight depression. The day was still dawning, but he had thought to bring a lantern, which he now held before him as he led us into the courtyard's center. Here he slowed and floundered. He bid Kálmán and me to stand still as he trudged in widening circles about us, looking to pick up the trail.

I scanned the outbuildings and wall walk. Pál must be here—but where? What little familiarity Kuszkol held for me was lost. The fortress was transformed. It appeared a different place, one we must search anew. Snow had softened the turrets and blunted the crenellations, but the fortress's gaping windows looked no less forbidding. Night still held in every cranny, each one filled with some dark potential. Nowhere could I see signs of another's passage. The white quilt laid upon the yard stifled whatever secret it might have told.

"Perhaps nearer the gate," I said. Jakab nodded and we trudged to the wooden doors that we had left open throughout the night. Snow drifted against the sides of the passageway beneath the gatehouse, but was thinner in the middle of the corridor.

"There," Jakab said. He squatted and pointed out the depression of a long stride, as made by one running through the snow.

"They deserted together," Kálmán said. "They made a common cause in faithlessness."

His voice was flat, as if he had expected nothing more. He had no trouble consigning Pál to outlawry. There was no use in telling him that Pál could not abide the Zalaman.

Jakab followed the trail out past the wall.

"They are young and scared," I said.

"Forgiveness is in God's hands now."

"But—"

"It is settled." Kálmán began to trudge back to the barracks.

I bowed my head. Pál had abandoned me after all.

"Wait a moment." It was Jakab. He returned, scowling at the ground. "I can find only one set of tracks."

"One set?" I said.

"One set."

"Do they belong to Ferenc or to Pál?" I did not know what was for the best. If Pál had deserted, I would never see him again. He had not even taken his blanket. I doubted he could have survived the night. But if Pál had not left this way I could scarce contemplate the alternative.

The veteran did not answer me. The knight said over his shoulder. "Perhaps they left at different times and the storm rubbed one trail away." He sounded as if he wished that it were so.

Jakab shrugged to show he disagreed. He walked past the knight, back into the courtyard, watching the snowy ground.

"Is there anything?" I asked.

Jakab stood in the yard's center and slowly turned around. "There." He began to march towards the ramparts. Kálmán and I joined the veteran as he hesitated at the bottom of a set of broad wooden stairs.

"A trail leads up there?" I asked.

Jakab pointed at the risers. At eye-level, it was easier to see the ghosts of footprints.

We ascended to the wall walk south of the gatehouse, where the new wooden hoarding had been affixed to the outside of the ramparts. The trail disappeared between the merlons into the covered gallery that ran outside the rampart's edge like a long shed suspended high above the ground.

It was dark within, and soundless.

We approached. The hoarding seemed to exhale a frigid breath and I could not help but flinch. Kálmán reached open-handedly, as if to warm his hand over a fire.

"What whimsy could drive him to go in there?" Jakab asked.

We both turned to Kálmán, as if he had the answer. He bore an expression I had never thought to see him wearing. He was appalled. Afeared. Later I wondered if this was the face of revelation.

"What is it?" I asked.

He shook his head. "I . . . this is wrong."

"Wrong? Did he enter or not?" I asked.

"These may not be Pál's tracks," Jakab said, "but somebody entered."

It was Pál. It had to be. My need for this cast aside the more rib-crushing question. *Why?*

"I think it best if I stay here," Kálmán said. He spoke absently, his brow severe, as if he needed to deliberate on this discovery before he could act.

"You will not enter?" Jakab asked warily.

"We should . . . let one of us keep watch. It shall be me."

"Why should it be you?"

"It does not matter," I said. "Sir Kálmán can stand watch." I turned to enter.

"Wait," Kálmán said. "Before you go further." He withdrew from his cloak a stick of charcoal the length of his finger I had not seen before. "Now raise your face to me."

"My face?" Jakab asked.

The knight took the veteran's cheek in one hand and with the other scribed a black slash on his brow. "Memento, homo, quia pulvis es, et in pulverem reverteris." *Remember, man, thou art dust, and to dust thou shalt return.*

"What the hell?"

"I adorn you with the cross. Now you."

I submitted to Sir Kálmán's ministration.

"Spare a thought for your sins," he said, "as on Ash Wednesday. Know as long as you wear this, your prayers shall reach God's ear. Now go."

Ducking through the embrasure was like entering the flue of a furnace. Here, though, instead of heat drawing tears from every pore, an indescribable cold enveloped every plane of my body. Stepping down into the wooden corridor I became aware of my loose cuffs and collar, of my lashes that stood erect and the thin-skinned globes of my eyes. Linger too long and they would harden into glassy marbles. When I exhaled, a cloud hung before me, dissipating sluggishly as though the very air had turned to slush. When I inhaled, my treacherous breath let the cold inside where it set its talons deep within my breast.

My cloak armored me not at all, so I clutched my arms across my breast to try to keep in what warmth was mine. I could not let the cold reach my heart.

It was dreadful that Pál had walked here. The low, pitched roof kept snow from our heads, though it had sifted through the inch-wide cracks that separated each plank of the outer wall. His tracks were still clear on the floorboards which ran two feet below the parapet.

The purpling sky spoke of a new day, but little light penetrated, and ahead the passageway disappeared into shadow. Despite the lantern I nearly faltered before it. I could not imagine what had moved the boy to enter the hoarding. Though we hung from the side of the ramparts, the timber and stone and the suffocating black made it seem more mine shaft than high gallery.

Within a few paces we found that one of Kuszkol's soldiers must have once waged some mad battle against the darkness and cold long before our arrival. He had scorched every plank of the outer wall by torch. The effort was scrupulous and surely intentional, as not one square inch of the wood had gone unblackened.

We paused to stare.

The deed was as impressive as it was incomprehensible. Perhaps the fire-bearer had thought he might overcome a ghost. Perhaps he had chosen this spot to make his last stand. Within a few paces I knew the answer was far less simple, for it became apparent that after scorching the planks, the soldier had gone through pains to etch the walls. We stopped for a long moment to study this work, for it was difficult to reckon. Across the charred surface, wandering lines, like the trails of boring worms, looped in great profusion. Some artisan had used an awl to scratch a vast and meaningless pattern with meticulous and unfathomable care. Yet it appeared this work had dissatisfied the artist, or another, for across the entire sinuous trail the black had been stripped away in clean, straight lines running from roof to floor. The width of these swaths varied from a finger's breadth to that of my palm. But if the purpose had been to erase the snaking tracks, it had been a poor attempt.

It was utterly confounding. We could make no sense of it at all. Not until we turned away.

After a single step, we halted once again. Seen askance, the scrawling resolved itself. The winding tracks, when viewed obliquely, showed themselves to be figures, crudely drawn but very clearly in the shape of men. The upright swaths, too, took on a new cast—that of branchless trees. The overall effect was of a populated wood, a forest in which men dwelt among deep shadows.

Jakab turned his face away. For a moment his bearded lip trembled, and I thought he might call for us to retreat, but he steadied himself, and we marched on.

I tried to keep my gaze fixed on the floor thereafter, but it was impossible not to see the scorched planks, to obsess over the bleak scene glimpsed only from the corner of my eye. For there was another aspect to this image that is difficult to put into words even now, but which rightly chilled me then. Looking sidelong upon the black woods, I formed the strong impression that the outlined figures stood in the distance. That is, the forest and the figures within it seemed no flat tableau. When viewed indirectly, the whole became a receding vista. As I proceeded down the wooden passage, it seemed that I passed not a rough sketch, but an actual forest, one locked in black winter. That if I misstepped I might find myself passing between those trees.

The days, if not weeks, the artist must have devoted to creating the vista was astounding. This strange scene offered a glimpse of the soldiers' final state of mind. They had left no note, but rather this testament, like a portal through which we later observers could contemplate the madness that finally overtook them. Those man-shaped fears that emerged ghostlike from a fog, from the colorless realms that exist just out of normal sight.

The ramparts turned a corner, and the graven work continued with remarkable consistency. And yet, slowly, I became aware the image was changing. The snaking lines grew further apart. As they did, the images hidden between them grew larger.

"They are getting closer," Jakab said.

So they were. The figures had grown and appeared to advance

towards us. As we walked further, the details revealed by those worming tracks changed. They became less indistinct and their lurid forms, awful to behold, began to resolve. Worse still was their familiarity. From where could I know those slanting shoulders, those whorled eyes and splayed tusks? In which dream had I glimpsed those bristled cheeks and swollen wattles? In which dream could I have wandered so near the rim of Hell's abyss?

I thought again of the soldiers who had abandoned Kuszkol. Or who fled inward, for surely, they had crossed the chasm and entered the keep. They had come under siege after all. They had retreated from these ramparts, from this second forest they themselves had painted within these slatted walls. But then why had they touched flame to plank in the first place? I struggled with this thought. Did they understand what they had wrought? Did they suspect their enemy lurked within?

Jakab halted. In the lamplight, he looked as haggard as the knight had that morning. The flame highlighted every sag and crease, but lent his flesh none of its glow. He whispered, "We must turn back."

I agreed. Though suspended high on a mountainside, this passage lay beyond God's sight. Yet I pushed past him and plodded on, forcing my mind from my own fear to Pál. Some nightmare must have chased him into this tunnel.

Jakab was slow to follow, and I had nearly marched into the darkness before he began to pace along behind me with the lantern. I succeeded now in keeping my eyes downcast, away from the fire-touched woods. I would stay ignorant of how near the figures approached.

"Pál!" I called, perhaps bravely, perhaps unwisely, perhaps only to re-affirm my purpose.

The hoarding rounded a wall tower, beyond which lay a final ten yards of rampart before the mountain fell away. I turned the final corner and the smell of a snuffed fire grew, as if I walked into a darkened oven. The cold gnawed my face pitilessly, so like consuming fire, that I could not help but recall the image over which I had obsessed these past six months. Annaka, in her final moments, as the rafters came roaring down.

By my echoing tread I knew the passage ended a few yards ahead. I raised my eyes and saw a shadowy figure at the corridor's end.

"Pál!" I lunged forward and reached out for him—and recoiled!

His utter stillness seized my soul. What had happened to my boy? He was so cold, so unyielding. I could not comprehend what my fingers had touched. Jakab came around the bend and the lantern's light flooded around me to cast my shadow against the wall.

I started, leaping back into the veteran to set the lantern swinging. Together we made a tripping retreat around the corner. There, with eyes wide and chests heaving, we stared at one another. Beside us, distant figures waited in the freakish wood.

"Is it him?" Jakab asked.

My heart was pounding. The figure I had taken to be Pál had disappeared into my shadow as if its edges had withdrawn from the light. It had resolved perfectly into my silhouette. I held my hand up to the lantern. A trace of soot clung to my fingertips. "I must look again," I said.

We rounded the wall tower, my hand stretched back to Jakab, should he need to haul me to safety. The light revealed the truth. The man at the corridor's end was no such thing. Here, the hoarding's unknown artist had taken up his torch to fire-paint a final image. Simpler than the forest, but no less arresting. The contour of a man, about my height, shaded solid black.

"Him!" Jakab shouted. My grip tightened on his arm. It was the same figure who haunted the ruins of the abandoned town. The same silhouette we had discovered among the simple outlines of men, women and children.

We stood facing the silhouette, rigid and dumbfounded, as though a highwayman had emerged from the woods to point an arrow at our cheeks. Or, rather, a nightmare that had crept from between the trees.

The figure was blank, empty of significance, and all the more menacing for it. A perfect phantom to stalk the fantasies of the madman who had transformed this hoarding.

At last I pointed to the path ahead. "Are those Pál's tracks?" I asked.

"Nay," Jakab said. "They are your own."

Sixteen

We left the hoarding through the nearest gap in the parapet, desperate to put the lightening sky above us. The snow fell, smothering the mountaintop, like a fog pulling the corners of the world close.

Kálmán had retreated down the wall walk to hover near the top of the staircase. We stumbled towards him like two who had just fled a collapsing tower, eyes afire, brains ringing. With every step I spewed details of our search. The forest on the walls, the figure of soot—these particulars fled my tongue like a deathbed confession.

Kálmán was alike a statue as I relayed my account. I stopped speaking and remarked that the cross he had drawn on his own brow was askew.

"What does it mean?" I asked.

"It means our prayers are not yet answered," he said.

"But what did we see?"

"I know not the likes of it."

"And what of Pál?"

"You must keep looking." He turned and descended the stairs.

I began to follow. When I saw he marched for the barracks, I checked myself. It was too early to retreat. I returned to Jakab on the ramparts.

"Pál must have returned along here," I said, pointing to the path ahead. "Can you see his tracks?"

Jakab stood, still panting, one eye fixed on the hoarding.

"Can you see his tracks?"

He looked where I pointed. "There is nothing."

"Perhaps the gatehouse."

"This mountain is cursed," Jakab said. "That forest."

"It is cursed," I agreed.

"Your boy."

"What about my boy?"

"Maybe he . . . what can we do?"

"We can conclude a proper search, is what."

"Very well." His concession sounded not like agreement. "Let us see."

We followed the wall walk to the gatehouse. It was empty. Peering down the murder hole, I realized how near I had come to the silhouette when I had passed through here the day before. I wondered what other corners and crevices we had overlooked.

I marched from the gatehouse to escape the notion. The wall on the far side was empty. Jakab walked alongside me as he had no tracks to follow. We came to the end, where the wall met the roof of the smithy, finding no trace.

With nowhere else to go, I climbed onto the roof. Jakab remained on the walk, watching me for some moments before returning to the gatehouse. I was glad to be left alone.

The roof was low-pitched and buried in snow. I crossed the inner slope and scanned the courtyard. I would search each of the buildings again—the stables, the chapel, the smithy beneath me. There was, too, the cistern. The path we had tramped across the bailey's center was now nearly erased by the ceaseless snowfall. Like Kuszkol's garrison. Like Pál. No. I must not let myself think such. I would continue to search. It did not matter if I did not understand. I would search in ignorance. I would ignore the caving pit, the sick worm boring through my core.

I climbed to the outer slope of the smithy roof. The valley was hidden by the white curtain. If Pál had not returned to the courtyard from the battlements, he could have descended in only one direction. I crept closer to the edge and looked down. A cliff dropped twenty yards to the upper reaches of the forest. Shadow filled every gap between the boughs, as wild and unneedful of Man as any place on earth. The forest appeared empty, but it was not. No forest was.

I felt the press of eyes upon me. Another watched. Or perhaps I felt only the dead gaze of Kuszkol's fallen. Perhaps all the mysterious paths of this mountain led there, to the place beneath those eaves. How many frozen bodies, I wondered, observed me from those slopes.

Sudden movement below pulled me from my reverie.

"Pál!" I plunged my hands into snow as I lowered myself to look over the edge of the smithy roof. I lay on my gut lest I slide forward, off the downward slope, and peered over the brink. I could just make out a thin outcrop of rock that ran like a ledge a few feet below the smithy's foundation. Upon this treacherous path, barely noticeable in the storm, perched a dark shape, now still.

"Stay there!" I called. "I will fetch a rope."

At these words, the form moved again and I recognized the hooked horns and black tip of muzzle. The ram regarded me from slit eyes before turning round with great care. I lost sight of it behind the next gust of wind.

No track led me to the smithy or chapel, to the kitchen, the stable or the watchtower. Still I kicked through the snow, searching under tables, beneath the altar, in trunks and even barrels. I scanned rafters and knocked on floorboards, probing for trap doors. Jakab paced beside me, searching less frantically and, I could tell, with less hope. His presence was a great irritation.

The day broke, but still we carried the lantern to peer into every nook of the lower bailey. When I dipped my head into the cistern, I swung it below me to light the cell. The water lay a yard below. A skin of ice had spread across the surface, and beneath it, the water appeared opaque, a solid shadow. There was no sign the ice had been disturbed in the night.

"Where else?" I asked. "Do any tracks lead to the chasm?" Jakab shook his head.

I had left the chasm to last. The moat to the upper bailey. From where we stood we could see the raised bridge on the far side. A thick, undisturbed layer of snow had piled on the platform's upright lip. Pál could not have crossed. Yet if we did not look for him there, our search would remain incomplete.

We returned to the barracks. I told Jakab to warm himself above as I cared for the horses. I returned to the cistern and freed the water with a crowbar to fill the troughs. I filled the feedbags and carried forkfuls of hay from the stable's loft. After mucking the storeroom, I spent some time patting the horses and rubbing warmth into their legs. Both seemed to have caught a chill. I rubbed them down again but they continued to tremble, so I retrieved spare horse blankets from the stable then went upstairs to fetch a coal for the brazier.

I suppose I delayed because I was reluctant to face the others. I did not want to know what they had to say. I did not want to endure their hollow words of courage, or to hear them deny that spanning the chasm was possible. We would have to try, even if we guessed our efforts were in vain.

I could hear the fire roaring as I climbed the stairs. Before I entered, Kálmán raised his voice. "Have a care. I must have a dry floor."

I removed my boots upon the threshold of the sleeping hall. Jakab sat on a stool before the huge blaze. Kálmán was kneeling, his open book in one hand, his other holding his stick of charcoal.

He had not been idle as we searched the fortress. In a sweeping arc across the floorboards he had sketched a diagram. I could not tell if it depicted a string of men holding hands or a looping thread from a foreign alphabet.

"Kálmán." I said. I stepped nearer. "You must explain this."

The knight leaned forward and copied, I recognized now, another sign from his book, which was no psalter after all. When he finished, he sat back on his haunches and fixed me with a long, unrepentant stare. "Yesterday's prayers were insufficient," he said. "We must try again. This time we combat like with like. I do not take this measure lightly."

Kálmán turned back to his drawing without further comment. I began to walk the diagram's circuit. It would be a circle when completed. The image both drew and repelled me. I was sure that he was writing, but in a language unknown to me. Yet I was equally certain that he illustrated a sort of scene, for as I studied the dense, cursive arc I saw men, beasts, even trees and fields of drooping barley heads. It was like a map of creation, I thought. One could almost pick out all the angels and their domains.

"Where did you learn this art?" I asked warily, as I might a drunken knife thrower. Or a feeding bear.

Kálmán leaned forward to trace another loop that resolved itself into a sorcerer's rod, half-transformed into a serpent—or perhaps some fancy from the mind of a mischievous illuminator.

"Did you learn this in the Holy Land?" I asked. The charcoal tip stopped. "You once told me some wisdom yet persists in the East."

"Wisdom whose seeds lie dormant through the long drought," he said. "Wisdom whose roots drink deep to survive the desert storms."

"Is this art not . . ." I hesitated but could find no better word, "wicked?"

I feared he might bristle. Instead he studied his charcoal thoughtfully. "No more wicked than fire."

"And it is not the invention of . . ." It took a tremendous effort to say the name. "Lucifer?"

"It is the invention of a wise king. I know you have read the Gospels. Perhaps you have some knowledge too of the older books of the Bible."

"Some."

"Then you might remember King Salamon. He built the Temple to house the Ark. His example is so wondrous he has inspired many a bedtime tale, as Jakab reminded us yesterday. Salamon spoke to no ants but he did speak to angels. This is his art."

The words to correct him were between my teeth. That it was she, Salamon's wife, the Ammonite, who had devised this circle as her own seal, in defiance of her husband.

I pressed together my lips to stifle the voice. At this sign he nodded, wrongly assuming I had no more questions.

He continued his drawing. Jakab and I continued to watch. From some corner, a draft collected itself and flit across our feet. The snow through which we had trudged had not been so cold.

At length Kálmán stowed his charcoal and made to put his green book away. Before he did, he paused to replace a loose page slipped from between the other leaves.

"In the hoarding," I said. "We saw creatures. Manlike things, reaching out for us."

"Yes."

"Is that . . . are they the spirits you combat?"

Kálmán shook his head.

"No?" I asked.

"I do not know. They might reflect the spirit's legion being. They might be husks of those it has conquered."

"That it has conquered? I think they were not men."

"There was a time before men."

"And what of the shadow? The figure of soot."

"Of that I would be wary," he said "Now again I will pray."

He stepped into the center of his circle.

"Shall we join you?" Knowing his exorcism had failed once, I was not eager to attempt a second time, but it was too late for half measures.

"This prayer is in the tongue of Salamon's court," Kálmán said. "You cannot help."

He held his hands to his sides. In one hand he held a small bronze mirror, in the other a set of finger cymbals. These so absorbed my attention that when he finally raised his voice, I started. He was not content to speak in the hushed tones that had become our custom. His voice built quickly, powerfully, like wind filling a sail. He spoke his prayer in a sing-song cadence, the likes of which I had heard in no mass before, using words I could not begin to transcribe.

This was a spectacle from far beyond any horizon I had crossed. Perhaps from a time beyond. From back when Nagy Sándor toppled empires, from before the gentile had made the Bible his own.

Jakab rose and left the room. This movement broke the spell and I was quick to heed his example.

We descended the stairs. He leaned against a barrel and I against the post. We did not speak.

Fejes blew. Her head hung down and still her flank was shivering.

"Poor girl," I said. "I will get this brazier lit."

I had forgotten to retrieve a coal from the fireplace. I could hear Kálmán almost singing above us. I had no interest in interrupting him. Easier to start a new one. I struck my flint and sparks flew into the pan.

Even as the fire was beginning to beat back the chill, Kladivo groaned. I turned in time to see him lower to his knees. "Easy now," I said, and moved toward him, but stopped short when the horse rolled onto his side. I could do nothing to slow him. He let his weight carry him, pushing over a barrel, which upset the hayfork, whose handle knocked a jar of sauerkraut from the shelf. It landed with a crash.

Kálmán's horse loosed another long sigh. I could almost see his strength abandoning him in the clouds that jet from his nostrils.

"That beast is failing," Jakab said uselessly. The song upstairs slowed but did not stop.

I stroked Kladivo's chest, searching for a cause. His flesh was cold to the touch.

Kálmán crouched beside his horse. Taking the beast's neck in his arms, he whispered secret encouragement.

"Do you know the words to cure him," I asked. I was trying to warm Fejes by rubbing her flank with a rag I had heated against the brazier's bowl.

Kálmán stiffened. "I am no country wisewoman," he said.

No, he was not that. When I had climbed the stairs to interrupt him, I knew for certain the draft that swirled across the floor had no source in some crack in the wall. The pattern the fire had thrown upon his face and the lids of his shuttered eyes—they looked too alike shadows cast from some sinuous grasping, thorn-crowned puppet. His eyes, when they snapped open and alighted upon me, too much a lion's.

"They have taken a chill." I said.

Kálmán continued to probe Kladivo purposefully. He pulled back the horse's lip, raised his tail, lifted his feet. He studied the hooves intently. He touched a shoe and withdrew his fingers as though they had been nipped by a goose.

He leaned closer to examine the hoof. He touched, fleetingly, the shoe again.

"What do you think?" I said.

The knight released Kladivo's foot, and stroked him distractedly. His gaze landed on the shards of the broken pot, but I think he did not see them. Then he rose. He did not answer me. Instead he strode into the bailey with forceful intent.

"What is it?" I was obliged to fall in step behind him for his answer. "Is it not just a chill?"

He made for the stable. Inside, Kálmán walked down the aisle, stepping into pens and crouching beside the dead beasts that lay stiff and enshadowed in their open graves. He spent several minutes in study, during which time Jakab entered to watch what we did. After inspecting the roan, the knight stood with an air of resolve.

"Speak." I said. "What do you think to find here?"

"That." I followed his outstretched finger. At the end of stable was a pile of iron I had not noticed before. Worn horseshoes and twisted nails, discarded in an untidy heap.

I stared at the heap for a moment before walking back to the roan. Its feet were bare. I looked into the next stall and discovered the same.

"We must unshoe the horses," Kálmán said.

"What?" Jakab said. "Now?" But Kálmán had already passed him and was returning to the barracks. Together, one hauling on a lead, the other pushing on the tail, we were able to coax Kladivo to rise. We led the horses to the smithy, pulling them onward through each grudging step.

Kladivo and Fejes were weakening. Given the carnage in the stable, what else did I expect? It was not men alone that Kuszkol conquered. I remembered once how Pál, still a little boy, asked to set Fejes free. I told him then that freedom from our care meant only freedom to succumb to the dripping jaws of the forest. Walking with one hand on her neck, I saw how shabby was my instruction. In the end, no beast in our care is spared the slaughterhouse.

Jakab complained, "This is madness. Why must you play the farrier now? Let us finish our search for the boy that we may leave well before nightfall."

"The horses are weakening," Kálmán said. Careful to pull on his gloves, he selected tools from the workbench and took up Kladivo's hoof between his thighs. He began to worry nails from the shoe with a pair of pincers, and with a little prying and tamping, had removed a shoe with impressive skill.

Jakab stared sullenly until the shoe Kálmán tossed aside clanged off the stone floor. "It is too loud!"

Kálmán ignored the veteran and took up a second foot.

"But why must we unshoe them?"

Without warning, Kálmán snatched Jakab's wrists and jerked the veteran forward. Before Jakab had regained his balance, the knight forced the veteran's fingers to press against Kladivo's shoe. Even as Kladivo started and Jakab yipped, Kálmán held it in place. "Are you so insensitive to the cold?"

Jakab tugged wildly to release his hand, until Kálmán suddenly obliged. Jakab staggered back against the wall. The veteran's face twisted into a snarl and for a moment I thought he would charge the knight. I did not like his chances. With his thin hair awry, his slight shoulders bent forward, never before had he seemed such an old man. Never had he seemed so impotent. For his part, the knight, standing erect, was a tower of vitality.

Jakab retreated. He backed out of the smithy without a word. I watched him stomp off and cradle his hand, which he turned before his face. I remembered the phenomenal cold that had seared me when I picked up the dagger in the chapel.

Kálmán had retrieved his pincers and was working out another nail when I turned back to him.

"It is the metal that injures the horses," I said. "As the soldiers' own metal betrayed them. That is why they abandoned their arms in the chapel."

Kálmán paused to stare past the hoof. "One should put no greater faith in iron than in gold," he said.

"And the hellish cold we found in the hoarding?"

"Speak not so carelessly of Hell. It remains to be seen whether my charcoaling is sufficient. The hoarding . . ." The knight shook his head.

"This is all too absurd," I said. We had come to a place as horrific as any from Alexander's travels. What chance did Pál have? "Why did you ever allow us to come here?"

"No one of consequence ever denied the truth of this mountain," he snapped. "You may have scoffed at the stories. I was milk-fed on them. My father won title to this valley through hard service, terrible sacrifice, and his prize was bitter tears. Land no peasant would ever till, timber no forester would ever fell. I have prepared my whole life to reclaim this land. I will leave more to my son than a promise."

He bent his head to examine the passage of his rasp. He blew a mass of shredded hoof from the bowl of Kladivo's foot. I asked, "Does the king know about your book?"

Kálmán dropped the hoof and pulled himself up. He stepped before me and, like Jakab, I felt small before him.

"A man must not put too much faith in iron," he said. "Nor should man put much faith in sketches on the floor. None of man's methods is infallible. An accusation sits on your tongue. Restlessly, for it is the very one others have hurled at your hearth. Your words are those of condemnation. A wise man takes a care not to damn his tools, no matter how they might grieve him. A sinner I may be, but all my toils, all my acts and the tactics I employ, I undertake that I might better repent. The better question, I think, is what you have to say for yourself and your boy."

"Myself and Pál? What about us?"

"What is the true reason you have come to Kuszkol?"

"The reason? There is no mystery. We were ordered to do so."

"By His Excellency Albert Vetési. That old fox." He studied me coldly, his scrutiny verging on disdain.

"I know nothing of His Excellency's purposes," I said. "But I assure you, Pál and I are the poorest of his tools. We know nothing of his interests here."

"Yet there is some aura about you. A secret. Some endowment, perhaps. Some blessing from your wife."

His words froze me in place, as one etched against the lightning.

"Do not mention my wife."

"Annaka was her name."

Annaka. To hear her name, uttered by this stranger, who presumed to look down on me, who cared not at all that his blamefulness destroyed my esteem for him. I felt I would sick. Yet the now familiar buzzing filled me with unlooked-for elation. It was all I could do to keep from laughing. Instead, I blurted, "What did you say?"

"You will not place your trust in me, but it is you whose past is suspect."

"Are you suggesting the lies they spread about my wife—that *destroyed* my wife—are more incriminating than the fact of your methods?"

"Were they lies?" he asked.

"Of course!"

"As you say, then." Kálmán returned to attending his horse.

I bent my face close to his own. "It is *you* who prevail upon invisible powers. It is *you* who knows the secrets of this fort."

"And I know little enough."

"Do you know at least if Pál still lives?"

The knight's scorn softened unexpectedly. "I cannot say."

"Where is he?"

He finished rasping Kladivo's hoof and said, "Now bring me your girl." I led Fejes to him as Kálmán let Kladivo nuzzle his head and whicker into his hair.

"Where is he?" I repeated.

The knight gripped the first of Fejes's hooves between his thighs. "No place that I know."

Kálmán marched through the knee-high snow, leading the horses once again about the bailey to assess their recovery. He did not speak to me, nor I to him. I stayed only long enough to judge whether Fejes regained her pluck. She had. Satisfied, I left without a word.

I went hunting for Jakab that we might resume our search for

Pál. He was not, as I supposed, brooding over a wine before the fire. Thus, I undertook my second round of the lower bailey that morning. The snow had not relented and little sunlight penetrated the gentle storm. Twilight still sheltered beneath every roof. I found the veteran in those shadows. He sat on a bench in the chapel, leaning forwards with his elbows upon his knees. When I entered, he did not look my way.

The pile of arms was no more. The abandoned metal was strewn across the floor. Jakab must have kicked through it as we worked in the smithy. I had no doubt as to why.

"How long have you been delivering those letters?" he asked when I took a seat at his side.

"Twelve years."

Jakab nodded. "This is my thirty-third year soldiering. It seems incredible now. To think I ever swore my life to a king who would never learn my name."

I had not realized that I had sought him out for companionship. It was the first time I had chosen Jakab over solitude. More surprising, he seemed to need my company equally.

"I was beguiled," he said. "Or so one might say. My family were dung-soled herders. Simple folk. We carry the blood of the khans, and our clan drove sheep and cattle over the plain south of Halas. I was my father's fourth son, the lone child of my father's second marriage. Do you know much of my people?"

"Some." We needed to soon resume our search, but I could see Jakab was in no mood to be rushed.

"We are a strong people. Proud. Crafty. My father was lamed when I was yet suckling and my elder brothers each took their share of his herds while he still lived. Those filchers knew to take mine, as well. I did not rightly understand this until I was nine years old. Far too late.

"One night I pulled my mother aside. It was the Feast of Saint Márton. All were merry, and I thought it a ripe time to make my claim. I sought my mother's counsel.

"She listened to my complaint, and when I finished, she said nothing. She just stared past me, at my nephews who climbed across my father's knee. I took her hand and said, 'Mama, what should I do?'

"Finally, she looked me in the eye—she never had trouble meeting my eye, no, not mine—and do you know what he said to me? She told me, 'Your father is weak. Your mother lives in fear of being cast out by her stepsons and you must never, never dispute your lot.' She said my destiny was rags and cast-offs, but if I did not turn to drink and if I watched my tongue, I would always have a place at their board. If I could not abide this, then I could seek out an unwanted, cross-eyed daughter and live a life indebted to my father-in-law. Or, if luck was with me, marry a blown-out widow.

"But there were no widows in my village in the autumn I was seventeen. So I traveled to Szeged. I figured the city was so pestilential, widows must be queued at the church gate, awaiting any man to save them." Jakab smiled.

"I found no eager line of widows, and as happens, I found my way to a tavern and fell into a game of dice with some soldiers. On that day I won my first coin. A silver groschen. Many times since I have wished I still held that coin. A lucky charm, well earned. But that day I betrayed my luck. I spent the silver on wine for my new friends and for the barmaid suddenly so eager to warm my lap.

"I was old enough to know better," Jakab said. "But I was a yokel, and embittered at that. So the next day I woke up in the gutter and I enlisted straightaway. All for a chance to win at dice again."

I had heard such accounts the country over. A favorite tale among old-timers was the story of how they lost their chance. I said, "Every man who has enlisted has gambled on winning a better lot."

Jakab laughed. "But I did not gamble! Enlisting has been a sure bet. I have won gold, and I have had a taste of widows and ugly daughters at every posting. I used to be a stallion. I like to think I have left whole broods behind, but that is not my concern. I am a simple man and I started with such few prospects that I cannot rightly say my hopes have been dashed.

"That first year though." He shook his head. "Well, some cowherds came to town to complain about rustlers. I knew the plaintiffs well enough. They were from a neighboring clan. Their headman committed a grave breach of tradition by coming to town. Such disputes have always been settled among ourselves. But . . ." The veteran shrugged his shoulders. "We caught the culprit. It was Uzur. My eldest brother. Do you know what the punishment is for cow thievery?"

"I can guess," I said.

"Well, I saved my brother's thankless head. Afterwards, he spat upon my name. He did not recognize that I was loyal where he was not. You see, I intervened with my captain, and he was persuaded by the terms I proposed. We confiscated Uzur's herd. We distributed half to the aggrieved clan, and the captain kept the other half for himself. My reward? I ate beef all that winter."

He spread his fingers and I noticed for the first time the silver rings he wore on nine fingers.

"Jakab . . . those are from the floor?"

"We must all take what we can, when we can. The army has taught me that. It is the king's own law."

Even in that dim light I could see how red his hands had become. "Remove them at once," I said. "You saw how the horses failed. Do they not freeze you? Do they not burn?"

"Oh, aye. It was worse at first. But with them all on together, it feels about right." He made two fists. "Now I feel like I have some ice in these knuckles. I just wish I could find a tenth."

"Take them off."

"I am so tired," he said.

"Take them off."

"I cannot see it making much difference. Besides, I have spied a fine ring on your finger since we left Veszprém. Remove yours and I will remove mine."

His smile unsettled me, as did the flashing glance that alighted upon my banded finger, too much like a serpent's tongue.

"It does not pain me," I said.

Jakab's smile broadened. "And soon I will be accustomed to these nine. I reckon one cannot truly escape the cold up here in any case. Did you come here to fetch me?"

I hesitated to speak. The change gave me pause. Jakab had never been reliable or bold, but now I doubted his wits.

"We tackle the upper bailey forthwith," I said.

Jakab rose and began to nudge iron weapons aside with his foot.

"Did the knight say you would find the boy up there?"

"He promises nothing."

"Do not be so soft-headed to think you can trust him."

"I am not," I said. "But it is the only place left to us."

"And how could the lad have conquered that gorge by himself? Do you suppose he walked on air?"

"Perhaps he had help," I said.

"Meaning he was abducted." I suppose this is what I meant. Perhaps, at this point, this is what I hoped. I knew no response would please the veteran, so I said nothing. "The knight probably assured you his kidnappers would be reasonable, that we will find the boy and he will be sound, if only we press ahead."

"No," I answered. "He said when we find Pál I must be ready for anything."

Outside the chapel, the gentle torrent smothered our tracks.

Seventeen

The mountain gave way at our feet. Below us, a chasm sheltering at its depth a seam of new snow and beneath that, no doubt, a sliver of dirty glacier. We stood on a ledge, on a shallow wooden balcony that extended from the rearward side of the lower bailey. The entrance to the upper bailey lay across the rift, out of reach, its portal clad by a raised drawbridge.

I could see no way for us to close that breach, to foil the will of Kuszkol's defenders to starve on that cold and final crag. The raised bridge presented an insuperable hurdle. How our three-man siege might ever hope to gain access, I was at a loss.

Kuszkol's upper bailey was built uphill. When lowered, the bridge would slope down to the balcony to form a ramp. This difference in height further disadvantaged us. So too, did the lack of any purchase a hurled rope might find. The merlon teeth of the far parapets were too distant, and what is more, buried beneath a thick sheath of snow.

Thus we stared at the drawbridge's upturned belly without speaking, and the longer the silence stretched, the greater my anguish grew, for I knew that whoever spoke next could only utter words of futility or defeat.

It was the knight who spoke the former. "We must fetch a ladder."

I suppose Kálmán's talent for fanning the hopes of men came from his training to command on the field, or perhaps simply from the privilege of his upbringing and his ignorance of despair. Whichever, his resolute tone unaccountably buoyed me even as I voiced my doubt. "No ladder will reach the top of those parapets," I said.

"We need not mount the wall," he said. "We need only fashion a new bridge."

I could see no reason to the knight's words, but neither any sense in contesting them. I had no better scheme. Jakab and I tramped back to the smithy and returned with the ladder.

The gap was ten feet across. The threshold of the far portal was ten feet above the ledge upon which we stood, and the raised bridge rose above that. Kálmán lowered the ladder across the gap and settled it against the far wall. The tips of the ladder's rails came to rest upon the narrow lip of the raised bridge.

"Now what?" Jakab asked.

"Now one of you must cross and lower the drawbridge."

"I would sooner try my hand at turning water into wine." The veteran cast about him, as if for a safe place to sit and wait out this misadventure.

I was no more pleased than Jakab. Perhaps less, for I had for a moment allowed hope to root in my breast. I had trusted the knight would devise a cleverer stratagem by which to close the gap. But watching the veteran's face twist, I recognized that this contempt could wreck us as fast as any failed crossing, and so I nodded and placed my foot upon the bottom rung.

Kálmán and Jakab knelt to brace the ladder's feet. It was propped at a perilous incline, and I began my ascent knowing it was their strength alone that kept the ladder from skidding. I climbed with caution, keeping my eyes raised from the unfathomable white below. The wooden rungs bit into my shins through my riding boots, and my cloak was an annoyance once it slipped to one side. I was glad, though, that I had chosen to forgo my gloves. Seeing my white knuckles clench every dowel gave me a false sense of control. The mountain wind chilled them, but I had known far worse cold that very day.

Yet midway across, my skin prickled and the mountain air caught deep in my lungs. I stopped climbing, certain that someone watched.

I studied the dark loopholes that punctured the far gatehouse wall. There were so many vantage points from which a stranger might watch me, from where he might spy me along the shaft of his arrow, I knew that death could come streaking without me so much as marking its swift flight.

"What is it?" Kálmán called softly.

I slowed my roving search and studied each of the slits in turn. I saw no figures moving, no one, and yet I felt the weird and invisible weight of another's watchfulness. I almost scrabbled backward to put myself out of reach. When I had climbed over the ramparts I feared another might catch a sight of me. Now I was convinced unseen eyes were trained upon me. I strayed through the deliberations of a wolf who contemplated whether its jaws might tear a fountain vein.

Still, the watcher only watched. This instinct gave me no peace as I examined the far windows. They were empty. The one who watched, the beast who anticipated me as I clambered into range, was not, in any sense of the word I understood, there.

Pál could not have gained the upper bailey by himself. For myself I could see no chance of success, and I had the help of the knight and the veteran. My wife would have counsel for this moment. I could hear her words. *Relent,* she said. *Go elsewhere. Our colt does not await yonder.* But I was done with her counsel, so I moved my hand to the next rung, and bent my mind to our boy.

I finally reached the far wall, and the precariousness of my place banished even these uncertain thoughts. The drawbridge was lightly constructed. Luckily, its planks were not flush with the wall, and I saw now a gap of a few inches between the bridge and the masonry, across which rested the ladder's rails.

Between this crack I could fit my fingers, perhaps my hand past the wrist, but if the knight had thought I might somehow slip through to access the upper bailey, he was mistaken.

I made the harrowing return to the others. "I see no way to lower the bridge."

"Does the bridge suspend from rope or chain?"

"Rope."

"Good," Kálmán said. "Return and cut the rope."

"Cut it? But I will surely fall with the bridge."

"Tie yourself off."

Jakab shook his head. I thought he waited for me to speak out against this folly, so he might lend his voice to mine, but I turned away and marched to the storeroom. I kept my eyes from the steps to the wall walk, drawing minor comfort from the knowledge I need never step into that forsaken hoarding again. I returned with rope that Kálmán tied about my waist and shoulders in a harness. He then clapped my shoulder like a good horse and sent me over the span.

My nerves were no better on the second crossing. Maybe worse, for I had a clearer idea of the slim chance we had to gain entry. Once across, I knotted the end of my own line about one of the bridge's ropes where it disappeared into the wall. I then withdrew my bone-handled knife and began to saw the other. The little blade, which I used for bread, was hardly up to the task. Yet on I worked, and after a time I struck upon a method that severed fibers with every stroke.

When the cord was halfway cut, I paused to inspect the strain in the last few threads. The rope had grown narrow, and for many moments I could not persuade my hand to move, for I could too easily envision the consequences. What finally allowed me to continue was a memory from childhood. Of perching in the crotch of a tree, staring at the leaf litter below, readying myself to leap. What compelled me as a boy was the insight that my fall was inevitable.

There was no profit in waiting, so I resumed my sawing and in a few strokes I made my final cut.

The rope snapped. The bridge juddered beneath my palm as its right-hand side skewed from the wall. At the same time, I felt the ladder slipping sideways beneath my feet. I snatched at the deck as the ladder disappeared beneath me.

I fell. My body collided with the bridge's underside. The crash knocked the sense from me, and I was aware of a mighty curse echoing behind me even as I lost my grip on the deck. For a fleeting instant, which my gut recalls even today, I was falling as my line let out. Then I struck the deck a second time.

Twisting from the end of my rope, addled by the fall, I saw a dark figure kneeling across the way. Kálmán, swathed in his black cloak, bent to lift up Jakab who had nearly followed the ladder over the edge. This sight struck me unaccountably. For an instant I did not recognize Kálmán, yet the scene became vividly familiar. I had viewed this event before. By some presentiment I had anticipated that dark figure leaning over Jakab, or maybe I had glimpsed its likeness in a dream. I chuckled through my locked teeth. The comedy of this sight delighted me. It was too absurd. The source of my reaction was opaque to me then, and the moment passed.

I watched as the shaken veteran rose to his feet. The knight, looked across the gap towards me and I witnessed the rarest of sights —a grin. He said simply, "Good."

And he was right. My knot had held and by some miracle I had managed to keep my grip on the knife. I recovered my breath and began to climb.

The right side of the deck now yawed from the wall, allowing me to slide a full leg into the gap between the bridge and the wall. It was still too slight for me to slip between, but as I peered down I found our first piece of luck.

On their retreat, Kuszkol's defenders had neglected to lower the portcullis. Once the bridge was down, we could walk into the upper bailey without any further barrier. The portcullis's grill also gave me a better anchor for my line, so I cut the knot and refastened it to the iron bars. Then, balancing on the two-inch deck, I began to saw the bridge's second rope.

Hope began to build as I worked. The only eyes I felt upon me were the knight's and the veteran's, my comrades on this unlikely expedition. I sped my pace and rushed the inevitable fall.

And fall I did. The bridge's supporting rope snapped. The bridge dropped, and I tumbled over its edge and skidded down the deck even as it gave way beneath me. The bridge landed with a crash and bounced, with me upon it.

I lay dazed, my eyes fixed on the barbed lower butts of the portcullis. Poised like fangs.

I heard footsteps. I turned my head, and the knight loomed out of the white day. He offered me his hand. "Very good."

We passed under the portcullis, through a narrow tunnel, and came into a high-walled court. Loopholes pierced each side of the enclosure, for this little square was conceived as a killing yard, a place where Kuszkol's archers might punish any assailants who had prevailed against the chasm. Staring at the slender cracks, it was too easy to imagine their arrows flying from every quarter.

We sidled along the wall, though I decided the archers' perches and niches could not be manned. The place was too forlorn. We passed through a small archway and out of the courtyard, into a small defile, where again, Kuszkol's last defenders might annihilate their enemies. No challenge was called, nor any arrow fired our way. We followed the path upwards and around a corner and emerged finally into a wide and sloping yard—the upper bailey.

The sheer face of Kuszkol's keep rose above us. A mason-laid cliff, as daunting as any of the mountain's escarps. A row of black windows perforated its upper stories, as remote as soothsayers' caves, and a white battlement crowned its head. At its foot a naked staircase rose to an iron-bound door.

Over the keep's western shoulder, I spied the mountain's peak. Among its hoary crags I could pick out a narrow path that led up to its summit and the beacon thereupon.

We stared long at the keep. Kuszkol's final defenders lurked within. Someone had closed the gates and drawn up the bridge. Though there was no sign of life, it could not be empty, for there Pál must wait. There was nowhere else he could be.

Even as I held this thought, doubt tugged at its edges. The mountain's slopes below the fortress's ramparts were vast. He may lay broken below countless wintering trees, and I would never find him, his burial unmarked beneath the oblivion of snow.

A touch settled on my shoulder. It was only Kálmán motioning for me to follow. None of us had spoken since we stepped from the drawbridge. The knight led us onwards, through another archway to the passage that ran behind the walls of the killing yard. Here we found a wooden staircase that led to a narrow gallery by which archers might access their eyries, and at the end of this corridor a doorway into the little gatehouse.

I doubted Pál could somehow have crossed the chasm only to have taken up refuge in this gatehouse. Still, glancing back at the keep, I did not object to the detour, for I feared I would soon exhaust places to search.

I ducked through the small doorway. Immediately a shocking cold bathed my face as rudely as a splash of icy water. So wicked was the cold that I did not immediately note the hint in the air until Jakab made mention of it. "Fire."

It was true. The air contained a memory of a fire that had burned in this gatehouse. It recalled to me the hoarding. "We must not enter," I said. "He cannot be here."

Kálmán strode ahead through the door. Next went I, but Jakab did not follow.

The knight and I climbed a winding staircase, and with every step it seemed the cold grew more bitter. So too, did the acrid sting of ash in my nostrils. With every step the thinness of the mountain air stifled us even more. So did my certainty grow that we would discover multitudes. In the killing yard I had momentarily convinced myself this place was abandoned. I had been mistaken. The feeling of being watched as I crossed the ladder, that had been real. My observer was near at hand.

A protest rose in my throat, but Kálmán did not slow and I followed him into daylight. We entered a narrow room that lay behind the archers' posts in the gatehouse. I caught a sight of scorched walls and nearly pulled back, but Kálmán suddenly grasped at my arm as his footing gave way beneath him. I steadied him, and I felt my own foot slide beneath me. The floor was skinned by ice.

The walls glinted in the light of the day, glazed like the floor. I had never seen the likes of it. The whole narrow room was encrusted. I kept my hands well beneath my cloak and leaned my face close to study this wonder. I peered through the ice and saw what lay beyond the frosted patina. Black walls, streaked and smeared as though by a rag. Evidence the stone had been coarsely scrubbed.

"Let us be gone from here," I said.

But I did not move. I peered at the ice and was sure that crawling behind it, across the smeared black, were the ghosts of worming lines. That if viewed obliquely, the image behind the ice would still reveal figures advancing through the teeming trees.

"Was it thus in the hoarding?" Kálmán asked.

"The same."

"Here they tried to erase the forest."

Tried and failed, for in the act, their wash water froze. The forest was still visible beneath the ice.

"Let us be gone," I said again.

Kálmán ignored me. Instead he moved his head so that he no longer faced the wall and crept forward a step. When he gasped I knew he was watching sidelong and had succeeded in penetrating the ice to look indirectly, as one must, into the forest.

"Look away," I said. "No good can come from those depths."

"I see it now." Kálmán rocked back and forth, changing perspective on whatever scene he could perceive aslant. In the hoarding, such a shift in perspective had caused the figures between the trees to seem to near.

Finally he turned to face me. I was not comforted by his glow of enlightenment. "You can go," he said.

"Let us search the upper floor," I pleaded.

"Do as you will." He waved for me to return to the stairs, as he resumed his position, peering sidelong at the wall.

I left him to investigate the upper floor—the guards' bunk, the windlass chamber, the small armory. What little there was to see, I barely noticed. I was consumed by the thought of him, alarmed that below me Kálmán stood so willfully gazing where none should look. He should be driven back by revulsion. He should be driven back by the tangible sense of *need* that pulsed through the cold. I could not imagine he was unaware.

I rested on the bunk for a while. My hip was sore from my fall. It felt good to sit. After a time thoughts of cold slipped away as I remembered how she would often rest like this upon waking. She was slow to rise every day. Countless times I found her sitting on the edge of our cot with her fine yellow hair hanging over her closed eyes. Her hands, one holding a comb, would rest forgotten in her lap even as mine lay quiet now. I would have liked to have fallen back asleep. My hands were unaccountably warm. My ring did have a goldish cast in this mountain light.

Perhaps I lingered overlong. I roused myself and felt calmer and somehow more indifferent to the chill. But I knew peace only for a moment. I went downstairs and there I found the knight with both palms pressed against the ice. Leaning close, as a child with his nose to a window, he stared straight into the wall.

"Kálmán."

He did not acknowledge me. I did not ask again. I pulled him away and he stumbled, then slipped and fell into my arms, nearly dragging me down onto the glassy floor. He did not complain of my man-handling him—did not even grunt as he fell. He was in a daze. I stood him upright and steered him through the door before he could object.

We descended the stairs. He proceeded with a stoop and touched the wall for support. When he turned his head, his face verily glowed from behind his stringy black locks, he had paled so.

"That was damned reckless," I said.

"I am unaffected."

"You gazed into a nightmare. What could you hope to gain?"

He paused near the doorway and laid his fingers to his temple. "To see what lays beyond."

He staggered out of the gatehouse. The wind had risen, driving the snow on, obscuring the rock above the keep. It struck me then that in this lofty height we truly trespassed the sky. The snow-clotted air seemed to banish daylight itself and the shadows pooled greedily in every wall's lee.

We found Jakab where we had left him, shivering beneath a rind of snow.

"It is a place," Kálmán mumbled.

"What did you say?"

"I have seen it. It is a place. Deep."

I did not want to know. I could not stop myself from asking. "Is Pál there?"

His eyes finally focused on me. "Pál? I . . . I did not see him."

Whatever else Kálmán thought to say in that moment was lost when Jakab suddenly clasped his cloak. "Listen!"

This brought the knight out of his trance. He failed to draw himself up to his full height, but the edge in his voice was not blunted. "Unhand me."

"Cannot you hear them?" Jakab asked.

"Hear whom?"

"Men."

Kálmán cocked his ear before saying, "I hear no men." Nor did I.

"They call to us."

"You are mistaken," the knight said.

"They are weeping."

"Weeping?"

"No. Laughing. Singing a merry tune," Jakab said, his eyes as wide as walnut shells. "What do they say?"

Kálmán freed his cloak and favored me with a look I could not interpret. Was I to be afraid? I heard no men. The knight made to step into the courtyard when the veteran took hold of his cloak again. "Take heed!" Jakab said. "Look there, upon the battlements."

"I see nothing," Kálmán said, now staring up to the keep's crown. I shuffled closer that I might peer between their shoulders.

"The man," Jakab said.

"I see no—"

"The one rendered on the hoarding wall."

And then, for a moment, I saw it. The parapets upon the keep mere hints through the blowing snow. Moving between them I saw, or thought I did, a figure. A man, perhaps. Wholly black.

Neither wind nor mountain sent the shiver that lanced through me.

"I see no man," Kálmán said.

"You see none?" I asked.

Kálmán looked at me again, and this time it was easier to parse the astonishment in his face. His cast was frightful. Ashen pale, and now his shock that I had seen what he could not left him slacker-jawed than I had ever seen him. He looked again at the battlements. As did I. This time I saw no one.

"Take heed!" Jakab cried, wrenching the knight away from the corridor's entrance.

"But why?" Kálmán asked. The knight's plaintive tone, so foreign to the man who only minutes earlier had willfully gazed upon the benighted forest, was as disquieting as the veteran's panic.

"They loose their arrows upon us!"

"They do?"

"Listen! Can you not hear their barbs strike the ground?"

Crouching beside Jakab, I strained my ears to hear. It was nigh impossible to hear else but the wind's mighty voice. Then I heard it. Dull beating. Snow falling from the roofs? Or perhaps, the muffled sound of drifts swallowing arrows as they fell short of our position.

The knight had stepped closer to the open bailey, and again the veteran pulled him back. "Can you not see their arrows? Look! Have you grown blind?"

Kálmán stepped back, and his face was now etched by true bafflement. I was no less confused than he, and so I crept forward to look once again. Then I saw.

Hundreds of darts flying my way. I scrambled back to Jakab's side.

"He saw them!" Jakab said. "I am not mad."

I crouched, panting, awaiting a flock of arrows to stake the ground within inches of my leg. The moments passed, and this sight that sent me sprawling was transformed before me. How alike arrows, I realized, resembled the speeding snow. Still I watched, but no shaft came hurtling out of the white, no fletching erupted from my tracks.

"You saw them?" Kálmán asked.

I closed my mouth. I could say neither yea nor nay.

I knew many moments of despair on that mountain. On that day those moments stitched together to make a fearful seam, a long, cruel and listless afternoon of cowering. The snow fell, the light failed, and we trembled at the end of the passageway. We left the door to the gatehouse unopened at our backs, refusing to risk its asylum. Jakab shifted his feet to keep them from freezing, while Kálmán squatted with his back to the stone wall.

My memories of that day are laced through with confusion. We remained there for hours, pinned down by our assailants. Or so it seemed. For what was most crippling, worse than the wind and the constant snow that swirled in our eyes, was not the certainty that an arrow would come flying between the flakes, but its opposite. Our deaths awaited us mere moments hence, or perhaps decades. I was undecided if it was real. Our angst mounted as the day stretched, to rise as a ridge between us, so that we became locked in our own mute valleys. We did not even speak of it. We simply waited, each a fate unimagined by the others.

When Kálmán finally could not support himself any longer, he sat cross-legged in the snow, and my dread of maddened spearmen charging out of the storm gave way to a more pointed concern. I had watched the knight weaken. He was changed, resembling no more the nobleman of proud heritage, but a vagabond freezing in the streets of Veszprém.

Thus I steeled myself, and though the gatehouse ceded its staircase and chambers to creeping dusk, I ventured upstairs again. If nothing else, the cold had lost its bite. I returned with bows and arrows from the armory and, from the bunk, all the bedding my wide arms could carry.

I made a nest for the knight as the veteran looked on with faint disgust. He had no sympathy for Kálmán, though I suspected Jakab suffered little less. He quivered like an axe-bitten sapling, and kept his hands buried deep beneath his cloak as the snow heaped upon his shoulders. His cringing bettered our position no more than Kálmán's disintegration. It worried me how the knight closed his eyes.

Finally, I shook his shoulder. "What are we to do?" He was yet our leader, and without him, I knew we would be well and truly lost.

He gasped at my touch. "How is your hand yet so warm?" he demanded.

I noticed then that I had forgotten to replace my gloves and indeed I felt no need for them. I watched a snowflake melt upon my knuckle. He took my fingers in his and I did not like the feel of it. Kálmán's face was all creases and sallow ridges. His lip hung so loosely, I thought spittle might drip from its spout.

"How might we evade their onslaught?" I asked.

"There is no attack," he said. "I must lie down for a spell."

"I will not move," Jakab said. "Leastways, not until the night has fallen. Then we might slip the way we came."

"We must gain entry to the keep," I said. "Pál is held within." I turned back to the knight. "You said they do not attack?"

"They do not."

"Jakab witnessed their barrage."

"And did you?"

"Of course, he did!" Jakab snapped. He had tried to nock an arrow. It was awful to see how quickly snow had dusted its shaft. By the timid way he gripped his bow and failed to place the arrow's notch to string, I guessed Jakab suffered frostbite through his gloves. Or maybe from those rings he had claimed as booty, if he was still fool enough to wear them.

"What is the truth of it?" I asked.

"Victory is one with suffering."

"What the hell does that mean?" Jakab asked.

The knight did not deign to answer. It sounded more like the wisdom of a flagellant than a man trained in the art of the sword.

"The night is near," I said. "Perhaps Jakab is right. We should wait until the dark covers us when we can move unnoticed."

"Very well," the knight said. He closed his eyes.

I shook his shoulder. "You must not sleep!"

"So be it," Kálmán said, grimacing as he unknotted his legs. "If I may not rest, then I would proceed."

He took my hand again that I might help him to his feet. His gloved fingers cupped mine and lingered unpleasantly, but a moment later he had thrown off the blanket I had draped across his shoulders and made a brave effort to stand erect. "I have seen what I needed to. I know how to defeat this mountain."

"How so?" I could not tell if I believed him. In our wretchedness, I no longer truly cared.

"My error was not venturing deep enough. My efforts last spring, yesterday and today—I was ignorant of that place where resides the *spiritus.*" He lowered his gaze. "To think of the men who have suffered."

"Deep enough?" I asked. "What do you mean by that?"

"I must venture into its province," he said.

"That is no answer," I said. "Our concern is Pál and your father."

"Aye," he said, simulating his old vitality. "I will save them both."

The knight began to totter from the passageway. "Have you gone daft?" Jakab hissed, but Kálmán had already stepped into the courtyard.

I followed on his heels. Jakab did not.

The storm had, if anything, worsened. I could not make out the keep's battlements, nor distinguish its row of dark windows. I could see, however, that no line of defenders issued from its doorway, and that the ground before the passage's mouth was not littered with arrows. There was no sign of attack.

The foul weather afforded us some measure of cover. Though I spied no watchmen, I had to assume guards were studying the yard before them. The wise course would therefore have led us around the bailey's edge, along the wall, that our progress might hope to go unnoticed. Kálmán denied us this advantage, however, when he stumbled across the center of the bailey. I hurried closely behind, and I admit, crouched that his shoulders might shield me from the wrath of Kuszkol's defenders.

When we had reached the foot of the staircase leading to the formidable door, the knight paused, and I took this chance to whisper. "Will we find them whole?"

Kálmán regarded me, his whiskers englobed by ice like winter dew. "That I cannot say." He put his foot upon the lower step and heaved himself upwards.

I followed. We stood before the door of Kuszkol's keep. I had little faith in our ability to sway the doorman if we knocked, and little idea how the knight might otherwise hope to gain entry. As I contemplated how we might batter in the door without facing an iron-tipped welcome, Kálmán took hold of the handle and pushed. It swung open at his touch.

This surprise brought no relief. No light washed our faces. The stone corridor beyond the threshold was black. The darksome keep was no final bastion, I realized, but a great and terrible tomb.

Kálmán stepped across the doorsill, and to my later chagrin, I was slow to follow. Instinct stilled my foot. It is no easy thing to be swallowed.

The shadow had already deluged the knight when he turned back to me. His riding cloak had become saturated and his face hung before me bodiless, like a sick lantern. He turned not, as I thought, to question my delay, but merely to take one last look. His face receded into darkness. The door swung shut. I cried out, but the moment before I leaned my shoulder to the planks, I heard the bolt slide.

Eighteen

Your master kept his heart veiled from all but one. When I saw him I said, "You are different than I imagined," and Albert Vetési said, "How so," and in my turn I said, "You are clothed as a beast." For though the sun had long burnt off the night's chill by the time your master walked across the palace ward he yet wore a fox's pelt upon his shoulders, for his bones foretold the warmth could not last and to him it seemed right to carry this fur as a talisman, for it was a gift from his one friend, the one man who knew him. The guardsmen swept their dice from the table when he entered the marshal's tower, but he only lumbered past them and swung open the cellar door, where he did not wince or pause at the stench of blood and vomit and soiled straw, these proofs of human frailty. He descended the dark spiral and as he came I listened. His gaoler had fled and no guardsmen followed and so he retrieved the key ring from its hook and he opened the banded door without peering through the grill.

You never knew your master. When at last he came I said, "You are different than I imagined," and Albert Vetési asked, "How so?" and in my turn I said, "I had not foreseen you had once known another like me. There is enlightenment in the way you point your beak." For your master had ofttimes been called upon to play judge and those with long memories know that early he was a prosecutor of heresy, but only those who know him best remember his first judgment involved the charge of *maleficium*. He said, "You are my messenger's wife," and I said, "More." He lowered himself to a stool and touched the spot where he had slipped his one friend's letter. The stranded lord had sketched a silhouette that leaned from the parchment with such crooked vitality that your master had stared long at it in hard wonderment. "My secretary carried your message that there is a shadow in my pocket. What does it portend?" He spoke with his hand upon this breast and I spoke the truth when I said, "Your heart is hard. Did you not know it was lurking there? Did you not know what Kázmér would find upon that mountain?" He straightened and said, "I would prefer you not say his name," and by this I knew the rest of him.

For every man has facets to him which I cannot know until I speak with him, and from my encounter with your master I learnt that I had a predecessor and her name was Panna and that she had taught him the hard lesson. In his youth, your master learnt this lesson well. He applied her moral to his own life and understood that he must make of others timber to build his ark lest he drown among their miseries. He was born of privilege but somehow was not made of the same skull-cleaving steel of old stock. He was soft, so soft that the lesson he learnt, which should have come as second nature to him, was like a revelation, an inner meaning, and since then he had never stopped hewing. Some mistook him for woodsman but his eyes were uplifted and he became a steersman. He became more awful than others. All men and women use one another, but they at least gain some human satisfaction from dominating their servants or undercutting their neighbors or extinguishing the lines of their enemies when they hold their children face down in the mud. But he had never taken such pleasure. Perhaps it was his empty bed that left him cold, but I think the reason is that he had become like a beast that no one has named. He lusted for survival. He was never so low as to take revenge. I said that I had been wrong about him. His fingers were fine. I thought they would be heavy, ugly things. Twisted by age and his callous deeds. I told him I thought he would be ugly because he was Albert Vetési. But he was like an angel, clothed in fur and stinking of ferocity. His heart beat like a stone.

Nineteen

I stood with hands pressed against the wood. It is a strange thing to be betrayed, no less so when the deceiver never held one's trust. The fury I thought might rise in me laid sleeping. Nor did I deny my senses, telling myself that Kálmán had erred and would admit me forthwith. No. I remained at that door because I had nowhere else to go.

When had I been betrayed? I thought perhaps Kálmán had decided just then, as he closed the door and darkened my hope as surely as a hood drawn over a convict's head. Or maybe it was the day prior, when he had insisted we surmount the fort's ramparts, already knowing what menace waited to consume us beyond. Or perhaps I had to seek further back, to some bright morning in the king's own hall in Buda, when the mission was conceived and an allotment of men's lives was committed to its execution.

When I finally returned to Jakab I did not speak of it. It hardly mattered. Yet he must have guessed what had transpired when he saw me trudging out of the storm, for he began to run, bounding as a fugitive sprinting from the sheriff's hounds. The thin bridge quivered beneath his hammering steps, and when he came to deep snow in the lower bailey, he bulled on, like a stuck elk lurching through a slough.

He slammed the door of the barracks behind me, and we two stood breathing in the darkness as the horses huffed nearby for a long and wordless pause. It was not until we were upstairs that he began to curse. He spewed a blasphemous stream, offending a calendar's worth of saints that played no part in our misfortune. I knelt before the coals to begin the mindless task of resurrecting the fire. His panic tainted me and the cadence of his pacing echoed in my mind. *What now what now what now?*

Once I had awakened the fire, I turned to find Jakab rolling his blanket and stuffing it into his pack. I said nothing even after he began to fumble with the laces on the knight's own bag. After losing patience with the knot he took a knife and bobbled it once before slitting the pack like a butcher in search of giblets.

Jakab withdrew the satchel's innards and began to pick through the spillage. I saw an ivory box held briefly up to the light before disappearing into the veteran's bag, followed by a silk keepsake from Kálmán's wife. By the wayside he tossed a rosary and a folded letter. Next his hand fell upon the knight's green book, from which he recoiled as if he had come upon a yellow-toothed rat.

"You cannot leave," I said.

"By God's bleeding wounds, I shall not spend another hour here!"

"What about Pál?"

"What about my neck?" Jakab leapt from his looting as he cried this, his chin raised to reveal a bearded throat.

"A force is sure to come," I said. "The beacon was lit two days ago. The storm has delayed them, but they are certain to arrive tomorrow."

"The king's support be damned."

"Night is falling. You will never reach the mountain's foot."

Jakab grunted, "The knave's horse will speed me."

This stilled my tongue. To take a man's gold was one thing, to take his steed, another. Kálmán had been disloyal, but such a theft did not sit well with me.

I thought of Kálmán's indecipherable face at the doorway and shuddered to imagine what task he thought to perform in that hushed and somber tower. He must have thought he could gain entry to the other place, groping around in the dark, where he would perform his exorcisms in the ghost's own lair. Perhaps he thought to lock us out to spare us. I did not know. I did not know if he bartered our lives or his own. Perhaps betrayal wore the same guise as sacrifice.

"Even should you take the horse," I said. "You will reach no safety. You will only succeed in killing a fine mount and dying beneath him."

Jakab dropped the laces he was struggling to tie. He rested his eyes on Kálmán's circle.

"We should never have entered this infernal fortress. We should have awaited the king's troops. I said as much when we sighted the beacon."

And so he had, and he had not been wrong. At the time I had sided with the knight, who said we must carry on. I had been anxious for Pál to learn that he could not thrive if he protested the will of his betters.

On the inbound journey, I had looked forward to taking my leave of Jakab. Now I sought to persuade the veteran to stay though I knew well his faults. Without him I would never have crossed the chasm, and whatever my next step might be, I could not defeat Kuszkol's defenses on my own. Nor could I imagine becoming stranded here with no other voice but that one which whispered loudest when I was by myself.

"Night is falling," I said.

"We are invaders here! Unwanted. If any madmen yet survive in that godforsaken keep, they may well be on their way to destroy us now."

"I think there is no one."

I turned my shins to the blaze to dry the meltwater that beaded on my stockings. Rather than resume his packing, the veteran lingered close to the fire. Eventually he pulled up a stool. I was tired. He was tired. We slumped, bone weary, but our thoughts were far from sleep.

"I will relieve you of one mystery at least," I said. "It was I who loosed Ferenc's bonds."

The veteran turned. "You what?"

"When I moved him from the stable, I bound him with a slip-knot. He must have discovered it last night and freed himself."

"You wanted him to run? After hectoring the rest of us to stay?"

"I gave him a choice. I warned him of the storm. I am not sure I did right by him."

"He escaped, did he not?"

"In that dark he could easily have wandered from the path and found himself at the bottom of a gulley."

"Or maybe he made it across the valley," Jakab said.

"I hope you are right. It is not a chance I would want to take."

"You will not come with me?" Jakab asked.

"I cannot."

"What will you do?"

"I will find a way."

"You are not wanted here."

"No," I agreed.

"What about that?" Jakab gestured at the green book that lay beside the knight's ravaged pack.

"What about it?"

"You might use it to protect yourself."

"I would sooner burn it."

The veteran looked warily at the book again. "Is it safe to?"

"I know nothing about it."

We shared a moment of silence. Each at a loss how next to act, how to preserve ourselves.

"Truly," he said, "do you think there is no one?"

"There is no one," I said.

"But there is the man."

I glanced at the veteran. The shadows had settled into every crease on his face like grit. He looked like a plowman after a day's toils behind the ox. "Which man?" I asked.

"The man. The one we found at the hoarding's end. The one we found in the town square among those outlines. The black one that Pál spied from the road."

"He is not real."

"That is the ghost," Jakab said. "It is real."

"It does not seem real. It is a drawing on wood."

"Just a drawing? It strode the keep's parapets."

"Perhaps it is more than a drawing," I said.

"Some of the old stories about this place tell that the commander who first went mad was sick at bed. That he awoke to find his shadow at the foot of his bed."

"I remember."

"I have heard this same account more than once. That the shadow with whom the commander spoke was his own."

I watched the flames shape and reshape writhing crowns. "What are you saying? Not that the old commander is haunting us."

"I am saying we cannot trust the shadows."

"Or," I said, "you are saying that we cannot trust our own."

I hated putting these thoughts into words. They obliged me to join Jakab in looking over our shoulders, to our doubles cast across the floor and onto the far wall.

"Perhaps that is the truth of it," Jakab said huskily.

"Or perhaps," I said, "we are about to let our imaginations carry us away. Just as our minds deceived us when we were in the upper bailey when we thought we were under attack."

Jakab scowled.

"Surely you realize," I said, "that there was no threat. There was nothing but wind and snow."

"Our enemy was there."

"It was a fantasy. Our minds deceiving us."

"Then it is our minds who are our enemies!"

"You are saying that we are going mad."

Jakab rocked forward, as if my statement had injured him. He plunged his fists beneath his armpits. "I do not know. I think it is more. Something more, in ourselves. Something within us that wishes us ill, that seeks our destruction, even. Many men give into this fancy. You may not have seen it, but I have, many times. Men who charge into the fusillade when cover is ample. Men who use bare hands to grasp at the cavalier's lance. Men who act when no act is needed, who would rather seek their end than to let another moment pass them by. These men embrace death. To escape their helplessness, or maybe to prove their strength. All men have this seed in them, I think. This impulse for self-murder."

This speculation sounded too reasonable, which did not please me. "But why this cold?" I asked. "And why these figures on the wall, fashioned out of soot."

"What is colder than a fire gone out?"

"What does that mean?"

"Is warmth found before the fire or in the shade?"

"Soot is not a shadow. It is the fire's footprint."

"A fire gone out."

"But how can any of this be real?"

Thud.

From beyond the room came a sound. Some collision. Muffled by the snow or perhaps the thickness of the barrack walls.

"What was that?" Jakab said.

"A loose shutter in the wind."

Thud.

"Aye," Jakab said. "A shutter."

"I am less sure. It did not sound like a shutter that time."

"A door, then."

Downstairs the horses whinnied. We met one another's eyes and both knew that he would not be leaving the mountain this night.

"Which door?" I asked.

"Must be in the lower yard. Otherwise—"

Thud.

"What should we do?" I asked.

"Nothing. It is just a door."

"It did not sound like a door." At first I thought it was a crash. Wood and hinges clashing. Now I wondered if it had seemed more intentional. More human.

"It did sound like a door."

"No." Knocking, perhaps. "We have to go see."

He shook his head.

"Yes," I said.

Thud.

I imagined the night ahead, sitting erect on this stool, powerless. Agonizing hours spent listening to the storm even as I had spent the day searching its every gust, wondering what it concealed.

"We have to go see," I repeated.

"You."

"I will go."

I crossed the room and peered down the steps. It was dark below.

"The lantern," I said. "To dispel the shadows."

I retrieved it from the table and returned to the steps. The horses blew in reply to the scuff of my boots on the steps. The light limned their twitching ears and glossed their great eyes as they tracked me.

Thud.

The sound came from outside. I stepped off the final riser.

"Let us get this brazier lit," I said. The horses stepped close to me. I struck a spark into the pan and the fire took.

Thud.

I opened one of the double doors. The wind reached in to rifle the hem of my tunic and dandle my forelock. Snowflakes brushed my lashes and the backs of my hands. I could see almost nothing. Only a few feet of snow, and a little further out the faintest outline of a square painted against the snow. Light thrown by the fire upstairs through the parchment-stretched window. That was the only light.

A whole sky of furious snow and cloud lay between me and the moon.

Thud.

It was difficult to know from which direction the sound had come. From the left, I guessed. The chapel.

I stepped into the yard. The lantern was wholly insufficient. The snow drifted silently and suffocated the edge of its nimbus only a few feet from where I stood, obscuring what lay beyond. I hooded its aperture. Night swept in. After a few moments I could just barely distinguish the stable across the yard. And there was the gatehouse down whose stairs I had first descended. The buildings' shapes were so indistinct I did not trust the sight. Was this the report of my eyes or my mind as it struggled to sort sense from this formlessness? Did the windows seem too dark? It was impossible to tell.

Thud.

The dark was too close. Too thick. I had to move. I began to push through the snow, revealed by the light that bled about the lantern's cap. I followed the furrow we had plowed during our retreat. Its edges were already blunted beneath the relentless snowfall. I looked over my shoulder. It was not my imagination. I could distinguish the stable's roof. Its shuttered windows, which were secure. Its open doorway, which still seemed to me somehow too dark. It had to be my mind playing tricks. Black is black.

Here was the chapel. At least three feet of snow had drifted against the door. It could not swing in the wind. No door could in this snow.

Thud.

Had the sound come from within? Maybe, but I did not think that was possible. I tried to imagine how the quiet chapel could be so breezy. I could not. I had to consider it was not wind. I did not want to know. I had to learn. It could be Pál. Maybe, somehow, he had escaped whatever bound him while we crossed to the upper bailey and for whatever reason took refuge in the chapel. Maybe he needed to take my hand before the ravenous shadow would release him. Or maybe it was Ferenc, crawling back to us after almost freezing on the mountainside.

Thud.

Perhaps they were calling for help.

I began to kick the snow aside. I paused only once when the sound came again to wonder why it seemed no louder than when I sat with Jakab before the fire. This did not seem possible.

I unhooded the lantern and opened the door.

Perhaps I was too eager for the light to flood the chapel, and this distorted my perception, but the dark was gelid slow to retreat. Not slow, but grudging. The chapel was revealed to be as we had left it. A sweep of metal objects. Empty benches. Only the barest draft through the high smoke holes. The darkness collecting in the corners.

Thud.

That did not sound right. If the sound had come from within, the dull impact did not echo from the chapel's stone walls as it should. But I was here, so I began to pick my way across the littered tiles. When next I heard the sound, I doubted myself again, thinking it came again from the chapel. From deep within. The altar.

An ornate table with a linen altar cloth embroidered with scenes from the Passion of Christ. A piece too fine for a garrison. My master and Lord Kustyer sometimes exchanged gifts. Perhaps this had come from Veszprém. I rounded behind the altar and held my lantern beneath it. I had looked here when I searched for Pál. It had been empty save for the tabernacle in which I assumed the chaplain reserved the chalice and host.

The tabernacle was open. It still held the Eucharist. Perhaps Jakab had pried it while looting and lost his nerve before he tucked the chalice beneath his cloak. I looked about for other cabinets. There were none. Nothing to explain the sound. Perhaps the tabernacle, its lid repeatedly dropped shut, could make such a noise, but it could not possibly carry to the barracks, and besides, no wind could have had such an effect.

Thud.

I stiffened. The sound did not come from anywhere near me.

I had no desire to come face to face with that shadow, with that figure of soot, stepped down off the wall. But I carried on, pursuing the sound, clinging to the belief that if I could at least catch sight of the thing it might lead me to Pál, or at least reveal some knowledge that would show me the way. For surely Pál's disappearance was linked to the figure. Thus, it was not bravery but a detached zeal, a sleepwalk towards abnegation, that took hold of my feet. It took every ounce of my will, and yet it took none, for my route was inescapable.

I chased the sound to the kitchen, where I found no shutters but a flour bin. I did not recall that it had been open when last I had searched there. Next I followed the sound to the stable, which I did not enter, for I knew I would find feed bins. When next the sound came from the door to the gatehouse stairwell, I did not follow it.

I stood in the yard and told myself there was no sound.

Thud.

Or that there was a sound, but not a person. Some loose shutter somewhere. That the storm swirled between here and yonder and I would never be able to track its source.

Thud.

And the tabernacle must have been open. And I was wrong that the flour bin had ever been closed.

Thud.

And even if there was a sound, it would cease wherever I shone my light.

I remembered the lanterns in the chapel's niches. I returned and lit these and carried them, one by one, to hang within the doorways of the kitchen, the stable, the gatehouse stairwell and the chapel itself. When I exhausted this supply, I walked back to stand in the middle of the yard and examined the points of light that shone around me. A miserly string of little beacons, weak through the downfall but strong enough to roll back some night. Each illuminated a patch of snowy ground before its doorway. If I could not catch sight of the ghost, then perhaps I could dispel it. I could perhaps sleep knowing these fires were burning.

I kept turning around, watching, waiting for the sound to come again. It seemed as long as I kept turning, kept checking each of the lighted doorways, one followed by another, I might be able to thwart the sound from returning.

I was not wrong. The sound did not recur as long as I kept turning. This surprised me, and I could not but wonder why. Because, I supposed, with the light shining within each of those doorways it was easy to believe that there was someone standing guard within each. Someone who stood just out of sight and in whose presence this phantom noise could not emanate, for the unreal cannot abide the real. Someone who had just stood in the doorway a moment ago and whom I missed. But of course, I thought, there was such a person. I had just stood within each of those doorways. Those lights were placed by me and as such it was I who stood guard.

This reasoning sounds fanciful, like the reckoning of a dreamer, but at that moment it struck me as completely sound. Indeed, more than convincing, I believed I had discovered some insight into my nature. It was I who stood just out of sight. I was the source of the light and it was I who had the power to keep the ghost at a distance.

But I was not dreaming and so my mind did not so easily skip over the consequences of this intuition. If it was I who stood within each doorway, did this then mean I was divisible? Were parts of myself hidden to me? Or rather, was I whole but this moment contained a multitude, such that I did simultaneously stand within each doorway? If so, why did I only perceive myself here, at my center?

In my confusion, I stopped turning.

Thud.

That had been further away. Across the bridge, which I could not see. I gazed at the place where the mountain's final crag rose in the upper bailey, the keep whose darkened windows and doorways remained invisible far beyond my lantern's reach. I wondered how, if Kálmán now wandered its passages, he could do so blindly.

An absence in my periphery. I turned. One point in my string of lanterns had dimmed. The gatehouse stairwell. I returned to the barracks and blocked the door.

Thud. Not so far away.

Jakab sat before the fire, his hands cradled in his lap.

"Well?"

I shook my head.

"But what is it? I hear it still."

"You know what it is."

I turned to the room. To the empty chairs and twisted blankets. To Pál's neat pack, Kálmán's gutted one, and the soldiers' lockers pressed against the wall. Among the lifeless things, my eye found one shape amid the carnage of the exploded pack. It lay half-hidden, as though trying to escape my notice. Or luring me forward, demanding to be extricated from the tangle. Once I took note of it, the book seized my attention like a harlot stretching in a window. I could not draw my eyes away. It was mine now to handle, as the farmer must deal with the dog that runs wild among the hens.

"I think," I said, "you were correct. We will need protection this night."

I moved near and stared at the book between my feet. Better to feed its pages to the fire. I picked it up, expecting some hideous weight or texture to it, and was offended it felt so ordinary. It was finely covered in green cloth, and I guessed fifty pages long.

"Careful," Jakab said. He remained on his stool.

Between the green covers was found true witchcraft, inculpatory signs that would move any bailiff and mob to bind a man's neck to ankle and drive him before a hail of stones. No trial need even be called. Kálmán practiced forbidden arts in plain sight. Yet by his lack of contrition, I suspected he never feared such brute justice. He was spared the snapping teeth and smut-caked nails of his neighbors. I wondered if he was sanctioned by the realm's highest power. He had escaped his due, and this wrong kneaded my tired rage as a potter limbers clay. It mattered not that Kálmán was most certainly damned.

My fingers parted the pages as if of their own accord.

Inscribed in perfect black upon the page was the twining wreath of man, god, scale, hoof, leaf, bud, hill, stream and word as comprised a full rendering of creation. An echo of the image Kálmán had sketched on the floor. Leaning more closely I saw the perch consume the minnow, the king raise a dripping head, wheat sinking roots through the fur of a fallen marten and the forest dashing itself against a mountain slope, attempting to pull down the airy peaks.

I turned the page. Again, the lacy circlet of a world was depicted. I turned another page. The circle I thought of as a map, once again.

I leaned close to study the details and found among the smoky ribbons of unintelligible verse the life which teemed among collapse was subtly altered from the first map I had reviewed. Again, kings and slaves, prairies of racing horses and pits of writhing snakes, and repeated with striking occurrence on that page, a lance. Knights stuck boars, storks pierced fish with dagger beaks, as did some monstrous creature that lived beneath the waves, while a slash of lightning split the oak tree's girth.

On the next page, the map appeared again. Alike the previous iteration, but as my eye followed the coursing path of the words, I perceived a strange prevalence of what I might name disgorgement. Rosehips erupted petals, waters gushed forth from the source, and from egg clutches burst whip-tailed tadpoles.

On the next page, peasants bound sheaves, sparrows wove nests, trees knotted wandering roots, and clouds spun into darksome funnels.

On the next page there were no figures of men at all, nor fish, nor fleet deer. The circle entire depicted only a forest with peaks rising above the canopy. The earth was covered everywhere by woodland, except where winter had taken hold, and here, through the barren branches, snatches of rocky ground could be seen between the trees. In other places, the forest yielded to flames that ate through the wood like a scythe. But even in these glades of ash, new shoots abounded at the base of the fire. Among the wintry scenes, I saw that as often as the leaves fell, the needled trees simply gathered snow upon their boughs so that the earth beneath remained obscured.

The page chilled me in a way the others had not for even the cursive words that formed the ring's spine were concealed by the shadows that deepened between the trunks. So little showed through the bush it seemed the forest had nearly succeeded in excluding light from touching the earth.

I peered so deeply into those dismal woods, wondering if I might not glimpse figures between their trunks, that it took some time for me to realize I myself had become plunged into darkness. Lost between the trees on the page, for a fearful, drowning time. Only when I noticed the glint of the near-spent coals upon my wife's ring was I able to tear my gaze away. I looked up to see the fire was nearly out.

The veteran had retreated to his blanket while the book consumed my attention. He snored softly, wrapped tight in his woolen cocoon.

I closed the book and noticed that the edge of the last page peeked above the others. Had it become unbound? No, from the edge I could feel the calfskin of this page was of finer finish than the other leaves of the volume.

I stirred the fire to gain a little light. I pulled the leaf free and was astonished to find it unlike any other page in the book. It was an official ecclesiastic certificate. It bore a seal. The seal of the Bishop of Veszprém.

My master.

At first I was perplexed, for I had never before seen an indulgence note. When I recognized what I held—a remittance of punishment for Kálmán's unnamed sins—I was amazed. In exchange for certain codices made in donation to my master's episcopal library, His Excellency had pardoned the knight's trespasses. Albert Vetési himself had sold Kálmán his absolution.

I replaced the note.

Pál had been correct. I had made excuses for my master. I had forgiven him, even, for my wife's death. Now I understood a little better his role in the world's duplicity. This discovery inspired more weariness than anger.

Thud.

I walked about Kálmán's circle. Viewing the ring from the outside, it was difficult to distinguish the figures, the capering bulls and spearmen I had seen Kálmán draw the day before. Rather, the inverted image took on a malign cast. Not unlike a forest, with eyes peering from the brambly fog that twisted between the trees.

I stepped into the circle to improve my vantage. Cold seeped through my soles. Despite the fire, a wicked draft pooled on the floor.

Kálmán's circle was corrupted.

I gathered buckets of snow and spread them across the charcoal circle. Like a scullion, I took up handfuls of straw and scrubbed. The straw I clutched sullied and tattered as the charcoal stained my palms and spattered the backs of my hands. Jakab did not rouse during my exertions.

Thud.

I returned to Kálmán's book, carelessly smudging the pages. I did not know the meaning behind these maps nor why they differed. I did not know if I should try my hand at copying the map that Kálmán had—which one, I could only guess. At length, I opened the book randomly three times and selected the one that looked simplest, despite its profusion of loops.

I found a charcoal stick among Kálmán's belongings. I chose a spot on the floor near the room's east wall where Pál had swept the floor, but which was unblemished by my scrubbing.

I studied the image. There was no beginning to it and so I decided it did not matter where I began. When I placed the tip of the charcoal stick to the floorboards, I was reminded that though I am literate in Latin and the mother tongue, I am a frequent writer of neither. Nor have I wasted any spare parchment that came into my possession by doodling upon it, as I have found some young priests do, as if parchment were as plentiful as sand. Thus, before I could pull the stick across the floor I was stilled by doubt in my mundane abilities.

There was no help for it. I moved the charcoal and the action was utterly instinctive. My hand and wrist knew how to curve.

I did not interrogate myself over this unimagined talent. *Impossible* talent. But I pulled the charcoal and it felt right, like this was a task at which I was much practiced, like reading the clouds or securing Fejes's straps, a task at which I had long proficiency and in which I could take some pleasure, not some task I had grown to loathe like rendering tallow or the laundry. I gave up on every stain.

The shapes that passed through my fingers were beyond strange and filled my eyes with yet more delight. I say not delight because of my transgression, though I was not unconscious of this, but rather for the pure outlandishness of that which flowed from my stick. I drew in a language that was undoubtedly Eastern and surely ancient. Some tongue that Sándor might once have heard, if not learnt from a tutor, or possibly in which he received some words of counsel from a savage sage come forth to his throne room. Learned men travel across the breadth of this earth and down time's well through their reading, and even I myself have sampled this joy through my Alexandrine. For the first time I wondered at the many rare and wonderful volumes that my master bid me fetch. I wondered at how far he traveled as he stood before his lectern ensconced in the comforts of his study at Veszprém.

It took me some time to recognize the curls and twists in the loopy script depicted twins and sometimes two halves partitioned. Here was the goat's cloven hoof stomping upon the hinge of the pilgrim's shell. A ram's stones cut and divided alongside lungs and kidneys on a butcher's board. Two stars shining with a valley dipping between them, the land that links opposed horizons. And here were figures, an entire court of coupled courtiers, and at its center a two-headed man bowing low before some other long-dead king, Salamon.

I was growing hot. I had shed my cloak already, and found I needed to open the throat of my tunic. This was not the sort of labor for which one paid with sweat, so I thought this odd, but even so found myself removing my boots and my stockings too that I might twitch my toes a little and let the night's breath graze the space between them. This reminded me of a time soaking my feet in a stream. A moment I could not quite recall. I continued on but had to pause again to wipe away the sweat that ran into my eyes. I also listened for a twenty count, but heard no more sound coming from outside.

I wondered why the room was so dim. Stools stood between my circle and the hearth. Even so, their intrusion did not account for how little light was cast by the fire. Had my fire burnt low again? But no, I could tell by the color and height of its flames that the fire was just now entering its prime. I looked about me and was taken aback by how thick the shadows seemed. How they massed in the far corners, which were invisible, as if a heap of black-dyed wool were obstructing my view. Indeed, the entire room was murky, as if my sight had grown cloudy. I rubbed my eyes but they worked no better, and as I looked about I noticed how the darkness seemed to almost coil in certain parts of the room, doubled upon itself like a great length of rope. It is a poor description, but the shadow contained *layers*, as if it was concentrated to stifle, to expunge the sight of that which lay within it. The book, for instance. At some point I had laid it aside and continued to draw the map from memory. It rested just outside my circle but I could hardly make out its edges. The darkness also seemed to smother the long hump where last I had seen Jakab sleeping.

The veteran. He was completely swathed. Or was I seeing a dark form draped over him?

"Jakab," I said.

I was not alone. I could feel that there was another, others, here with me. I felt no eyes watching. Not from where Jakab lay. Not from anywhere. No one was watching. Instead, I sensed a presence.

From beside me. From the brinks of my vision, left and right. Others who recalled the figures in the woods that could only be viewed obliquely. I was suddenly thankful for this darkness. That I need not cry out in recognition, for I was certain that I was bounded by only the familiar. By those with whom my shadow overlapped— the furthest figments of myself that receded into black. That if I searched among those who leaned just out of sight, explored their necks and faces with outstretched fingers, that I would find Pál among them. That Pál had joined that host.

Yet the presence behind me was another again. I could smell her hair. I could feel her breath on the flesh behind my ear, in that place only she had found. *You are wasting time.*

"Jakab!" I hissed.

What if he did not answer? What if he was claimed already? How could he not be?

"Jakab!"

Movement from that form.

I sprang from my circle and barged through the impossible shadow. The cold that met me was alike the hoarding's, alike a sigh from frozen earth. I shook the veteran's shoulder and heard him groan. The sweat that sopped my tunic grew chill and my teeth began to chatter.

I pushed aside the stools and approached the hearth. It burned high but not brightly. I added wood. I took the poker and beat at the coals. The new wood did not take. I could not remember the last time a fire had so resisted my efforts. This knowledge, as much as anything, made me afraid.

"Day."

I nearly dropped the poker upon hearing Jakab's croak. I turned to find him sitting up.

The room was not gloomy at all. The shadows that had consumed it only moments before had dispersed. The room entire was bathed in firelight. The window parchment glowed with advancing dawn.

"I fell asleep," he said.

"Yes."

"Did you?"

"No. I spent the night . . ." I gestured at the floor.

Jakab rose, the blanket draped over him. "You erased his circle."

"Yes."

"And this over here?" He stood above my own. "You replaced his with this other one?"

"Yes."

"This came from the book?"

"Yes. I am not sure what it means."

"What could it mean?"

"I am not sure what the writing means."

"What writing?"

"The—"

Upon the floor where I had crouched for hours was inscribed a circle. A single stroke, unadorned. A ring. Perfectly proportioned, as through guided with a fretworker's compass.

Jakab returned to sit before the fire.

"I have been dreaming," I said. Yet I walked barefoot. My tunic was clammy.

"Is there broth?"

"Broth. Yes." I set the pot on the hook.

"I am leaving," he said.

I was still too baffled to protest. I glanced over my shoulder at my circle. Beside me Jakab splayed his fingers to warm them. The glint of metal caught my eye.

After a quick look, my gaze turned to the safety of black and seething coals. Silver banded nine of his fingers. Ill-begotten, to be sure, but it was not his pilferage which repelled my eye. Frostbite had left his fingers blue and bent and swollen like carrots. I looked sidelong and marveled that he did not mention them. The pain must have been tremendous, and yet he endured without comment.

I could not help but steal a glance at his face to gauge whether he was brave or oblivious. His brow was creased, but the contorted lines of agony I expected, I did not see. My study drew his notice. "What is it?" he asked.

"Nothing."

We ate. I did my best not to watch how he gripped his spoon in the web between his finger and his thumb. He said not one word about his pain. He did not remark upon his own inept eating.

When his spoon fell clattering to the floor, I waited a full minute, watching as he tried to grasp it with dying fingers, before I retrieved it for him.

He grunted as I placed it between his bottom knuckles. I did my best not to flinch away from his ravaged flesh.

"I must be tired," he said.

This was no dream. Nor was the night. He had been captured as he had slept beneath those shadows.

"Must be," I agreed. I kept my eyes fixed on the ground after that. I did not want to watch him fumble another spoonful of broth into his lap. I could not tell whether his unearthly fortitude was a blessing or a curse. I could not tell whether there was a difference. He could not have sat so calmly if he knew that he would lose his fingers, if not his hands, even if he stayed. I had once helped an old woman who flagged me down with a half-handed salute, and she had told me all about the ruination of frostbite as I helped round up her baying kids.

"How do you feel?" I asked.

There was the slightest hesitation. "Fine. Better now."

"You were right about this mountain," I said. "It is not for the likes of us. If I could leave I would."

The spoon stilled in his bowl. We sat silently. The fire popped. At length he said, "He was a good boy."

I spoke no more about Jakab staying and, with his belly warmed, his mind turned back to flight. I struggled not to stare at his damned fingers, and so when he told me he was taking a chain of sausages, I gladly fetched and wrapped them that my eye had somewhere else to rest.

It was an act of betrayal on my part to saddle Kladivo. When Fejes and Kladivo touched noses before I led the knight's animal into the snow, I nearly abandoned my faithlessness. But, in the end, it held. Kladivo was only a horse, and if the price of ushering Jakab from my camp was the beast's life, I was in no position to bargain. The veteran had been corrupted, as Kuszkol's garrison must have been, as perhaps had been Kálmán, too. The mountain had conquered them all.

I had decided. Better for Jakab to break his neck descending the mountain than for him to crumble next to me. This is the raw truth. I trusted him less than solitude.

Twenty

I sat before the fire and stared at my fingers. Ruddy and hale, no cold had pierced me. The silver of my wife's betrothal ring drank the fire's light so that it appeared transmuted to gold.

I was ill with fatigue. I needed to sleep, but still I sat and wallowed, incredulous at what I had endured. I began to understand why Pál had wandered off. The night had lured me from the fireside. When I was hanging those lanterns, I had almost strayed into its clutches. I wondered how close I had come to losing myself. Close, I thought, for the night had chased me all the way back into the barracks.

Kálmán's book provided little shelter. My real protection had come from the betrothal ring. From she who had never left me.

After Kálmán's exorcism, Pál had asked me whether the knight had succeeded. What he meant was whether I was free. What the boy did not understand was that no exorcism was needed. To be free of my wife I must only be faithless.

I pulled the ring from my finger and the warmth left me the way sunlight leaves a meadow when a storm cloud rolls in.

The fire seemed suddenly a very tiny shield. A hellish draft caressed my feet. I remembered how the cold had finally touched me at the night's end, and wondered how close she had come to being defeated. I held the ring up against the fire and the flames gathered perfectly within its circumference and glistened all round its inner rim. A hearth to carry. It was not concern for my own welfare that spurred me to slip the ring back on my finger. Neither one of us could ever completely give up on the other. The chill was forgotten even as a veil of contentment warmed me.

Six months before I sat in Kuszkol's empty barracks I had come home to an abandoned house. The reek rising from my cottage already foretold the worst before I crossed the threshold, but it was a misdirection. The house was abandoned save for the swarm of flies that circuited above a joint of rotting mutton like a wheeling heaven.

I would discover later that Annaka had died in prison and Pál was safe, sheltered by my eldest sister. For a time lost to me, I joined the flies and walked circles about the table. I was as purposeless as those pests, perhaps more so for I was void of their lust and hunger. Time restarted only when I noticed the glint from between two chimney stones.

She had stowed the betrothal ring there, like a miraculous vein of looping ore. At first I thought this a renunciation, one a long time coming. I supposed she had divorced me. But as I rolled the ring between my fingers I knew otherwise. I understood I would never see her again, and knew too that she had not forsaken me. The ring was the final link in a chain she had cast to bridge our separation.

The months following her death I pitied her and I resented her, too. I despised that she had not let me drift free. She had cast this ring about me, and on that lonely morning in Kuszkol, alone with this link, I brooded. I wondered if she knew we would end here. Since climbing the mountain's slope I had felt her presence more strongly than at any time since her death. The old knots tightened. For the first time, I wondered if she was to blame.

For all I had given her, I know she viewed me as a disappointment. In our early days, she adored my tales of the road and those I would read about Great Alexander. Where Pál loved the story of how Sándor befriended Bukephalosz—how he took the bucking beast's ox-wide head and tamed it by turning it sunwards so it could see its shadow no more—Annaka preferred the tale of how the king ensured his future conquests by sundering the Gordian Knot. She had once asked me, "Why cannot you be such a hero?" I did not know what she meant, but it was shortly after this she began to press me to make more of my position. She insisted that I heard so much on my travels and in the private salons of the powerful that I should be a proper spy. The bishop made poor use of me, she said. If my master could not recognize my worth, then perhaps his enemies might.

My mind has turned again to the strands that snapped in our marriage, by which our marriage finally came undone. I would prefer to dwell a while longer on the happiest days. On our beginning and how she came by this ring.

Our pact was sealed not long after our meeting outside the nunnery. I had left the castle on account of Ökör. My dearest friend had not regained her strength since she flagged on my return from Buda. Her gait never quickened beyond a trot and she ate sparingly, refusing even the burdock I bid the stable hands collect. We had horse doctors in the citadel, but I put my faith in Márton, who had a plot in the woods above one of the bishop's vineyards.

Márton told me Ökör carried a foal. I am no slave to temper, but as I rode her home I seethed. The deed likely occurred at some farmstead where I had found lodging and a stud had found poor Ökör.

My mood was not improved by my hunger. I had left early in the day and had neglected to fill my stomach. It had rained that morning and the leaves dripped and the path's ruts had filled.

Ökör clopped homeward and my mind wandered, as it does. I rounded a bend and came upon the girl, right there, standing in my path. Her hands held the handle of a basket. She had slipped her kerchief down around her neck.

"Hello," I said. "Were you waiting for me?"

"Me?"

"Are you alone?"

"Why do you ask?"

The girl's lightness touched me. I dismounted and already I was shedding my dark mood like a damp cloak. I was pleased to see her, though after our last encounter I was less sure of how to proceed.

"The forest is not safe," I said. "You told me yourself it is filled with rogues."

"I do not scare easily."

She stepped closer and tilted her basket towards me. It held a loaf of black bread, eggs and an earthenware jar of pickles.

"I boiled these eggs before I left home. Too many for just myself but I am often seized by such fancies. Ask anyone." She pointed off the path. "I waited out the rain yonder, beneath a great fir, beneath whose skirt the rain never kisses the earth."

Ökör bowed her head to drink from a puddle.

"Perhaps you are the rogue who waylays travelers," I said.

"I have done it only this once."

"Did you follow me from Veszprém?"

She smiled. "The others never cease with their questions and they are such bores." She then lifted her hem and stepped into the undergrowth.

I followed. We came to a sunny glade where thistles grew and dragonflies buzzed about the rain-pearled blooms. Among the beech and yew grew up a great, drooping fir, between whose branches she ducked as if entering a hovel. I hobbled Ökör and followed and it was as she had promised. A dry, dim den I could nearly stand within.

We sat and she peeled an egg and handed it to me.

"My reputation is very poor," she said. Outside our bower the forest dripped.

"I know." And so I did. Since the nunnery, tongues had flapped. My eldest sister, spooked, had rushed to deliver a stern warning. She gave me the girl's measure—an unwanted fosterling, a bad luck charm widely mistrusted for her queerness and the cruelty of her words, which sunk like harpoons in any who would leash her. Many a spiteful rumor was told about the girl. They said she knew too much.

"If you have heard my tale, then you must surely know my name."

"Yes."

"I would hear you say it."

"Annaka."

The effect this had on her was unexpected. She set aside her basket and rose onto her knees and moved towards me. I could smell rosehip on her breath, intoxicating in that grotto of resin and dried needles. She moved within my grasp and thus I reached, but she caught my wrists as though I were a boy who snitched her baking.

"Say it again," she said. "Say 'Annaka.'"

"Annaka."

She drew my wrists apart and slid forward into my embrace and for the first time my fingers spanned her back. My face bent forward, but she placed her hands on my shoulders to keep my lips inches from her neck.

"Again," she said.

"Annaka."

"Now say, 'wife.'"

I drew back but she had locked her hands around my neck.

"Wife?"

"You have called and I am here. Now name what you would have from me."

"I want that which you have come to give."

"I have come also to take, and thus must you give in kind. You may have all of me, far more than any other, but take me entire and I will take you in full. There is a name for such exchange. I would not have you deceive yourself, horseman. No matter what the priest might say, if you draw any nearer, you will wed me on this day."

"I want . . ." My voice failed me. My limbs ached for her, as she well knew, but marriage? It perhaps says much about me that I had not contemplated this even after weeks drowning in my obsession. Even though my sister had described to me my entrapment and told me the girl would make a terrible wife.

"What do you want?" she asked, running her fingers down my neck. "You are a smart little rooster and you please me so much. Do you understand? This is your chance. Bind me to you before I drift away between the trees."

I made my choice. I knew I would never meet another like her again and so I said the word. A week later I slipped the ring on her finger. A token only, I had thought, until years later I found it waiting for me wedged between the stones of our hearth. The truth is I wed her beneath that fir tree.

Twenty-One

I awoke well after midday to a room bright and cold. I rose and stretched and eyed the kettle when I remembered my poor horse below.

I descended and my faithful Fejes nuzzled me straightaway. The quiet morning without Kladivo was no doubt misery. I stroked her side and recalled a day nine years earlier, not long after my new wife and the little boy had come into my life. Pál had embraced the shivering foal. Annaka never cared for my horses, but that day her brother fell in love.

I filled Fejes's trough and rubbed warmth into her haunches and considered the day ahead. I had but one place to search for Pál. If he was not in the keep, then he was not on this mountaintop. How I might enter I could not imagine, but I needed to find a way.

I had little hope I would succeed or that I would even return to these lonely barracks. Perhaps today the arrow would bite as I stood before the keep's locked door, or I would find myself dangling one time too many and slip. These thoughts weighed on me, as did my decision about Fejes.

I had failed Pál, and though the reasons eluded me, I was certain I had failed Annaka as well. I had lost both. All that was left was this fine, patient beast, and today, if I did not return, I would fail her too.

If I did not return and I had locked her in the storage room, she would suffer horribly, slowly starving, her tongue cracked by thirst. I did not blame the soldiers of Kuszkol for falling to the mountain's curse, but I did blame them for the deaths of those horses. They must have known, as they lost themselves, that they betrayed those in their charge.

The Lord did not fashion horses for mountaintops. Neither did He shape them for stables, for at first horses wandered a garden. But if I did not lock her in the room, what then? Should I leave her untethered in the yard? She would wander off, and on the slight chance I stumbled out of the keep with my brother-in-law thrown over my shoulder, I would need her for the downward journey.

I was not leaving the mountain without Pál, which meant I would likely not leave the mountaintop at all. I would die on Kuszkol, if not on this day, then on the morrow.

I decided to set her free. Pál, whatever had become of him, would approve. If she wandered through the gate and stumbled from the mountain path, at least her last view would be of the valley and the tracts of field hewn from the forest below. She might not even fall. She might make it to the bottom. Her odds seemed no worse than mine.

I ran Fejes around the yard through knee-high snow. After a few rounds of the lower bailey, I climbed onto her bareback that I might sit astride her one last time. I did not guide her and she continued to walk the circle, and then, for her own reason, left the path and made a new channel through the snow. I thought of what path I must strike in my own search, and knew that if I did not find a new approach, I had best lay down now. I was at a loss. I remembered, then, an augury an old courier taught me that he practiced when he lost his path. He would let his steed wander as he recited the *Ave Maria*, and the way viewed between the beast's ears at the prayer's end was the way desired.

I looked between Fejes's ears, and smiled when she seemed to linger before the privy. "*Ave Maria, gratia plena,*" I began, and to my surprise, Fejes immediately began to walk again. Her muzzle swung from the main gate to the stable to the drawbridge to the upper bailey. As I spoke the last word, she dropped her head and swung around. The staircase to the wall walk was framed between my guides.

I leaned forward to rub her neck. "That is a poor joke," I told her, before dismounting. I tied open the storage room that she might find shelter should she choose to stay. I then laid my head against Fejes's jowl and whispered that she was a good horse.

I needed no conjuring trick. I knew where to go, and that I must search more diligently for a way into the keep. I stood on the balcony before the drawbridge. From here only the day before, Kálmán and Jakab had held the ladder's feet as I crossed the span. Remembering, I already knew the day's search would be futile.

I looked over the edge, down into the crack that clove the mountain's summit and which served the upper fortress as a moat. Pál could have just as easily broken on that narrow ground as on the mountain's slope. I squinted, anxiously searching for a sign. When I found it, I nearly toppled over the edge.

At the crevice's depth, a fresh furrow through the snow.

Whoever trekked the trench's depth had passed not long ago, for it had snowed in the night. A cry built in my chest. A simple, *Come back!* Common sense stilled my tongue.

I had to investigate. I judged the distance to the bottom to be forty feet. Once again, Kuszkol could only be conquered by rope.

I returned to the lower bailey to forage for cord from the storage room. Fejes stood in the yard and watched. She was sanguine at my second farewell, as if she accepted I would come back again.

The drawbridge's severed ropes swung from iron anchors at the foot of the platform like strands of spider silk. I cut one free and threaded my own rope through the loop and tossed the coil over the edge. It unwound in the air unlike any sight in nature, its end piling messily on the trench's floor.

About the descent I will say little, but that it was exhausting and exhilarating both. Fatigue and elation warred, but in the end fatigue won out, so that when I reached the bottom my arms ached and I hated to think I might need to pull myself up again such a lofty height. At last my feet sank into snow. I stood between two rock faces, as though I had fallen down a crack in a giant's kitchen floor. The cleft at the crevice's depth narrowed so that I could touch both walls with extended arms. To the east I saw sky where the passage opened above the slope. To the west the passage turned. The tracks ran in both directions.

I had peered down the eastern slope when I stood atop the smithy roof, but no vantage from the lower yard had offered me a glimpse of the mountain's western flank. I went west.

As I trudged in the steps of another, I wondered at the slenderness of the path. I am no tracker, but it seemed the man I followed must have placed toe-to-heel. The westerly defile turned, and for a few paces more I rounded the upper crag upon which rose the keep. The view then gave way and the afternoon sun spilled upon the path ahead and I emerged into the western sky.

Forest consumed the distances. It rolled hill upon hill interrupted only by the few forested crests between me and Moravia. I had come to a narrow strand of meadow. Through the winter blanket sprouted the downy heads of dead plants the winds had left standing. The tracks split into manifold branches that churned the new snow.

A herd of wild goats raised their beards to fix their keyhole eyes upon me. Their hooked horns carved blue heaven.

I have faced many a wild creature in my wanderings. Always it has been my good fortune that after a moment of recognition in their dull eyes, even the fanged and clawed turned and fled. These goats did not. I was neither bear nor lynx, and what was more, I was but one while they were a multitude. Not one made a step to retreat.

Could Pál have somehow climbed down here? Had he descended to shelter in some secluded cave? This secret meadow was the only hope I had had in a day, and yet, warily viewing the pasture, it was not hope that filled me. The goats ranged to my south, some stepping forward to fill the gaps in their defensive front. I backed away, towards the north, noticing too late the yearling kid behind me, and him only once he bleated noisily.

The lone kid stood a little way up the side of the mountain's summit crag, its clever hooves gripping a ledge I noticed only now. A snowy shelf perhaps a handspan across that ascended the rock wall. A path? I turned round and saw the herd was strolling towards me, a nanny among them bleating in response to the kid.

There was little wisdom in my decision to chance the newfound path rather than retreat to my rope. I suppose desperation is its own species of wisdom. The yearling nimbly turned about and climbed. I did not trust I could match its speed, but I hoped that if any goat dared follow me such treacherous footing would steal any chance for it to charge and ram me with its horns.

I placed my heel to toe, so that I might walk slantwise. The ledge seemed chipped out in places, widened by the pickaxe. My hands sought purchase in the rock face. I groped at a thin ridge upon which snow heaped, and nearly leapt away when it shifted beneath my touch. Dislodged snow revealed rusted links beneath.

A chain. I hooked my fingers behind it and pulled. The whole line swung out. Snow fell from its links, and I saw where the chain was pinned to the rock by great bent nails. My doubts evaporated. I stood on no goat run. I had found a secret path.

The mother goat bleated again. She lowered her head as steam gushed from her nostrils. I saw that, even if she could not knock me down, she could still gore me with those horns and pitch me from the path. I forgot about salvation and began to clamber upward.

With the chain as guide and helping hand, I climbed with reckless haste. Though my view of the world remained unchanged, the distance below me grew precipitously as the slope gave way to sheer drop. At the bottom, humped snow concealed, no doubt, broken rocks that hungered for dashed brains and which, I thought, must count even the bones of these goats among its treasures. Ahead of me, the kid bleated as a hoof slid, sending a little chute of snow over the edge.

I was gaining on the kid. It began to mewl, crying as a child might when Turks come foaming through the gates. The nanny behind me blared like a tolling bell. I made a mistake then, I turned my head to see that she was gaining.

It was here the chain disappeared. My hands slid along the links, over a nail, and then nothing. The line beyond the staple hung plumb, gnawed through by winter storms.

The nanny bleated again. The beast was nearer than I had guessed. Those slit eyes understood no mercy for my kind, and as I hesitated its head bowed and I saw it would ram me. I clung to the wall so dearly that I scraped my cheek when I turned away.

My fingers did not find a hold as I shuffled sideways. If I did not fall, it is only because I did not sway. I moved and tried to ignore how the kid's rump retreated. To ignore the sound of the nanny's huffing and the smell of its animal breath. I scuffed forward until, beyond the next nail, the chain reappeared.

I grasped at it and leaned my weight into it as I kicked blindly, gracelessly, behind me. In a tavern brawl, such a feeble boot would cost me teeth. But I was on a cliff and my heel glanced against the goat's muzzle, and this sent her skidding.

Her back legs went over as her haunches twisted. The kid must have seen its mother, for it bawled like never before. I felt a twinge of pity as she trumpeted in answer. Somehow her front feet clung to the ledge. It is a thing of sadness to see a life so desperate to not slip away. But the infernal creature refused to fall. Her back hooves clattered against the cliff face as she pumped her legs in a gallop and, by God, she regained the ledge.

The kid had stopped and twisted its neck around to watch, but it set off when I redoubled my scrabbling pursuit. It rounded a bend, followed closely by me, where the chain gave way suddenly again. Here the cliff folded back into a flat shelf where the pathmakers had not bothered to pin a chain. I loped through the snow and heard the nanny snort on my heels, but when I glanced up to see a masonry wall, my spirits lifted. We neared the summit.

Another bend, and the shelf vanished while the path became as wide as a man and steep. I climbed on hands and feet. I ascended a staircase buried beneath the snow. The kid ahead bounded up and over the wall.

I tripped the final step, but soon righted myself and dangerously paused, taken aback, after all that, to find myself on the mountain's summit.

Too late it occurred to me the beacon mount might be manned by one of Kuszkol's missing defenders. This fear dispelled when I saw the only path cut through the snowfall was the kid's, which looped around the beacon's stone platform.

This base was a dais upon which wood was normally kept stacked and ready. Today snow heaped upon the unspent fuel of the last fire, riddled by cavities and with charred sticks poking through. I recalled the conflagration had leapt high into the sky, but because it had been stacked poorly the fire did not incinerate the entire mass. An entire side of the snow-smothered fuel still rose above my head, giving the whole the look of a tumbledown tower.

I leapt upon the charcoal mass and began to climb the fire's remnants as the nanny mounted the wall. Burnt wood spilled as I pulled myself up the pyre. From the top I dared look behind me.

The she-goat faced me from the ground. She dipped her horns and rubbed them against the edge of the dais. Only once the kid had raced around the platform to join her did she raise her head.

In that look I saw indifferent hostility. This was the face of the Beast. I had seen Him depicted so only months ago in a manuscript I had fetched for my master, a tome penned by a Hussite heretic. In those pages I had seen this same face of the Enemy, gazing from those faraway eyes from beneath his crooked horns. I recalled in that image how scrolls curled from the Beast's fingers, upon which the bishops had inscribed indulgences for the kings who slaughter innocents in the name of their sons.

But in this goat's eyes I saw also a reflection of Fejes. I had always mistaken the tranquility I found in her gaze for warmth. Now I saw that the same gulf that separated me from this goat separated me from she whom I had thought most faithful. I saw that, though I might weep for Fejes, she would never weep for me.

I pulled a blackened stick from the heap to brandish before me. I shouted, a tiny wordless voice in the sky. Not enough to frighten, but the kid retreated, and after dipping its horns once more, the nanny turned and followed it over the low wall.

I remained upon the beacon to take in the world below. I could see the valley and the loopy string of a flowing river. Somewhere along its path it would pass out of the king's realm. The parchments in the king's chart room no doubt demarked this border with a red slash. Those maps were false. The earth knew no such partitions. The mountain ridges rolled away like waves.

My eyes drifted down the length of my weapon. I wondered why the tip of my club bulged so perfectly, as though it should be fitted to a socket.

I turned this strange baton over. Recognition was slow to take root.

I held a bone.

My instinct was not to hurl it aside. Commandeered by epiphany, I fell to my knees and began to shovel. I dug through spent fuel that seemed too coarse to have ever housed spirit. But my eyes were not liars. My excavation revealed cloth and skin and the churned-up flakes of burnt men.

Some were whole, others little more than grit. Here was one, once a soldier, now a shriveled thing with jaws drawn wide to expose fire-cracked teeth. Snow had settled in its hollows, in place of eyes and along the grooves of tendons. Here was another, his flesh pulled tight across erupting bones, squamous and bubbled like pigskin. And another, reduced to wisps of crinkled hair and the remnants of cloak and a boot, from which splinters slid when I turned it over.

Still I shoveled, begriming myself with their cinders until my arms and legs were black. I drove my fingers into cracks that clove brittle leather. In my haste I tore the arm from one of my countrymen. I broke the spine of another above the hips. I took these pieces and set them aside, one by one.

I stood upon bodies and bodies. I had found Kuszkol's lost garrison.

I sat on the unholy pile, resting my feet in the pit I had dug, scales of ashy skin falling from my fingers, overcome by a surge of relief. I felt myself a survivor of this slaughter, though I had missed it by days.

To ask why the dead were piled here was senseless. Up at this height I was beyond explanations. But still the old tales swirled in my mind. The stories told how Kuszkol divided men against one another. Perhaps one among these soldiers had become a murderer, strangling his fellows one at a time, dragging the evidence of this crime to this spot as a cat hides his lifeless prize. Or perhaps enmity had exiled each man from his brothers. Perhaps there was havoc, total war for supremacy of this hill to become Kuszkol's king. A children's game turned to ruthless frenzy. Or perhaps the answer was worse yet.

I pulled my cloak tighter. Sit too long here and a man could die of the cold. But I would not die of such, of this I was certain. If anything my feet felt warm. The residual heat of the fire, I realized, seeping up from the pyre's heart. How great the heat must have been once the fire was lit.

The sky stretched about me was as mute as ever. I stood. I scanned the world below, desperate suddenly to drink some vivid sight that was neither black nor white. A sign of life rather than its ashes.

My eye found it. A garish splash of red on the mountain's lower slope, along the path to Kuszkol's gate. Dark forms writhed about it. I squinted, and saw wolves working their craft. I saw, too, four hoofs pointed skyward.

Kladivo, his belly opened.

Twenty-Two

Steps descended from the beacon to a plain wooden door. I grasped the handle and pushed. The door swung open onto a winter-bright corridor. Before me stretched a passage.

Doors opened on the right. The floor was dull, touched by the wash water light. To the left the fortress backed onto the mountain and my courage ebbed to see no doors but a wall defaced. They were but black outlines, man-shaped and unshaded at their center, and they overlapped like horseshoe tracks in sand. I did not want to count them but I guessed they numbered some twenty-five.

A man is erased in death, so I cannot say why I quailed before this sight, but seeing the edges of those figures so carelessly lineated so they seemed to merge, to lose their distinct edges, filled me with a sort of revulsion. To lose one's very shape in the lines of another was an indignity I had never contemplated, but one that now struck me as intolerable. And yet, after the uncountable faces I had seen in my life, I would be the first to agree that Adam had populated this Earth with empty impressions.

The keep sighed frigidly across my brow but the cold could touch me no longer. I loosened my scarf and stepped inside. In the first room snow had drifted beneath the open windows. A reminder of how long this place had crumbled, slowly dissolving into the mountain's crags. Where the snow ended, dirt and scabs of bark covered the floor of one side of the room. A wood pile had stood there. Magnificent cobwebs adorned the bare wall against which the wood had rested. Across the room stood a stool and a watchman's brazier that some fool had filled past its brim. The wall on this side was scorched where the fire had leapt, and on the floor, among the ash and fallen cinders, I observed singed tatters of cloth as if the watchman had used rags as fuel.

The windows offered a different vantage on the lower bailey. I sought out and found my Fejes. She stood as though listening near the main gate which I had left open. My doubts returned. Why had I not barred it? I had thought to give Fejes the chance to wander, but any wolves that followed Kladivo's scent up the mountain path would find her already encircled by the bailey's confines. I had been wrong to think she might ever find her way. Kladivo could not and he had had Jakab guiding her.

I entered the next room. A sleeping chamber. Again it was empty and I began to resent the light. A bright room is empty in a way a darkened one can never be. The dark hides unknowns. It is itself an unknown, and thus, for the desperate, it secretes hope that light dispels. The desolation of this place was too clear. It was becoming more difficult to deceive myself that I was not too late.

The garrison was lost. My only hope was lost with them. Deranged they might have been, but I had counted on treating with men. I had no understanding of what had happened to Pál, but I had supposed my search would end with me pleading with my countrymen.

Panic returned to me. What if I did not find him? What if I walked home from this fortress alone, to return to the empty cottage in Veszprém? I found myself thinking of my grim work in the stables, of Pál's harrowed face. Perhaps if I had not inflicted mercy on those doomed horses, Pál would have found the strength to resist the mountain and stayed at my side.

This simple idea stuck me as surely as any phantom arrow. I nearly choked.

As I stood lost at that window, the snow lost its sparkle. The world dimmed. The clouds thickened and it was growing late. Night would come again.

This was a riddle. The garrison's pyre, the forest on these walls, the man-shaped silhouettes. Even poor Kálmán. Somehow they strung together. It was the kind of puzzle Annaka would have unknotted before I had even asked the question. My wife would have understood. That was her gift. She always knew when the world would shift before it did, and thus she was never put off balance. That was why others found her so odd. She adopted a different stance than all about her, a footing to withstand the quake yet to buck the land.

I stepped into the dimming corridor. At the end there was a tower. It held winding stairs that led down. Slits in the wall sifted snow upon the steps. I had little stomach for this descent, but Pál was the lure that called me deeper. I came into a passage illuminated only by what weak light trailed me. As above, doors lined one side of the corridor.

I opened the first and saw the seams of a shuttered window etched into the far wall. I slipped around the shadowed furniture and pushed, but the shutters would not budge. Snow had piled on the ledge and blocked the way.

I felt the dark behind me. I felt the darkness at my elbow, leaning close. Whispering silence in my ear. I began to hammer, like the fisherman who slips beneath the ice, until the shutters swung outward and I gasped for a taste of the failing light.

The room was unlike any I had entered since I last stood before the bishop in Veszprém. A heavy table claimed the room's middle, its scrolling wood richly finished but scratched by wear. Behind this a cushioned chair with a fox's fur draping its back. In the corner, a dummy wore polished mail and a plumed helm. At the dummy's foot, a coffer, its latch sealed by a heavy padlock. At the dummy's elbow, a florid tapestry, woven by northern hands.

The room bespoke an authority interrupted. The floor was papered with fallen pages, many about the brazier's iron feet disfigured with singed and curling edges. A shattered pot on the table's edge radiated long tendrils of frozen ink, a splash doubled on the floor where it had dripped. Beside this lower spatter, an upturned bowl spilled frozen pottage. A meal. Someone's last.

Not someone. Kázmér Kustyer. That was the name of Kálmán's father, and this was his chamber. Here he must have retreated to contemplate his charge, to contemplate his failings as Kuszkol slipped away.

I sat upon the chair and pulled the fox pelt across my shoulders. I had a clear view of sky. Charcoal churned in cream. Upon a tray rested quills, sealing wax, and a stack of rolled parchments. The only way forward was to claw through the ashes of dead men. I reached from my mantle, pulled a parchment towards me, and unrolled it. My heart nearly stopped at the sight of blunt black strokes. The crude form of a man in charcoal. The commander had fastidiously shaded it so that no hint of calfskin showed through. But this was not his own shadow he sketched with such care. This was the figure of soot. The silhouette I had encountered at the end of the hoarding.

Kustyer had a keen eye. The shape tilted off the page, its shoulders humped with menace, its fingers spread. I balled the page and threw it towards the brazier.

The second parchment also held a familiar image. The same black figure, but surrounded by the simple outlines of others. All sizes and shapes, as though each held a void at its center. Men, women, children, strung along in a chain.

These were the scrawlings we had passed in the deserted village at the mountain's foot. The ruins that returned to the wild. In the left margin Kustyer had written a date. The twentieth of September.

I reached for another scroll. Kustyer had drawn a peculiar image on this parchment. Two irregular boxes. At three points he inscribed tiny circles beside a date. I puzzled over this for a few moments before I recognized the contours of the upper and lower baileys.

A circle at the end of where the hoarding lay in this diagram was dated the fifteenth of November. A circle in the upper gatehouse was dated the first of December. A circle, somewhere in this keep, was dated the eighth of December.

He charted a progression. I recognized the first two points as the sites of the unnatural cold and the abyssal forest. The last circle was near to me, inside these very walls.

I set this parchment aside and with reluctance took the final scroll from the tray. At the top of the roll, in letters as bent and compact as bludgeoned candlesticks, the commander had set down a single word—*DISCIPLINE*. Below he had recorded a diary of transgressions.

> The 1st of May. Péter Tóth & Antal Ferenc have been drunken. I have pilloried them.
> The 3rd of July. János Balázs has been drunken. I have pilloried him.
> The 14th of September. Péter Tóth has been drunken. I have pilloried him.
> The 26th of September. János Balázs has taken the name of the Lord in vain. I have pilloried him.
> The 4th of October. István Fehérvári has been drunken. I have pilloried him.
> The 18th of October. Péter Tóth & János Balázs have gamed on Sunday. I have flogged them.
> The 27th of October. János Balázs has been drunken. I have pilloried him.
> The 1st of November. Péter Tóth has been drunken. I have flogged & pilloried him.
> The 2nd of November. János Tóth has spoken in defiance. I have flogged & pilloried him.

The 4th of November. Vilmos Vadas has slept at his post. I have fined him 1d.
The 8th of November. Péter Tóth has stolen wood. I have flogged & pilloried him.
The 12th of November. Péter Tóth & János Tóth have deserted their posts. We have searched paths and the town. Profusion of shadows smirch ruined walls. János Tóth fled from hideaway back into our arms. I have hanged him.
The 13th of November. István Fehérvári has stolen wood & has cursed me. I have hanged him.

In the span of two days he had hanged two men.

The 14th of November. Vilmos Vadas has slept at his post. I have pilloried and fined him 1d.
The 15th of November. Vilmos Vadas has slept at his post. I have fined him 1d & have suspended his pay while he is abed. He is sickly.
The 27th of November. János Balázs has taken our Lord's name in vain. I have pilloried him.
The 4th of December. Péter Tóth has fled forest & returned to beg clemency. I have hanged him.

A third.

The 5th of December. Antal Ferenc & L. Kiss have defied command to fetch wood. Will not enter forest. I have flogged & pilloried them.
The 8th of December. János Balázs has stolen wood. I have fined him 1d.
The 8th of December. János Grósz has stolen wood. I have fined him 1d.
The 8th of December. Péter Molnár has stolen wood. I have fined him 2d.

The 8th of December. János Grósz & László Turóczi have insurrected. I refused them the stake & I have hanged them.

A fourth and a fifth.

The 9th of December. Péter Molnár has stolen wood.
The 10th of December. My men are guilty. I must heed them.

The tenth of December was the last entry. By then Kázmér Kustyer had managed to hang one fifth of his command. The last two only four days before we arrived.

I reread the ledger and still could not make sense of it. The men burning wood faster than they could split it. A breakdown in order. Men sent to the gallows ... who had asked for the stake?

I pressed my palm over my eyes.

On the day we departed Veszprém, Kuszkol had already turned feral. The commander had already lost control. Pál had been destined to replace a hanged man. If he had arrived even one day earlier, he may well have joined the others on the pyre.

It was pure accident he had not shared Annaka's fate.

To believe what they say, she too started the fire.

So they say. Everything about the end of my marriage is hearsay. I was abroad those last days. I did not see her degraded, though I have oft envisioned her cell. The sodden straw and rats. Her tangled hair and soiled skirt. A lamp left too close.

They arrested her the very day I set out to Temesvár. They had waited for me to leave to move against her. Her crimes included knowing too much. Spreading truths that should remain unspoken. Reciprocating contempt.

She despised and was despised. I had been aloof from it, even as those around me exhorted me to have a care. But I have never liked to study a problem I have no means to solve. Marriage changed my ways only slightly and that is why Annaka was such a fine match for me. Her expectations were unlike any other woman's, at least until our last years together. Towards the end of our marriage, through her looks and silences I understood she willed that I change my ways. Never did she insist, but I felt her unspoken wishes as strongly as if she had trimmed my cloak with stones. I put no store by this want of hers. In that last year together I lost my tolerance for home. Now I wonder if she had foreseen her own end and needed me close. It is hard to say, for she never voiced her fear. Whenever others cowered, her attitude was condescension. She scorned all outside our home. She never said she was afraid to be alone.

There had been whispers. From the first my sisters told me I must master her. That only I made such distinctions fine enough to sort willfulness from wickedness. I ascribed their warnings to hysteria. My sisters, born like me to penury, had found dull husbands with sturdy cottages, to whom they had born ten-fingered, two-eyed, unremarkable children. That they refused to come to my house I reckoned meant... what? I did not regard it as serious nor did I seek remedy, for what did I need with company?

Besides, what could I have said? The rumors were that my wife had a knack for healing poultices. That she had sharp ears and a sharper tongue. That if one looked at her askew, she was liable to wield that tongue to slice one to the bone. Scandals shot from her mouth, unspoken disgraces, outrages so irresistible they must be passed along.

My sisters said there was a word for a woman like that, even if no one ever accused her of causing soup to burn or milk to curdle or an unborn child to quiet in the belly. One day Pál heard us. He heard my sisters and I argue. I drove my sisters from my gate and told the boy to believe none of it.

He looked at me, eyes laden with unearned regret, and said, "You alone are deceived."

My Pál had never been a wise boy. Never had he demonstrated any of Annaka's perceptivity. But those words . . . those words rocked me.

Yet I pretended they had not been said. I refused to understand and when I was told to ride east, I rode east. And while away my life came undone. Some believe I knew what was to happen and that I slipped away to spare myself seeing her manacled. This is untrue.

She was tolerated, in a way, until she was not. Her end did not unfold as many predicted. She did not offend the wrong person. She was used. By a parish priest, no less, who had been diverting a sliver of the tithe to keep a woman for years. This woman's circumstances had been a secret, though not tightly held. Then one day it was on the lips of all in the parish. I am not even certain it was Annaka who lifted the veil on his deceit. Either way, the priest seized on her disrepute, pinned the slander on her and thus attempted to shield himself by lodging a charge at her.

He relayed the charge to his masters. The Church took matters from there. The bishop intervened to stay her trial until I returned, out of respect, for I still command my share. She was imprisoned for a week that I might speak to her one last time.

But then she found a lamp, left too close.

My wife took away that last chance three days before my return. She became one with the flames. I feel like I know what she would have said to me. She would have said, I am beyond redemption so what difference does it make? And so she spared me. I was never forced to forsake her. I was never forced to fight for her life.

Why did she have to act as she did? Why did she have to be as she was? She was a mystery no one could abide. Towards the end, not even Pál. Certainly not I.

Twenty-Three

YOU KEEP PICKING THESE SCABS. You keep them fresh that you might peek beneath them for insight where there is only blood that should have dried long ago. You think you will find my treachery but I practiced none.

I could never remove that stain. Yet day after day I squatted upon those rocks and I scrubbed and beat the cloth and lost my flesh to vicious lye, until one day I caught another watching me. I raised my eyes, grateful to stare him down, thankful for a reason to dawdle and let the cloth stream in the water like river weed. There, eyes invisible in the briar, a young fox newly separated from his mother. Flesh draped from his ribs. He needed to eat and there were grubs that burrowed beneath his toes and yet he did not paw the ground to free them. His ruin poked from his little face, a quill lodged beneath his eye. The wound had festered and the fox could not open his mouth at all and so he would die there in that briar, pining to taste the stream. A cousin of the one who marched beneath his feet would be the first to wander down the fox's ear to feast. There it would multiply until the host waxed and waned and at length the dusty pelt collapsed onto bone. Ugly Borbála had turned to follow my gaze, and I was eager to meet her eye, to stare her down, but before I did I glimpsed a pit in the shadow she cast on the surface of my stream. A pit, leaning out, reaching out to devour what will ever be mine. Thus I knew my purpose and knew that I must speak.

I did all that I did so I might speak. So I might face your master and draw out his tale of gold and dark water. So I might hear him tell that when the castle's lord searched the pit's entrance, when he thought he was drawing near, that the forest closed before him like granitic teeth. "He wrote those very words." Your master and I spoke and he said, "I have erred by speaking to you." And I said, "You erred by letting Kázmér go to that mountain." And your master said, "He was not ignorant." And I said, "Nor were you." And he said, "I have erred by speaking to you."

And I, I said, "Yet here you are. Seeking my counsel."

Twenty-Four

I wandered into the next room. I could have slipped between the cracks in the walls, I felt so insubstantial.

This room was darker still. And cold. I neared the window and placed my fingers in the thin line of light that seeped through the shutters' crease. Even in this gray thread, my ring gleamed. As in the last room, these shutters were stuck with ice.

Thud.

They rattled beneath my blow. I raised my fist a second time.

"No."

It was not I who had spoken. Not she. I looked at my fist hanging mid-air.

"My eyes will not abide the light."

I turned and saw what I did not when I had entered the room. A bed heaped with covers. A head upon the pillow.

From where I stood I could distinguish little. The face was coarsened by the half-light, like a weathered idol hewn from wood. Sharp cheekbones and brow, sockets and nostrils brimming shadows above a wild beard.

"Sir Kálmán?" I whispered.

"Not my name."

I lingered near the shuttered window. "Then who are you?"

"Who are you." It was not a question. Just my own words thrown back like an echo.

"My name is András," I said.

"Do I know you?"

"I think not. I arrived only three days ago. After the beacon was lit."

"The beacon." Recognition. He shifted his head on the pillow but I could see his face no better.

"I say again—who are you?"

"Who am I? I am." From beneath the quilt fingers emerged. They ran over the beard, as though it were unfamiliar. They caressed the nose and cheeks. "I am Vilmos."

One of the men Kázmér Kustyer had disciplined. He had turned sickly and was put to bed.

The man moved his face. Perhaps he stared, I could not tell. No surprise or fear distorted his simple features. "Year after year," he croaked, his voice dried and hollowed by neglect. "I promised Magdolna I would put down my shield. I would pick up the plow and fill her yard with squealing whelps. Year after year even as silver threaded her braid. This time I will keep my word. I will not leave her again. You have finally come."

I had no answer. I was not who he thought me to be.

He understood soon enough. "You are a figment after all. You are not my savior."

"I will do what I can, but I have come to find another. A young man. A boy. My brother-in-law." I looked dubiously at the man. "Have you seen him?"

"I know you not so I cannot say. He is with the others, probably."

I thought of where I had found his comrades.

"We came only after the beacon was lit, which was four days ago."

The head shifted upon the pillow. "Are you real?"

"I am real. I came as a messenger."

"Ah," the man said. "Kázmér cursed you often."

"He cursed me? How could he have known about me?"

"You were to come sooner."

I recognized his resentment. Cooled to pre-dawn embers, but smoldering nonetheless. The garrison's last days must have been as bitter as they were desperate.

"And how could I have helped had I come?"

"Not you," Vilmos said. "The message you carried."

The message. In my satchel, until now forgotten on the barrack floor. "How could word from the bishop of Veszprém illuminate the plight of your lord?" My master and Kálmán's father were cronies of a sort, but even so.

"He did not say."

"One of my comrades entered the keep yesterday," I said. "Have you not seen him? He entered and he locked me out. Perhaps he passed this way."

Vilmos turned his face and sighed. He was a husk of a man, as sure as dead before I had arrived. I thought about backing out. Leaving him as he lay. I should have.

"There are only shadows here," he said. "Come closer."

"Tell me what happened."

"What happened?" he rasped. "Our iron spurned us. It snapped at our touch like a rabid cur. It did the mountain's will. It siphoned off our fervor so our heat oozed from us like sap. We shed our mail in exchange for blankets. Men wandered draped in them, clothed like specters. The sight of one another's eyes became unbearable. The speech of others unbearable. The commander could do nothing but bar the gate and call for more prayers. But the saints did not heed us. Our faith had gone. We did not pray, we only repeated words. I clutch my rosary still only because it was gifted me by my wife."

"Why did you not leave?"

"Leave? We were trapped. Are you not trapped? Why do you not leave?"

For all his apparent feebleness, this head upon a pillow was still filled with insolence. He had as much cause for anger as I. "Do you know the fate of your comrades?"

"I heard their groans."

"Then you know they are gone."

"I saw them before they departed. Saw enough to feel envy."

"Why envy?"

"Come closer and I will tell you."

I felt no desire to leave my place beside the window, but I did as he asked. I walked to his bedside.

"Closer."

"Tell me why you felt envy."

"Our discipline was broken. We had become crazed by cold. So cold, we burnt all our wood. We would refill the woodshed and burn it just as fast. Eventually the thoughts of my comrades leapt to the hoard upon the beacon mount."

"They sought to plunder the beacon's reserve?"

"Kázmér was busy hanging them when László pled instead for the stake. This was a profanity that could not be unsaid. The notion spilled from mouth to mouth. It could not be put back again. Word spread. They had found their means to release themselves from the cold. A chance to feel heat one last time."

"They murdered themselves?"

"They mustered. They gathered, and climbed in single file. They rushed upwards, pushing one another forward, for this new idea was akin to salvation. The last words I heard any of them speak were, 'We could be like moths.' I heard nothing more after this but their release, but for days now I have dreamt of how it must have come to pass. Of how they tore at the edge of the tarpaulin that covered the stack of wood. How the flame was kindled, coaxed until it threw up fiery blossoms. Maybe they shoved it deep. Maybe my comrades pushed closer. Maybe they planted their hands on the edge of the beacon's bowl and whispered congratulations to one another and said, here she comes, here she comes. Or maybe I am wrong. I cannot decide. They were a mixed lot. I can only say I have dreamt as well that they said nothing at all. That they twitched silently, like crows waiting for a fox to open a hen on their behalf. They twitched and from time to time a caw went up, no words, just impatience, though none doubted their turn to come for they could see the treasure within the pile, illuminating all its plunging fissures. The fire took. Alive, it scaled the pyre from within, unto the summit, where it roared. I could hear that for myself. All the while my brothers pushed closer, holding out their hands to the flames that erupted and tumbled from the woodpile's flanks. Closer, for warmth had come."

I stood above him and said nothing, matching his tale to the evidence I had found. I could find no cause to naysay him.

"In this place men become indistinct," Vilmos said. "You have seen what became of my brothers. I have seen it too, for one cannot so easily keep one's thoughts to oneself here and your thoughts are not quiet. In the end they became confused. One cannot say where one begins and another ends. The little fragments of them count for nothing. One can only make sense of their remainders as a whole."

I studied the invalid. He was no different from those men who had died. He admired them. The most Christian way to treat with him would be to drag him from his bed and return him to the barracks where I might nurse him to health. The memory of Jakab killed the impulse. I did not want to sleep next to one who had been corrupted. "Tell me how you survived."

"For a long while I thirsted. Then a cup appeared beside my bed."

I saw the shape of a cup on the floor.

"Who brought it?"

"Who brought it."

"Yes, who brought it?"

"Did you not?"

"I did not bring it," I said. "I have only just arrived."

"My fever has broken. Come closer."

I stepped closer. "What is happening here?"

"I have been abed for weeks. How am I to know?"

I looked down upon the man. He could read my face no better than I his, I reckoned. "You can tell me nothing, then?"

"If you place your hand on my brow I will tell you."

"I would rather not."

"Come closer."

"How can I come closer? I already stand at your side."

"Touch my face."

I hesitated. He was spent and I felt little sympathy for him. Still, I reached out. I put my hand across his brow and was shocked by the chill of his flesh. Like a slab of pork left on the counter overnight, he felt more meat than man.

"That is good," Vilmos said. "Kázmér would sometimes creep in here as I lay in my fever and touch me as you do now. To steal my warmth."

I withdrew my hand. "I have felt your brow. Your fever has broken."

"Put your hand back," Vilmos said. "It soothes me."

"Where is Pál?"

"The boy for whom you search."

"Yes."

"I will tell you."

I waited as he shifted below me. "Then do so. Tell me where he is."

"Come closer."

"Why?"

"Kneel beside the bed and come closer."

"But why?"

"Do as I say."

I stood over him, indecisive. He had lain here for untold days. His patience was greater than mine. I knelt beside the bed. He struggled for a moment to free his hand from his covers then placed it on my arm. He was alike a corpse reaching out from its winding sheet.

"Pál was taken."

"Taken by the spirit that haunts this mountain?"

"He was taken to show you the way."

"To show me the way to Pál? I do not understand."

"The boy will show you the way. He is your beacon. You must follow."

"I am trying to follow."

"You are doing well."

I could not grasp his meaning. He could not know anything of my search. If he did know, he should know it was not going well. "Why must I follow?"

"You are the messenger."

"The ghost awaits the letter I carry?"

"You are to go."

I had had enough. Perhaps with some warm soup in him he might begin to make sense.

"Come," I said. "Get up. I will set you before a fire."

"I would rather you lie next to me."

"What did you say?"

"You are more real than fire. Come. There is no shame in huddling for warmth."

I stared at his face. Too close. His fingers tightened on my arm.

"I will not."

I pulled his hand from me.

He said, "If you do as I ask I will tell you where to find the boy."

"So you know where he is?"

"Come. Lend me your warmth and I will tell you all."

"I will not."

"Why will you not?"

"You are mad, I fear."

"Is that the only reason?"

"I think perhaps you are dreaming still. Can you not see I am a man?" I asked.

"It is you who is the dreamer. And you are no man."

The voice, almost forgotten this last day, buzzing so softly on my tongue like a fine velvet, suddenly filled my throat. I had to gnash my teeth to bite back the laughter that threatened to spill between my lips. I managed to bark, "I do not trust you."

"What harm can I do? I am only a shadow of the man I was. You are full of vigor, not I. It is you who commands here. Now climb in."

"No."

"You love the thought of who you are more than you love the boy. Yet you do not even know who you are."

I could not account for my lack of disquiet. The need to grin behind my fingers. "You speak without sense."

"Then let me embrace you." Two arms emerged from beneath the blanket. White flesh. A shift that smelled like cold sweat.

"I will not embrace you."

"I want to tell you about the boy but you must do as I say. I know where he is."

I held myself out of his reach. "Have you a weapon?" I asked.

"As you see, my hands are empty."

I looked on.

"I am a man who thought himself passed from the world. But you have come. Come closer."

I watched until his arms began to tremble.

"Why would you have me embrace you?"

"I am cold. It is no trick."

I watched until his arms began to droop.

"And you will tell me all I wish to know?"

"I will tell you no lies."

I leaned forward and he clasped me to him. I could not believe he could still stir, he was so cold. I felt his fingers clamp across my back. His beard scratched my neck.

"Now tell me," I said over his shoulder.

"I have not seen Magdolna in so many months. I fear I might never see her again."

"You will see her. Now unhand me and tell me where Pál is."

His grip tightened. "No. I will never see her again. Climb into bed."

I began to pry his arms from me.

"Climb into bed and I will not shame you."

"This is unseemly."

"I said I will not shame you."

I threw him off me.

"Where is he?"

"You have a womanish aspect," he said. "You are more woman than man."

"I am not." I pinned his wrists between my hands to stop their questing.

He said, "But you are. You burn with a beautiful light."

"I do not burn," I said. "You have caught a chill and you are addled, that is all."

"You do burn, and I cannot help but reach for you. Perhaps you are invisible to yourself. Perhaps you lack the courage to acknowledge you are alight. But I can tell you your hair is up in streamers. Even now when you are silent I watch your mouth open and a flaming snake reaches forth and I can hear the quiet thunder of your speech. I do not understand, but I am not blind. I can parse its promise. The shelter you offer beneath your fire-billowed skirt."

His words failed to astonish. If anything, they piqued me. As if he harped on details that were not relevant.

"Perhaps you will soon see things as I do," he said. "We two are alike. We two are about to be cast aside. Let us bring each other comfort."

"We are not alike. Tell me were Pál is."

"You still care to find him? He is somewhere cold. Colder than this. Somewhere dark. Darker than this. Somewhere quieter than this, somewhere lonelier. Though he is not alone."

"Where?"

"Somewhere deep."

"Deep? He is in the cellar?"

"The forest."

"The forest?"

"You know which one. Now climb in with me. Your pride is no match for this place."

"You are raving."

"Am I? I am filled with need and I put voice to it. Perhaps I have misled you. I apologize, dear messenger. I am truly sorry. Perhaps you will survive. Another has paid for your life."

I did not know what this meant, and yet, like everything this survivor had said, his words rang with a kind of truth, if mad things can be true. I was not yet dead. I was not cold. Not in my marrow, as the stones beneath my feet demanded. Even so, at his words a shiver shook my teeth. My flesh erupted in prickles.

I looked up across the bed, to a soot black face, hanging just feet from my own.

I leapt back. The figure was there, across the bed, looming over the man I was about to abandon.

Had he been there before? No. Or perhaps he had. I cannot decide. It could be he had been there the whole time. I could not tell then and I cannot tell now, and of course, it does not matter. It made no difference, for I was already running.

My last sight of Vilmos was his pale hand reaching towards me. No plea escaped his mouth. I stumbled across the threshold, towards the steps and then down. Down, around and around within the tower, down into the keep's lower, black corridors. Forward, I searched blindly for the exit, breaking my nails on unseen stone, barging through the shadows, fleeing the cloak folding behind me. And the face. The one who stalks the battlefield, straddling the madness and the cold. Like my double looming out of nightmare.

I burst through the door, dazed by fading daylight, dazed by that intuition. The black one was no double of mine. Why would I think that? The black one had a face and it was a face I knew. He had once had a name too. Before he had entered the keep I had called him Kálmán.

Twenty-Five

I awoke to Fejes's breath upon my mouth. I opened my eyes and yet I did not see. It must be night, I thought. The sky was black as a coffin lid and seemed just as near. I raised my hand with difficulty, as though my arm had been stuck fast in place, until it broke the surface and grasped at air. Fejes passed her nose across my mouth to sweep aside more snow that I might be revived, and thus I understood where I lay.

I sat up. It was night, but not quite so black as beneath the layer of snow where I had lain for who knows how long. The glittering stars revealed by their absence the now familiar and despised outline of the gatehouse and stable. I had run as far as the lower bailey before my legs had given out, as had my mind, and I had plunged into dreams. Dreams that were not my own.

Here I had lain as the snow piled upon my limbs and brow, as the mountain gently prepared me for death. I rose and discovered recompense for my toils knotted in my neck and arms. But my lips did not chatter, and I felt no numbness even in my fingertips. By rights I should have turned to ice. I felt the cold, but it was beyond me, like the howling tempest beyond the battened shutters. I had survived. I would never be cold again.

I began to walk. Fejes rubbed her head against me, nearly toppling me over, and I wound my fingers in her mane. She, who alone was left to me. She, who had not forsaken me. I was so thankful for this beast with whom I had traveled leagues uncounted in wordless concord. My truest confidant. My only friend.

Behind me, the keep. Vilmos, stranded in his narrow bed, forage for famished shadows. Behind me, Kálmán...

Kálmán had become another. I knew it even then, though I could not will myself to contemplate the transformation. I did not fear he would follow me, but I resolved never to set foot in the keep again.

I had no right to set foot anywhere. I should have frozen to death. But Fejes led me on, and I followed, to the only place that had seemed safe.

Up in the barracks, in the dark, on the floor, I had left my satchel. Within it, alongside spare hose and my sewing kit, my portfolio. Within this, a letter. Handed to me by the bishop's clerk the morning I left Veszprém.

Night reigned within the barracks. Fejes did not follow when I stepped inside.

The cold intensified. I felt the mountain redouble its attack, sinking its slender knives. I remembered the cold that had assailed Kálmán's circle. Though it bit, though it made my eyes and nose run, I carried on. Armored and impervious, like a bear who shakes off bombardment as he raids a beehive.

It was thus not the report of my flesh which prevented me from venturing further, but of my ears. In the dark another stood near, breathing roughly.

"Reveal yourself." I said. My hand sought out my knife's hilt.

"It is only me."

"Jakab?"

The veteran shambled from the darkest part of the storeroom. The weak starlight from the doorway showed me no more than his shape.

"I am glad to find you," he said.

I stood rigidly, wondering if he could be real, unsure if it was better to flee or clasp his shoulder. "Why are you here?" I asked.

"I . . ." He stood there, improbably, my lost comrade, swaying. "I came back."

"Why?"

"I did not want to leave," he said. He added nothing of Kladivo failing him and being torn apart by wolves halfway down the mountainside. "Let us sit down." He trudged towards the steps and onto the treads, already marching up.

This was not right. Jakab's return was as unacceptable as it was unexpected. If he were keeping tally, if he understood at all our parting, then he should know better than to trust me. Though it was he who had fled, it was I, sound of mind, who had abandoned him.

My satchel was upstairs and so I followed. I heard him creaking the floorboards ahead of me. Something about his gait, his posture, suggested he was more battered than I despite my fatigue and the aches from the day. I followed, knowing I was the stronger.

The starlight was not bright enough to shine through the parchment windows. I could not make out my hand in front of me. The room's few furnishings were revealed by memory rather than by sight. Ahead, Jakab knocked into a stool.

My satchel was to the left of the hearth, with my bedroll. I would need to feel about in the dark, but I thought I might be able to find it quietly. It was the prudent course, to retrieve the satchel and to read the letter elsewhere. I was not sure where in the fortress I might find such peace, to wait out first light. Jakab spoiled my plans when he spoke.

"Will you not sit with me?"

Though his mind was unsound and though I was not sure what else he had become, the plaintive note in his voice was only too clear. Whatever else Jakab was, his travails on this mountain had made him an old man.

So I found a stool in the dark and I sat with him. The wrong decision, perhaps, but a man can only turn from the damned so often. We sat for some moments, not seeing one another. His breathing was so labored it sounded like he hauled every breath by hand.

"Do you know where Pál is?" I asked.

"No."

I had not expected him to say otherwise, and yet he gave no hint of objection to the question, which was itself disquieting. The man who sat across from me had unmistakably lost his old temper.

"I will light the fire," I said.

"Do not." I ignored him and crouched before the hearth. By feel I built a tent of straw and kindling. "Do not," he repeated as I drew my tinderbox from my pouch and touched flint to steel.

I have said before that I am a master fire starter. Never before, though, had I lit a fire as simply as on that night. From one strike sparks gushed from my fingertips, as surely as sweet water from a spring. The kindling burst aflame as though I had first doused the scraps in pitch, while behind me a low whine rose in the throat of Jakab, an exhausted wail like a mourner's last keening at the end of a wake.

I added more wood to the fire and flames wreathed them just as hungrily, dispelling the room's shadows and repelling the noxious cold.

"Why have you done that?" Jakab asked. His tone was curiously injured, as though I had somehow been disloyal.

I turned to behold what had become of him.

His nose and ears were black. His eyelids and lips were black. His cheekbones were smudged as though by soot. It was not soot, but his flesh corrupted, destroyed by frostbite. His fists sat balled in his lap, mottled by gangrene below the last knuckles as though by some sick lichen. Embedded in the ravaged flesh, silver gleamed from nine fingers.

I believe I cried out. He did not respond, though his face was frozen into a sort of grimace from the pain to which he gave no voice.

My satchel was within arm's reach. My legs were doubtless swifter than his. I could have run. A day earlier, I would have. But I had not found Pál yet and there was nowhere left to go. I did not know the way forward, but I suspected this revenant would stumble after me regardless of which direction I chose.

Best to treat with him as a man. "Why have you come here?" I finally asked.

He tilted his head in puzzlement.

"You were making your escape. What happened to Kladivo?"

His confusion deepened. "The horse? I dismounted and . . ."

"And what?"

A smile split his lips, a dreadful thing. "I came back here."

"Why?"

He was silent for a time. I watched as the question rippled across the surface of his confusion. For a few moments it worked on him, like a pebble dropped into a pond, and doubt nuanced the deep lines of his face. Then it passed, and he said only, "You should not have lit that fire."

"You were to cross the valley," I pressed. "You sought an escape from the mountain."

"I did?"

"You had given your all to this mission. You had done your duty and departed. A reasonable and honorable path."

"My duty?" He grimaced. A glimpse of his old, sour self. "I have never cared for duty."

"Then why did you return?"

"Me? I came to fetch you. I came to tell you to extinguish this fire, that it is time you left the mountain."

Whatever grasp I had on him was lost. His face resumed its suffering, non-expectant cast.

"Why should I leave the mountain?" I asked.

"It will not have us. Its stones rumble in fury. It recoils at the weight of our step. It abhors the fire you carry."

I remembered Vilmos's story of the iron stealing the soldiers' warmth and it occurred to me that Jakab lied. The mountain did not abhor my fire, it coveted it. I waited for him to say more. His wasted hands shifted in his lap. "Why would you say that?" I asked.

"That ring. I must take it."

I heard the old hunger in his voice. The old lust of his. "Why must you take it?" He did not answer, he just leaned further forwards in his seat. "Who told you this?"

He raised his eyes to meet my own. I could see the question reflected there, as if he might ask me the same thing. Then that horrible smile burdened his face again and he shrugged. I would get no better answer from him. He did not know. He did not care.

"Give it to me," he said.

"This is my wife's betrothal ring."

"It is her last curse."

I folded my other hand over the ring.

"Then why take it?"

"I offer to relieve you of it. I will rid you of it. I will take it deep."

"This ring graced my wife's finger. She bequeathed it to me."

"Your marriage is ended. Your wife ended it. She forsook you."

"I will not remove it."

Jakab shrugged again. "You must."

He stared unbearably for a time, before his eyes drifted to the flames. I let his words settle before asking, "Do you speak for the mountain?"

He slid his stool forward a half-foot.

"Mountains do not speak."

"This fire," I said, gesturing to the hearth. "It does not warm you?"

"I feel it."

"Do you not feel the life in it?"

"A life fed on bones."

"What life is not?"

Perhaps he found this too clever, or perhaps he simply tired and wanted this final task of his to end. He rose slowly from his seat.

"It grows impatient," he said.

I rose to face him. This man, for whom I felt no love. Who somehow stood instead of twisted on the floor in his final throes. For him too, I realized, there was nowhere left to go.

"Come with me." I turned and walked through the door. I was near the steps' bottom before I heard him lumber after me. I went outside and awaited him in the snowy night.

He asked no questions when he emerged.

I turned and strode to the main gate. There I did what I should have done before I entered the keep. I swept snow aside with my feet and pulled the great doors shut. Jakab arrived and said, "Do not close these doors."

"There are wolves," I said. By rights he should have been warming their bellies. I hefted one end of the crossbar.

"Do not bar these doors," Jakab said.

I dragged the timber and struggled to fit the end into the cleats. Jakab trudged to me and swayed at my elbow. I ignored him. He raised no hand to stop me, only said, "Do not."

"Perhaps the wolves followed you," I said.

"None followed."

"Perhaps they have already slunk into the bailey."

"They have not."

"If they have entered they will have found an easy meal." I turned and crossed the yard again. At the stable door I turned to see him plodding in my tracks. "In here," I said.

"There are no wolves."

I stepped into the darkness. The room was utterly still. In the unseen stalls the horses laid in their final repose, tongues lolling and throats slit.

I watched as the veteran hesitated upon the threshold before stepping into the darkness. Once inside, he paused again. I said nothing until he approached me where I stood halfway down the aisle, deep within.

"In pagan days," I said. "There was a king who took his nation entire to the barbarian East that he might unite the world. But of all those who followed, the one he loved best was his horse. When the horse fell in battle, the king's grief was such that he built for it a tomb. Upon that tomb he raised a city."

Jakab said nothing, but I felt he was listening.

"A city upon a tomb. A tomb for a creature with no soul in need of curing. Imagine that. I think I understand. I understand such a futile work. For futile it was, for the memorial did not ease him. The horse's death defeated the king. Heartbroken, he joined his friend months later. Perhaps he should have remained to dwell in that new city. Regardless, he did not and his grand vision failed. The earth was not united, not before the king fell. Where he fell was Babylon."

Jakab stirred. "Great Babylon," he said.

"I have never cared before. But now I wonder—what if our exile from the Garden is everlasting? What if none of us return home? No end of days. No resurrection. No hellfire or paradisiacal waters. Instead we might sleep."

"Sleep," Jakab said.

"Or so we might hope. To slumber, at peace alongside our brothers, all quarrels forgotten. I do not fear this. Do you? You have earned your rest. Thank you for the kindness you showed Pál."

I laid a hand on his shoulder then passed him. He hesitated in the dark even as I exited the stable. Even as I closed the door and placed a bar across it.

Fejes blew softly, beckoning my return to the barracks. But I delayed. I waited for Jakab's muffled knock, those ruined hands raised in protest. I awaited the veteran's voice raised in final argument.

But he did not knock and he did not call, and at length I turned away.

Twenty-Six

I RETURNED to my seat to watch the fire. The flames flowed upwards over logs in fluttering cascades. Orange seeped into wood grain, into its seams to slowly transmute fuel into dust, a new layer of silt to fall upon the hearthstone. I fed the fire and prodded it needlessly so that it might eat its fill.

Dawn lifted the apron of night. The chamber's unseen corners were revealed, but I was content to rest. When was I ever allowed to rest? I heated some water and held the cup in my lap.

I wondered at my lack of doubt. How was it I felt such calm in place of revulsion, unsoiled by the filth of my guilt? I did not feel as I knew I should, as I knew I would. I could imagine my wife feeling such indifference. She was a hard woman. No thing and no one elicited her pity. This was also my vantage on Jakab, my one-time companion. I felt above it, removed from his fate.

I studied my ring. I could no longer pretend it was silver. It gleamed like sunstruck amber, a night-time pyre. Gold. It captured but would not release the light.

Something was amiss. I no longer recognized my edges. My conversations with Vilmos and then Jakab left me suspect, though I had carried these suspicions long before Kuszkol. I was never alone anymore. I no longer felt to be only myself.

She was with me. More than a voice, she was inside. My fingers, wrapped around the cup—within them were her own. Body and mind, I was a glove to her. I did not care, not very much. It was just good to sit here, to spread my legs wide knowing I need never worry about modesty again. From this day on I would wear stockings instead of skirts. It was incredible to be so far from home, to see for myself the world.

When had she done this to me? Was her trick so simple as convincing me to accept a ring on my finger? I held up my hand and admired its rich gloss, so familiar yet completely wrong.

She was my wife. She would be forever more. Why should I feel anger or harbor ill will towards her? It was my duty to carry her. Her life had been so short. Was it that I did not trust her? I did not like the thought. I pulled away from that conclusion, which led to panic and the drumming heart of captured prey. What I needed to do was to stop worrying, to banish these misgivings lest they lead me to true regret.

I was exhausted, yet I did not sleep. It was too good to simply sit and rest. I watched the fire, the dependable, insatiable flames. I looked about me at the strange, forlorn world of men. No loom in sight. No quern or mortar. It was breathtaking to think I was here. I was really here. I would carry no washing to the river today. I need not sting my hands with lye. I could forget those biddies and two-faced cows who spoke so cruelly behind my back and sought every day to humiliate me.

I enjoyed a grotesque satisfaction in wasting time. I was transfixed by an impulse that was not my own. It tasted like poison. It tasted like an old resentment that had not troubled me since her death, one which had taken root in my marriage just a few years after we created our home.

I took exception to her greed, her envy for the freedom to which I was born. She had gone to such lengths to claim this freedom for herself. It is wrong to be bitter. Woefully uncharitable, for she could find no contentment in the little frame that was her lot.

And somehow, by burning, she ensured I lived. I was alive because she had ignited the fire. The mountain might gust its stone breath upon me, but I was warm and snug in this chair, in this far-off place, while my companions had been taken from me one by one. The things they said about her—not one word a lie. She saw what others did not. Maybe she had foreseen this, and had given everything away, given herself away, that I might live.

I sipped some water. The thought was the only one that mattered. Her sacrifice was immeasurably larger than any small suffering I had endured. Her immolation put my troubles on this mountain to shame.

It was so like her to burn and yet refuse to reduce to ash. In her pride, she chose sacrifice but spurned repentance. She chose reconciliation through conquest.

I tired of sitting. It was her dream to while away the daylight hours, not mine, so I splashed the water onto the floorboards and rose. I saw to Fejes, and my girl brought me better to myself. I stepped outside into a dazzling day, a day so white and lucid blue that I nearly swooned in the clarity. I walked Fejes around the bailey, fed and watered her, brushed her mane.

Back upstairs the fire burned, but it seemed redundant now and I did not feed it. The water I splashed had run across the floorboards to fill the ghost of Kálmán's charcoal lines, just as the first trickles of spring wet the beds of drowsing streams. A pleasant effect. I admired it for a moment before crawling beneath my blanket to catch some sleep of my own while it was still light.

Twenty-Seven

Plenty of day remained when I pulled my satchel close. Kálmán's father awaited the letter it held for weeks, and I realized the absurdity of it having arrived, finally, only days too late.

For more than twelve years I had served the bishop of Veszprém, and for more than twelve years I had safe-guarded his seal. In my years of service, I had only ever broken a seal at the direction of the bishop's correspondents—illiterate captains without staff of their own. To break it otherwise was treachery, worse than abandoning my post.

I reached into my satchel, prepared to break the seal. My hand swept the bottom of my portfolio and came up empty. I opened the bag to peer inside.

The letter was gone.

I cannot say how far the sun traveled as I sat there in silence. I had exhausted all my ideas, all my companions.

I turned to the empty room that was left to me. The soldiers' long table and abandoned game of chess. The vacant stool beside mine where Jakab had sat only hours before. Pál's twisted blanket, from whence he had risen to stumble into the night. Kálmán's burst and pilfered pack, its contents lying in naked disarray.

Peeking from beneath the knight's crucifix, folded pages.

I rose. I walked to the traitor's things and retrieved the letter, my temples throbbing for want of his blood.

With a trembling hand I unfolded the letter, its seal already spoiled. The sight of my master's swooping hand brought tears to my eyes.

To Kázmér Kustyer at Kuszkol,

My dearest friend, I beg you forgive the late hour. That is two letters you have sent to my one. A first and I should think a last. I delayed not because you passed from my mind but because I knew you needed more than soothing words. It has taken me some effort and time to contrive my poor solution.

The difficulties you describe with your men are appalling. I agree the report of your hardships matches that of your predecessor sixty years past. It is no surprise that in such a tempest the weakest timbers split. I urge you to remain steadfast. As for that which you sketch in your letters' margins, my appalment is doubled again. I am dizzy contemplating it. It is utterly beyond me but not, perhaps, everyone.

Thus I send the best solace my poor imagination can conceive—your son.

I am not unaware of how he spoke to you in Szatmár this Easter. I am not unaware you forbade him from joining your company, and it is true that I have not always looked kindly upon his researches. Still, I am at a loss to recommend a better lieutenant. I have eaten crow and have begged he forgive my former skepticism. Some of the more outlandish precautions he had advised now seem prudent. He and I have discussed his stratagems, and while I will not say they give me great confidence, without them we are empty-handed.

I have presumed upon you but I have come to believe he was the least mistaken between us three. I believe, too, that Kálmán has grown into a capable leader of men. He could rule with a firm hand in your stead should you have need to travel in the months ahead.

I pause here to implore you to consider just this. You will not want to winter in that solitude. You are ever welcome in Veszprém but should you rather be bound for Buda, know that I have a new townhouse in the capital that has a full cellar and is at your disposal.

Should glory be your desired fare, your blade need not stay dry. Since last I saw you the borders of our nation wax. The king has marched into Moravia and even now he cuts through the heretic. Alas, as you predicted, the Bohemian throne will not fall as easily as in our strategists' designs. It is difficult to guess the outcome. Meanwhile, the Sultan is consumed with discord on his own southern frontier. I fear those voices arguing that Mátyás should turn from his course and redirect his wrath towards the heathens—that next year he might retake Constantinople and become a new Emperor in the East, no less—only grow more strident. I am as ever wary.

Finally, I must turn to a matter of which I am embarrassed to write and yet which I am compelled to share. Some months ago, I found myself in conversation with a woman who was much alike P. She was cryptic yet wise in a Terrible manner and though she has since died—I am certain of it—her cunning words, which I much misliked, have weighed upon me. The subject of Kuszkol arose. She had knowledge of your travails and foresaw that which lurks in your letters' margins.

Her two sooths—

First. She said a boy will come to Kuszkol and that he will bear her favor and shall brave the darkness. This confounded me. I ignored this bit of prophecy until, on the very day I located Kálmán, her own brother came to my attention. He is the youngest man I have sent you.

Second. She knew of the mine and that its entrance has remained hidden. She offered a riddle for locating it. I cite her verbatim. "Heed the bearing of the beast unshodden. Shine a halo on the path well-trodden."

I cannot begin to parse sense from it. It seems a frivolity but I think it is not. This woman gained some infamy before her death and Kálmán has pressed me about my interview with her. I have said less to him than I have to you. I have never spoken to him about P. and if he must learn of her, I would that he learn from you.

It pains me I have nothing better to send. Nor do I like this strange crossroads at which we have arrived, as if somehow we have gotten turned around.

Forgive these poor scribbles. I beg you be well and that you consider my counsel. Leave before the winter will not let you.

In friendship,
    Albert Vetési
    Written at Veszprém, the 30th of November

He spoke to her. My master spoke to her in her cell and he did not offer to commute her sentence. She spoke of Kuszkol. She had sent a message to the future, one I had couriered myself. All those months ago, Annaka already understood Kuszkol's place in our lives.

Kálmán had studied this letter as well. I reread my wife's words and wondered what he might have made of it.

Two sooths. A boy and a riddle.

I had the urge to take up a stool and dash it against the wall. To take my knife and eviscerate every pallet. To throw her ring into the fire. *She knew.* She knew Pál would come and face this peril. And she did not prepare him. She did not prepare me, or take any steps to safeguard us in this cruel future that she foresaw.

A boy will come who will bear her favor.

This cursed ring. It was meant for him. To offer him protection.

I could not have known. How could I have known? Why would I think it was meant for anyone but me?

I stoked the fire. Her clues were meant to offer hope, and yet I was out of options. I had searched everywhere for Pál, except, perhaps the lower floors of the keep. Except—I reread the final passage—the lost mine.

Heed the bearing of the beast unshodden.

Her instructions to find the mine. We had found many an unshodden beast here. Did those dead horses point in any direction? Perhaps their stalls aligned so their heads pointed vaguely towards the gate. Perhaps I had to search the lower slopes after all. Or . . .

I clapped my head. We had already unshod Fejes when I augured to find my bearing. Fejes had pointed toward the hoarding. Where Pál's footprints led.

I read the letter yet again. The page trembled in my fingers. Here, in my master's hand, her words had waited. Instructions intended not for Kálmán's father, but for me. Spoken across months and leagues and the veil of death itself, through the pen of another.

Shine a halo on the path well-trodden.

I turned my fingers so as not to see the golden band, for suddenly it glared too brightly.

Twenty-Eight

The lower bailey was at peace. An abandoned cloister. Days of snowfall and scouring wind had obliterated Pál's trace. If he had somehow passed into the forest, I thought of how cold he must be.

Vilmos said Pál was also somewhere deep. This deep place was a mine. I did not understand, nor could I quite believe. The forest was a cursed image on the wall. Yet this was my path. I stepped into the snow and followed the lost footsteps. Across the yard, up the stairs and onto the wall walk again.

From the ramparts, I scanned the valley below. The north of the realm, now clad in white. I could make out the swaths of field cut from wood. Across the valley, smudges of smoke from charcoal fires. Little different than before, but I was too high to know how those small folk fared. Whether the children still squealed as they leapt through drifts, whether milkmaids cooed to resting cattle. Perhaps such happiness sounded no longer. Perhaps the same fear that gripped this peak had slid into the valleys to taint every whisper.

The wind carried me mountain sounds. It told of creaking boughs and impatient crows. And another message, coded in tramp and muffled jangle. The report of men ahorse.

I leaned out from the parapets. Upon the mountain path, a

hundred yards down. I saw soldiers decked in dull armor. Some dozen of my countrymen, returning my gaze. No hail was raised, no hand held high in salutation.

They spurred their horses forward, kicking through the snow. Still, their eyes remained on me. At first I thought they took me for the enemy, or that they had expected to find no one alive. Then I grasped the reason for their astonished faces, for their rigid postures and still fingers that did not so much as twitch from their reins. The sight of me unsettled them. I glanced at my hands, still soiled by the dead men I had quarried on the beacon mount. I was covered in soot. I had to wonder—did I loom like a phantom? Whose face did I wear?

I turned away from the parapets, to my quiet citadel. My stomach rose, ready to heave.

"Friend!" Rang a forceful voice, accented by privilege. "Let us speak!"

"Friend!" He switched to the Slavic tongue of those mountains, "We have come to parley."

He did not know who I was, perhaps even which side I was on. I stared at the glistening snow at my feet, unsure what to do.

"Friend! Show yourself!"

"No!"

"Friend! We are your countrymen! We come under the banner of Mátyás, your king. Word has traveled of your beacon fire. Open the gate!"

Knocking echoed below. They stood beneath the gatehouse.

I had not begun my search for a way into the forest. "Not yet!" I cried.

"We have come to your aid. Open the gate."

Again the knock, heralding the end of my solitude. "I cannot receive you. Not yet." I eyed the entrance to the hoarding as the men whispered furiously below.

Then a harsher thumping. "Open this damned gate!"

It was too early for rescue. I had no need of them. I darted to the hoarding and ducked inside.

Immediately, voracious cold gnawed at me, plunging its chisel tips to pry me open. The cold was utterly malign, the mountain's wrath, the fingers of the ghost seeking to undo me.

I swayed for a moment, under assault, steeling myself to fight for my next breath. The breath came easily. The chill could not touch me, not even to make my skin rise in gooseflesh, for I carried the very fire that still burned her. Were I to walk this passage bare-chested, my blood would course as hotly in my veins, though death be a hair's breadth away.

The fire-marked wall was as I remembered. Black but for the meticulous bands, from top to bottom, and the mad snaking lines like worm trails between. I averted my eyes and from their corners saw the hidden vista. The vast forest and the figures massed between the trunks, beneath dark roofs, like me. As I began to walk, the figures shifted. When I quickened my pace, they heaved and lurched. When I sprinted, they raced towards me. Shoulders rolling, chins bobbing, arms reaching. Forward, faster, they sought to cut me off.

I rounded the tower and sped toward the hoarding's end. So near did my pursuers draw that I could hear their steps resounding in my own as I pounded the boards. They almost had me. At the last gap in the parapet, I turned aside and hurled myself through, back onto the wall walk, tearing myself from the fantasy of pursuit, shocked awake by the still-dazzling day. I filled my lungs with clean air and loathing. For myself. For my stubborn weakness that I would not resign.

I could never go back into the hoarding again. Thus I swore even as the image of Pál suddenly resolved in my mind, as though summoned by another, lying in pale repose. My boy, lying in the darkness. Unable to move, unable to call out, like one mistakenly interred beneath the cathedral floor. It was this vision of his helplessness that drew me back in.

I stepped into the wooden corridor and regarded the torched planks. There were no trees, no devils to be deciphered in the charred surface. This comforted me not at all, for the illusion was to regard it thus, face-on. I just need adjust my vantage. Sure enough, I turned towards the hoarding's end and they were there, surging forth. The figures so near, snatching at me, seeking to pull me in that I might lope among them, forever in that night.

I kept my gaze forward until I came to the end, to the black figure who awaited me. The one who had ventured out from the trees. My witness. My accomplice. Man-shaped soot. My height. My width. Hands held at the ready, for the moment had come. To reject this stain would be to reject my shadow, to renounce the acts by my twin on the ground, on my behalf. To renounce the one who stalked my every step.

More snow had collected through the slats since last I had come, but the ruts of my earlier passage were still evident. My footprints and those of Jakab, and before us Pál.

A path well-trodden but no halo. What did I expect? The lunacy of this place had broken me.

I bowed and studied the footprints. Wholly mundane. I touched my finger to the snow and, in the light slanting through the slats, her ring gleamed.

I was at a loss. This was the very end.

"Please," I said, and more. And if the words that followed should be named a prayer, they were addressed to her. If my promise to yield all be named a vow, my fealty was pledged to her.

I touched the snow and my finger began to trace a circle.

My finger traced a circle.

Not I.

She had heard my plea. She commanded more than my tongue now. I whimpered as the circle circumscribed me.

There, there, she shushed. She told me to close my eyes. So I did. I saw the sun burnt into the gum of my lids. There was a way, a radiant circle, a yawning disk at my feet. I felt a flush of heat and the cries of my countrymen were no more.

Twenty-Nine

Most men aspire to be rooting boars, to bury their snouts in wet leaves, gorging on dropped fruit and the little grubs that seethe beneath the rotting canopy. Not you. You wandered the wildest paths, beyond this stinking dark and green, to follow corridors of sunlight, to vistas opening beyond until at last the wind found and flounced your mane. There is more to this world than wood and hilltop, as you discovered, and you became more than other men. You were the wind's adopted son, galloping on your plain. The wind is greater than any pile of rock, greater than vine and reaching stalk, for it is imbued with invisible weight. Weightless weight. I liked you best on top of me, pressing down like a thunderhead and at first that is all I craved. I longed to shudder beneath you. I longed for you to press down so hard my back would break, my trunk would crack that I be severed from the leafy floor. Only later when you nuzzled my hand for apples, when you huffed upon my needles and galls did I imagine them as wind-whipped lash and gouging hoof. I imagined I was you. I had to have you. The others warned but only you were wrong, I set a trap for you. A trap but no cage. I never caged you. I was content to feed you from my fingertips then let you run off, as long as you came back so I could lean in close and smell the strange scents that had settled upon your head. As long as I could hear your happy snorts that spoke of far and wide. Oh, I longed to ride you, to play your parable king. They were right and you were wrong. It is the wind that makes you deaf as it roars past those ears. Or perhaps so much world fills your eye you are blind. You always mistook me. I never wanted a child. A babe would have burdened me, an anchor hanging from my neck. No doubt it would have slipped from my grasp and bashed on the laundry stones. Besides, I gave you a little one, one I hoped turned more colt than shoat, who huddled in the open paddock I fashioned for you. I hoped you would teach him to race far off, teach him the hidden byways that lace across the land. I have not abandoned hope. Not for him. Of you, I tired. You neither listened nor saw. You left me behind, rooted in place, but then again you never promised me escape and mine was the fault of dreaming. And then one day I knew you were close to never coming back and I, a better watcher, a better listener than any other, learned what was to be. I saw a war of no concern. I saw our colt stumble on his first gambol. Down he fell, down deep. So came the time of suffering, and I gladly gave myself away, for at last I saw my path to victory. My boughs turned to flame, and for precious moments my reach extended. I finally spread beyond myself. And to whom did I reach with those ropes of fire? I reached for you, for at the last I saw you from my tower of flame, charging across your plain. I never meant to shower you with sparks. If I injured you, if I singed your fetlocks so that now you are lame, forgive me. Forgive my lack of tears, but they have boiled away. You never understood your luck. There was never any genius to you, only restlessness. By this inconstancy you became beloved to others. My unrest condemned me. You wonder how we passed through solid rock? If you had known me you would know. Roots that run so deep have no trouble piercing stone.

Thirty

I HAD ENTERED ANOTHER PLACE. No sight filled my eyes but the fading image of the circle that had for a moment burned before me. This place was silent save for the far-off sound of running water. And it was cold. Hideously so. My inner flame flickered and I was able to draw breath. The air held no hint of embers, no residue of the smoke that had permeated the hoarding. This came as a surprise, for nowhere at Kuszkol had I experienced anything approaching such frigidness without also stumbling across the signs that fire once raged.

This place was not as void of smell as it was of light. There was a stench of mineral, that sickly jaundiced powder the alchemists call brimstone, which is the yellow bile of the earth. Having awoken to this taint, the task of breathing became onerous, and for a long moment I stood pinching my nose. Were I to linger long, I thought, I would no doubt suffocate.

Allowing my thoughts to ramble this path was an error, as was interrupting my lungs' rhythm. A powerful urge for open sky seized me, for clean air, which made my next breath that much bitterer. I reached out. I felt nothing. I took a step, two, then many. The ground was uneven. I was at risk of tripping, of falling on some hazard unseen, yet I quickened my pace. I ignored how my steps sounded. I stifled the cry that lodged like a bolus in my gorge.

Finally, my hand struck stone. I spread my fingers across a column, thankful for the touch of what was surely my enemy, this mass hidden so well that not once had it been warmed by the sun. I bowed my head and struggled to curb my nerves. With my fingers splayed across the stone, I discovered a rumble deep in the rock. It rolled up through my hands and set my marrow atremble.

I stood in a subterranean chamber. The heart of the mountain. Of how I had entered, I could make little sense. How I might leave again, I had no idea. I had no bearings and no faith that fumbling as I did would lead me anywhere before thirst deprived me of wits or a chasm should swallow me. This was no mine shaft. I doubted there existed a travelable path that led back to light.

Above me, a mile of rock. Its weight, incalculable. Greater than every man, woman and child in Christendom stacked upon my shoulders. Greater, perhaps, than every splinter of the northern wood. This was a place from another time, from the first chapter of creation when all was war between wave and gust, between ray of sun and implacable stone.

You are a runner, she said, *fleet of foot.* But her murmurs were senseless in this place. Here I was as good as dust. My only task was to settle upon the floor.

She countered. *The elements you revere are not separate from you. You are their interpolation. You are but one part dust. Do you not draw air? Then so too must there be the possibility of light. You carry a light. You are a fire starter.*

I withdrew my flint and steel. I struck a spark and for the first time since the birth of days, the chamber was revealed.

I was in the forest.

A wood made of stone. The trees pressed close on every side like a half-constructed palisade. Some boles were slender, the width of my forearm. Others were conjoined and formed ridged composites wider than my chest. Their skins did not share the texture of bark, but rather flowed like melted wax. The canopy ran together an arm span above me. From this ceiling depended stone vines and branches, toothed and tonsiled as if I trod a dragon's tongue. If one might call a rock face diseased, then so I shall name the crusts and dark veins that pocked and spidered those trunks, tumored like clots of suet and splintered honeycombs of bone. The cave that opens near Zavala Monastery in Bosnia is the closest I have seen to it, but that cave was as modest as a little chapel next to this most lavish basilica. The nearness of the lobed and thrusting stone did not ease my suffering. Nor did the rumble which filled the air after the spark had died. The mountain protested.

I struck a second spark. I glimpsed between the columns vaults receding like crypts in the nightmare of a deranged church builder. I did not test a third spark, for again the earth growled, so alike thunder following a lightning flash. I groped towards that gap I had seen. The path I found brought me some slight comfort, a sense of direction, when in truth I had none. This comfort was countermanded by the nearness of the trees and ceiling, which pressed so closely, unseen, and which threw back the drum of my footsteps. The passage seemed also to condense the frigidity so that I was certain the stillness of the air was not due to a lack of wind, but because the very air had frozen. That the only possible way to traverse the solid ice was to filter through, to become as light.

I wanted to stop. I wanted the menacing dark to finish this punishment, for I was not a ray of light, I was blind and lost and whatever purpose had brought me here was forgotten.

I did what I knew I could not. I pushed on. The cold did not topple me, though I staggered. The harder I pushed, the faster I walked, the greater the echo that filled my ears. I must have taken the wrong path, for no chamber opened about me, but a passage between the stone trunks. It recalled to me another passage. The hoarding where I had run and those other steps that had shadowed mine, those other steps which lurked in the echo of my own. The figures in the woods matching my pace.

This notion of the figures took hold of me. I was seized by the thought that even here, there was too much echo in my steps. I began again. I quickened, feeling my way forward with my hands. Again, I heard it. Behind me? Yes, I was stalked. I was not alone.

There was another in this place, with no need for light, as nameless here as me. Yet whatever haunted me was familiar, so familiar, a name would fit if only I could unstick my tongue. I thought of the one I carried. No, it was even more sinister than she.

I stopped to still the echoes. To no avail. I felt it creeping closer. I agonized over whether to risk the mountain's appetite with another spark. Of course I must. I had grown more fearful of what black lurked within the black than the colossal weight of stone overhead. So, again, I struck flint to stone, and oh, how that glimpse filled me with regret! For I did not find an empty tunnel. On the edge of the meager flash loomed the shape of a man. Cloaked and at least as tall as me.

I turned. I ran. I bashed my shoulder on a tree. I struck my head on a low-hanging growth from the roof and nearly crumpled in a daze of swinging stars. Still I stumbled on, for there would be no release in slumber. I was already exiled to blackout, already locked in dream. That awful dream where another haunts. Not an infernal other, not as the priest supposes, but something more like oneself—one's own soul in rebellion. Released, unconcerned for its master's fate, if not hostile. In the dream the spirit is cold.

A shiver set my limbs twitching.

My outstretched hands confirmed my worst fear—the path between the trees narrowed. Even as the passage grazed both shoulders, I pushed on. I had no more wits than a scurrying beetle, my legs driven by terror's whip as I sought a crack in which to take refuge. I came to none and the path continued to narrow. Inevitably, I would become trapped.

I pushed on, sidling sideways. I had no chance, yet I shuffled forward for as long as the passage failed to close on me. My cause was hopeless. I was quarry. My enemy knew this territory better than I. Yet I pushed on. On until the rock scraped my spine and breastbone. On until I became lodged.

A knob of stone jutted into my belly. My belt was hooked. I threw my weight into displacing myself, but only managed to squander the little freedom I had to withdraw. My only latitude was the ability to swivel my head, in futility, for I could see neither forward nor back.

Then, finally, I heard its approaching steps, no longer concealed within the echo of my own. Faint, soft, as though my hunter trod a path of ashes. I strained uselessly against my rock snare. Still closer the steps neared. I stilled myself to better listen to the dark. But there was no other hint to its nature, not even the slightest of breaths.

Stand aside.

The steps ended. Very near. I gaped uselessly as the frigid air finally stung my lungs. That is when I first felt its touch. Moth-wing light, a dry fingertip in the web of my thumb and finger. I snatched back my hand with a shout. The hunter was so close, but I no longer sensed its presence, not in a material way. Yet it was there. I knew it. I folded my arm to my side and balled my hand into a fist.

The touch came a second time, skimming the hair upon my wrist. I pulled back, as far back as the rock would allow. Yet my hand was locked on the side of my assailant, and the questing touch returned. Faintly caressing the back of my hand and the ridge of my knuckles.

I lashed out with a cry. I battered empty space. The mountain's cold, so long apart, drove deep its needles. The touch returned, mindless of how I thrashed and heaved, this time on the elbow. A sob burst from my mouth. I was helpless, like a chick who had failed its first flight, doomed to the snake between the stones. The touch grew less timid. More than one finger slipped up my arm. And when it surpassed the cloth of my sleeve, again contacted flesh, the groping became more assured. Stroking my forearm, enveloping my balled fist, then pulling my hand effortlessly from my side.

Move out of my light.

The violator's hands were not human. They worked with implacable strength, but their surface felt friable, as though made of crust and powder. My fingers were peeled back like the petals of an unblossomed bud, and I understood at last the object of the thing's pursuit—the ring.

I tried to strike out a second time, but so sure was my enemy's grip that my arm barely trembled. It squeezed my wrist without mercy. I loosed a wordless plea.

The ring was the only thing of value, more valuable than my life. Claim the ring, and the black one would claim my fire. The creature slipped its wicked nails behind the thin edge of my metal band and began to work it from my finger. The ring started to slide. If it were parted from me, it would be lost forever, as surely as had I dropped it from a ferry traversing the river. The knowledge of this imminent failure bloomed bitterly in my chest. The blasted one worked the ring another quarter-inch down my knuckle. Sickened by my impotence, all resistance fled my limbs.

The other part of me, the one whom I carried, was not so resigned.

The flame casts no shade.

Perhaps it was she who thrust the memory upon me, the story of pride set aside, but remember it I did. As the shadow worried the ring down towards my fingertip, I vividly recalled Father Péter's tale of Alexander and the wise man. The sage who wanted only for the king to stand out of his sun.

I understood. I was alike Alexander in that moment. I was naught but a barrier to the light.

Pride has value. One needs pride to be. It was no longer my time to be. I could confine her light to dream no more, and thus I acquiesced. I stopped clenching that inner fist I had held since first slipping on the ring. I became open-handed, so flat that I was reduced to an edge. I set myself aside, and she became more alive than me. Then, at last, I properly knew her rage.

I cannot describe to you what it is to burn alive. To lose one's hair in an appalling gust, to hear the fat sizzle beneath one's crackling skin. To have one's vision filled with red and then black as one's eyeballs burst. The pain is indistinguishable from the flames. The flames, they are a scream. A chorus roaring from every pore, singing agony. Agony—no, the notion is too bounded, the name inadequate for that mystery which transmutes a life, layer by layer, to matter.

I had known this sensation once before, and as my ring slid towards my nail bed, I knew it again. Fire erupted through my nerves like a flock of shorebirds. My howl articulated grief beyond sense as my pith ignited and I combusted from within. Through the flames, flames like sunlit water, I saw my aggressor. The creature withdrew like a black sheet. And if I had to put a name to that ancient face, to the soul-sold visage that peered from the fuliginous cowl, I would name it Kálmán.

But it was Kálmán not at all. The knight had had clean whites to his eyes, where this thing had fire-cracked marbles. Kálmán's teeth had gleamed, whereas this thing's grimace brimmed with charcoal tiles. If the fire within me had not banished my shadow, perhaps I might even perceive these eyes and teeth as my own.

The earth rumbled with baleful force, as though a herd of bulls stampeded about me. My vision jumped. I rattled from within. I was sure my bones would pierce my paper-ash skin.

So I stood, helpless, wedged deep in the mountain's belly, aflame. How could I blaze? How could I see by my own impossible flames when there was no light? I could not be on fire. She was on fire. I was not stranded. It was she. Not beneath the earth, but elsewhere. This was her last moment. The thunder I heard was the rafters as they came crashing down. There was no knight's silhouette, it was her gaoler, his face by turns ecstatic and bleak, glimpsed through the clouds of smoke.

This was not happening. This was her last moment, the moment she failed to die.

Perhaps I had grown woman-thin, or perhaps the juddering stone had freed my buckle. Either way, I came free, and slid onwards, deeper down the path, to its end.

I stumbled into a stone bower, a little dead-end cellar, and all my seeking was done. On the ground, laid out as though for his burial, was my boy. My Pál.

Did I really see this? Was I truly aflame? No, not me. The flames poured from my second skin, the one beneath. No fire shot from my arms and shoulders. I was still lost in the dark. And yet, he was before me, on the floor. I know because I saw him there, illuminated by my own ghost light.

I knelt beside him. He was cold. Cold, yet his chest rose and fell shallowly, as though he savored his last sip of breath. I found his hand and squeezed. It lay so inertly in my grasp, harboring so little warmth, I doubted myself. Perhaps he was dead. Or perhaps the question was meaningless here, so far from the life-giving sky, in this realm that had never known life.

She had one last task for me. I was happy to comply. It was time to pass on this fire.

I removed the ring. For only the second time since I found her band cached between the chimney stones, my finger was bare. And with it, the light and heat left me, as surely as had a candle snuffed out.

The dark bore down. The cold, which had never ceased to claw at me, now struck my chest with the force of a sledge. I could barely draw breath. It was all I could do to slip the ring onto Pál's finger, to convey the fire, as every inch of me began to quake. I nearly fumbled my rescue in that dark. As the bones in my hands rattled, the ring nearly rolled away. I twisted the band up over the first knuckle, then the second. His fingers twitched in my hand but I was too weak to hold them. The mission done, I toppled onto my side and buried my hands uselessly between my thighs.

I closed my eyes. It made no difference now. I prepared to freeze. She had chosen to be with the boy at the end. I was content with her choice.

She was not dimmed by the handover. Nay, she would never be dimmed again. The fire took. Pál stirred. I opened my eyes and could tell that he had sat up. Not only that, he had sprung to his feet. This last I knew by sight, for the flame now flowered deep inside him. I saw it as all the phantoms of this mountain must have seen it carried in me. His features were lit from within, as though he were a vessel. A lantern, his flesh aglow.

His face so illuminated was newly revealed to me. I saw for the first time how dour were the lines alongside his nose, how firm the jaw, how determined the brow. The face belonged to an older man, to one more wearied, so much sterner than the boy I knew.

The earth rumbled again. Treble-fold. My head soon ached from rebounding off the floor. I thought my icy teeth must shake from my mouth as dice from a cup, that at any moment, the ceiling must surely give.

I lost sight of him briefly as a shadow intervened. The shape of Kálmán, the black thing, strode overtop me as though I were a spent husk. Before Pál could even gain his bearings, this blight ambushed him, assaulted him, questing again for the ring.

Pál recoiled. My boy was helpless, buffeted by the grappling touch, snared between those implacable, mantis arms. I had not saved him, I had condemned him by leading my stalker to his cell. The fright of Pál's inner-lit face was a terrible thing to see.

Worse was when those features distorted again. They hardened, set into a mask I could never have fathomed—a man, indomitable. A hero from some fireside story. A king leaning into a battle charge.

Pál shoved the thing aside. I watched, overcome, barely recognizing this man who was surely my own age, though much harder, much grimmer and more menacing than I had ever been. I wondered if I finally saw as she had exhorted, if now, as my vision iced over, I saw through the moment and glimpsed his future cast. Perhaps I had discovered Pál for the man he was always destined to be. If so, it grieved me. To witness him thus must be what it was for an old man to peer up from the deathbed to a beloved son. I longed for the little boy, but found instead this stranger, remote and vital, who spared no thought for the winter's weak, locked as he was in his own life's struggle against mightier forces.

For such my Pál was. He combated one far stronger than himself. The black one swooped again. By some miracle, Pál dodged and, without pause, took two fistfuls of cloak and bashed the monster against a stone tree.

The shadow reeled back from reaching fingers, from the betrothal ring that would assure its mission and set the mountain alight. Pál grasped it by the cloak and withdrew the creature's own blade.

Pál put the knife to work. Not as a bumbler, as some accidental murderer in a scuffling brawl. Rather, Pál stepped around the staggering figure and bided his time. He gripped the shadow by the scruff and with a deft, merciless stroke, slit the black thing's neck with as little compunction as a riverman opening a fish.

Kálmán dropped in a dusty heap. Pál stood above his foe, drawing a deep, living breath. I watched his face twist, and wondered if he received the same revelation as I. If he understood, in that instant, his fate. His destiny to be no mere soldier, but a warrior. A killer of men.

"Am I in the dark?" Pál finally asked.

"The mountain has us," I croaked.

"I tried to turn away. When I saw it, I tried to turn toward the light, even as Sándor bade Bukephalosz but . . . how can one not follow one's own shadow?"

He said more. The words became indistinct. I was fading. With the last of me I tried to whisper that if he did not turn he would remain untamed. Pál hesitated, and then either he or Annaka acted on his behalf.

He dragged me from where Kálmán sprawled. I wanted to

reunite with that shadow, to cradle up alongside him and finally join my predecessors, for I had earned the right to lie down with them upon the beacon pyre. I was so cold, so ready to become one with my comrade and those never-known brothers, that to be sacrificed to this mountain would be a pleasure. I need not burn again.

Pál bent down, or perhaps it was she, and traced a circle about us. As he drew, light, like a spray of gold, shed from her ring and bathed me again in impossible fire.

Thirty-One

Our rescuers discovered us as we emerged from the hoarding. The faces that greeted us were wary and numbed. They had explored the fastness by then.

I felt no gratitude in finding them, arranged on the steps and in the bailey, so alert in their proud uniforms. After so many days above the clouds, their solidity confused my eyes. An affront, surely, to the great smothering sky. The ruddiness of their cheeks, the naivete in their searching looks, seemed unreal to me.

Among them were two minor knights of Kálmán's own order and one of his cousin's. They questioned me at length, but in the end were left unsatisfied by my tale. Nor were they tolerant of Pál's sullenness or the hostility that shot from his glance. When I begged leave for us to depart, they would hear nothing of it.

Aside from our interrogators, the soldiers who made up this foray spoke only in hushed tones, if at all. The row of dead horses, the echoing corridors, the scorched fragments of men—they had no words for such sights. They had found Vilmos dead in his bed, his blanket pulled up over his face. Jakab, they found curled in the hay, as if he had nodded off to sleep.

That night, when the officers supped in the keep, Pál saddled up

Fejes and set me atop of her. I leaned onto her neck to say things she would never understand, and I knew she had missed my weight. I rode out with Pál walking at my side. One of the soldiers made to bar our way, but when confronted by my glowering brother-in-law, he backed away. The other guardsmen watched us march off without protest. They accepted our defection, even if they did not heed my call to join.

Our descent followed their upward tracks. The only point we slowed was where the wolves had done their work. Kladivo's ribs poked through the snow like a giant's bloody fingertips. I would have spurred Fejes onward, but Pál insisted we linger that he might take in the starlit carnage.

We passed the night in the forest. The dark beneath the trees was as dense and gnarled as the deadfall tangled beneath the snow. Something was wrong out there. A rage flew down the nameless paths, cohering, drawing itself together for another assault, or perhaps to run riot across the pastures of the northerners. The next morning, when we passed through the first village across the valley, we could see plainly that the peasants felt it too. They knew something gathered in the night beyond their fences.

It was not only the forest that harrowed the country folk. The war had finally touched that land. The enemy had crossed the border west of Biccse. Word traveled of winter stores plundered and horses commandeered. Those farmers with any wisdom already stowed their daughters in haylofts and sheepfolds.

Pál showed little interest in any of this. When we first rose he would speak and move like the boy I knew, but by the time we broke camp, he had grown surly. He would say nothing of his ordeal and asked me no questions about my own. He was filled with a restlessness that crowded out words. At the end of every day of travel, he was anxious to push on further. When we stopped at night, he would stay up to watch the fire die, reluctant to re-enter his dreams.

Back in Veszprém, we spent a day skulking about the house, him sitting with Fejes in the stable, me by the fire. The next day I felt strong enough to trek up Castle Hill, but I delayed. Instead I spent time with Terézia, who fussed over my complexion and placed the first of my great-nieces upon my lap. Pál spent the day grazing Fejes in the woods. Thus another day passed, followed by another. Listless, aimless. I cannot recall clearly of what we spoke when our paths crossed, if at all. The moat that yawned about him was all but impassable, and what little talent I had at traversals had been exhausted on the mountain.

Still I delayed in climbing Castle Hill. I knew the words I must speak to my master might spell my end, but it was not fear that held me back. I was trapped in an eddy, transfixed by the flow of all those happenings and the other lost leaves that spun around with me.

It was Pál who freed me. I entered the house one afternoon and found him leaning against the post. He glanced at me, then at the table. There, at its center, he had left the ring.

I picked it up and held it in the cup of my palm.

"I will not wear it," Pál said.

It was so light. It held no warmth at all.

Pál waited on me. I nodded. "I understand," I said. "You need not worry. I will carry her." So I came to wear the ring again, for I am faithful.

That night I lay in bed, listening to Pál toss in his loft, turning the gold about my knuckle. I thought about loyalty and I thought about sacrifice. I thought how they were often the same, and often one another's opposites. Perhaps some of her fierceness came into me, for I worked myself into such a temper that I could hardly sleep. I was up, dressed, and across the threshold shortly after dawn.

The dim morning air was full of little flakes. Our first snowfall. The arrival of winter pressed on Veszprém, a reminder of miserable days to come. The cocks were subdued in their calling and the Castle's gatekeeper did not even look up as I passed.

I waited outside the bishop's apartment for an hour as he broke his fast with an emissary from Vienna. The steward said I looked tired and offered me a stool. I asked after the widow Sára, but she was at home tending a sickly child.

I leaned further into my corner when the emissary finally parted. Afterwards the bishop conferred with his clerics before I was let in.

When I entered, Albert Vetési regarded me for a long and wary moment before finally rising from his seat. He had never done that before. "András? What news do you bear?"

His eyes darted more than once from my face to my ring.

"What they say of Kuszkol is true."

He leaned on his desk. That powerful, blunt face was buffeted like a breakwater. He knew enough to believe me. "I have received reports of a beacon."

I opened the flap of my satchel.

He took the pages and set them down without asking about the broken seal. I listened to him breathe. His composure eroded before incredulity, and then dismay.

"And Kuszkol's lord? Kázmér Kustyer?" he asked.

"I brought my boy home. We are the only survivors."

My master staggered back. He fell into his chair as though I had slung arrows into him.

This was not right. This is not what I had meant to say. I had meant to accuse him straightaway, not to answer his questions, not to dismiss his lingering doubts. I had prepared words. He had let Annaka burn. He had known of Kálmán's precautions, and still he had allowed me and Pál to walk through Hell. I wanted him to know he was my master no longer, that even one so lowly as I could repudiate him.

He dropped his head into his hands. He raised his face to study the ceiling and I was amazed at how bright his eyes were. Burnished by tears he did not shed. He struggled to find his voice. "But you are whole?" His throat had closed up on him.

Whole? He studied me and I him, and I wondered at his scarcely masked revulsion.

I said, involuntarily, "I told you we would speak again."

He sank further into the chair leather, as though pushed, as though struck by another volley. And I, I stood like a man who had lit the cannon's powder. With all my might I willed myself to remain on my feet.

"I did not counsel you to send Kázmér's son," I said. I was faint and yet I spit the words with a venom I could not taste. "You tracked Kálmán down and wasted weeks. Had you sent me even days earlier, Kázmér would not be dead." He covered his mouth. Age spots trembled. Even so, his eyes were hardening. "He died because you did not honor our bargain."

"I did not dishonor it."

"You sought to betray him on your own terms," I said, unsure why I spoke with such intent.

"I did not betray him."

"You were far from forthright. If you had truly wanted to save him you should have set all aside. You should have ridden to Kuszkol and pulled Kázmér out yourself. He would have followed. But your pride outweighed your love for him. You thought yourself wiser than me and so you amended my direction with your silly little scheme."

"That is called prudence."

"You hedged your bets and still lost. I call that failure."

Albert glared. "Kázmér would have done the same."

"He would have gambled your life?"

"If you must ask then you know nothing of the two of us. We led a life of daring."

"And you dared all."

"Should I be satisfied with less?"

Of all the arguments he could have made, it was this that quieted the voice.

His Excellency picked up the letter to Kázmér Kustyer and re-read his own words. He winced only once.

I felt dizzy. I began to turn my head, sure my heel would follow, for I would march from the chamber. Instead I clasped by hands behind my back and said, "The mine for which he searched is lost.

Let Kázmér's dream die with him. From now you will better heed my counsel."

He set the letter down.

"And what is your counsel?" I thought he would sooner lock me away than hear another word.

"Replace your secretary."

"My secretary? What has he to do with anything?"

"If he had his way, everything. Your secretary is a spy for Chancellor Várdai, who has promised him a position in court, perhaps one day a canonship, in exchange for evidence about the state of your mind."

His Excellency's eyes drifted to the door. Even now Father Lajos was lurking near, deciding precedence among the bishop's daily supplicants.

"I will make some inquiries," he said.

"Make also inquiries into your master of vineyards."

"Why?"

"He commits fraud against you. Did you not think last year's market tolls were high?"

The bishop's creased brow revealed that he had. "What else?"

I pointed to a parchment on his desk. Another letter. "The Archbishop of Esztergom writes to you in confidence."

The flush left my master's cheeks. He placed a hand over this half-folded page, as though to conceal the seal of Archbishop János Vitéz.

"We have much business in common," he said.

"Vitéz grows disenchanted with the king. He complains that Mátyás no longer bends to his will. You erred by replying to his last message."

"His letter demanded a response. He is my primate."

"Your words were too subtle, for he will whisper you are a part of his rebellion."

He pressed his lips together.

"Do not join him. In four years, Vitéz will be dead."

My master's scowl cracked under the weight of this revelation. "How can you know this?"

A nameless sensation rolled through me. The testimony of my eyes and ears, of my fingertips and tingling nostrils, *swelled* momentarily, rippled like light through water as I recalled truths I had never known, some yet to be. "I hear whole annals from how a daughter clinks the crockery when speaking to her father. I hear whole famines from how a head of barley brushes its neighbor. And I," I said, pointing at the archbishop's letter, "see whole knotted strings of traitorous resolutions in the way ink bleeds into stretched skin. János Vitéz will be dead."

My master looked as if he would like to snap me across his knee, but he had paled. On his back foot, desperate for a moment to spring from his defensive posture. That moment did not come. Instead, I saw inexorable ticking behind those eyes, registering everything I had said, calculating the future. Finally, he said, "What is your counsel?"

"Send me with a message to Eger," I said. "Express your concerns to Bishop Beckensloer. He is due to rise. With the king you must be more circumspect, for he yet loves the archbishop as a second father. Far better than he will ever love you."

He put his hand in his chin for another minute of silence. All this while I burned, but somehow exhilaration had substituted for the anger that had chased me all the way to his door. At length he said, "It shall be done as you say."

I nodded and took my leave. "I will be ready when you need me."

Thus I left the bishop's palace remade. She had always wanted me to become more than a tool. She had wanted me to become indispensable. Suddenly I was that and more. I was Albert Vetési's collaborator.

But if I felt some distortion of pleasure, it was fleeting. When I arrived home, Pál was gone.

I believe he made his way to the front, to fight in what now appears to be a long and pointless war. If not the west, then perhaps the south, for the Turk tests our border again. There are no safe places. The war grinds on. Yet every war is made up of endings. Thus my days are filled with dread, for I have heard no word from him. Wherever I travel, I ask after him.

Some part of me thinks I should pursue him no longer. I should put my search to rest. When Alexander wandered, he had the bravery to never come home again. She thinks the boy is brave. She is content that he is free.

In any case, I am rarely home. I live on the road now. I will not protest if she has of late grown bold. As I see it, if she sometimes takes hold of my tongue, she has spared me the effort of speaking. If she sometimes commands my steps, she has spared me the effort of choosing my way.

So I will ride forward and I will let her be. She may presume to rule, but she will never possess this last piece of me. I learned how to gird myself against her, under that mountain, where my heart froze mid-beat.

Acknowledgments

First, thanks to Susan Hung for her love, support and always incisive critiques. *Mountain Fast* was years (and years) in the writing, and she never begrudged the hours (and hours) I needed to hide myself away to finish it. She made the novel possible, and so much better too.

Thanks to Nick Mamatas for his fantastic editorial feedback. I overhauled many aspects of the novel after receiving his insightful comments, and once again, the result was so much better.

Thanks to Caitlin Sweet for her encouragement, and to Michael Johnstone and Jerome Skeete for all the writerly conversations and friendship on the journey.

Finally, thanks to Raven Daly for his haunting cover art. He beautifully translated my vague concept into a work that perfectly reflects the story's winter-dark soul.

About the Author

S.J. Shank is a lover of dead languages and collapsed empires. He is the author of the science fiction and fantasy collection *Rare Specimen and Other Stories*. He can be found online at sjshank.com.

Printed in the USA
CPSIA information can be obtained
at www.ICGtesting.com
LVHW042054130624
782774LV00001B/2